BAGGAGE

OTHER TITLES BY
S.G. REDLING

Flowertown
Braid: Three Twisted Stories
Damocles

DANI BRITTON THRILLERS

The Widow File
Redemption Key

THE NAHAN SERIES

Ourselves

BAGGAGE

S.G. REDLING

THOMAS & MERCER

Redling

Published by Thomas & Mercer, Seattle

www.apub.com

Amazon, the Amazon logo, and Thomas & Mercer are trademarks of Amazon.com, Inc., or its affiliates.

ISBN-13: 9781503950603
ISBN-10: 1503950603
Hardcover ISBN-13: 9781503952201
Hardcover ISBN-10: 1503952207

Cover design by Stewart Williams

Printed in the United States of America

This book is for my mother.

CHAPTER 1

I would already be home if I would stop turning around to stare. Cold drizzle soaks through my jeans and my ponytail has taken on so much water it whips like a sprinkler when I turn my head, but I keep turning to look. I've seen it nearly every day for six months and I still try to take it all in. After all, the world ends tomorrow. Again.

I'm standing on a hunk of slate that juts out over the culvert at the hairpin turn on Everly Road. From here I can see most of campus—the glassed-in wing of the library, the dome of the student center, and through the bare branches of the oaks and sycamores that line the wide green, I see the Jenkins Building where I work.

When I took the job in September, this vista exploded with reds and yellows. My boss said my walk home would get a lot less interesting come winter. Well, it's February 16 and I can't think of a thing I'd rather stare at or anywhere I'd rather be. I'm in no hurry at all to get back to my dark apartment and rental furniture. I'm certainly in no hurry to get home to my neighbors.

Mostly I'm not in a hurry to see what's waiting for me.

Messages on my answering machine. Letters in my mailbox. No

matter where I go, they find me. No matter how often they find me, I won't hear or read any of them.

Unfortunately, I can't stand here forever and I continue my trek home. When I cut across the road to Everly Place, the ugly, sprawling complex cuts off my view of the town below. Here it's just a parking lot and dumpsters surrounding the squat two-story collection of inexpensive college housing.

My mailbox fights me again, like it does every day. I'm tempted to not struggle with the sticky lock, to leave the envelopes and flyers to build up until the mailman has no choice but to refuse to deliver any more. Would they do that? Would that work? If you ignore your mail long enough, does it just stop coming? Tempting, but I don't put a lot of faith in that plan. The thing about messages you don't want is that they are stunningly persistent. I don't read the writing on the envelopes I pull out. I'm not careful and a few of them catch and tear on the inside lip of the box.

I climb the outside stairs to the second floor, my ears peeled as always for signs that my nightmare neighbors are home. At the landing, I pause. Silence. Thank god. At least I'll be lucky for a little while. At least I'll be able to face today's messages with a little less aggravation. Purse down, shoes off, mail tossed onto the coffee table. I head to the kitchen and see the message light flashing on my answering machine. Maybe it's just telemarketers. I bargain with myself: If it's just telemarketers, we'll have a salad and hot tea. We'll treat ourselves to something healthy and spend the rest of the evening in soft pajamas with one of those good books we've been meaning to read. I push the button and listen.

"You are receiving a call from an inmate at the Jefferson City Correctional Center. Press one to continue this—"

I hit delete and reach for the corkscrew.

. . . .

There's no point in putting it off now. I flop down on the couch, trying not to think about how much I hate this furniture. Seriously, I need to get a new couch. Just because I'm broke and this is a rental doesn't mean I don't deserve a couch that doesn't feel like burlap and smell like a German shepherd. Let's not even discuss the hard wooden arms, covered in drink rings and cigarette burns from the fabric to the uncomfortably sharp edges. The good news is the couch matches the scuffed and scarred coffee table that completes my living room suite. I have no easy chair, and there's a TV in the corner I've never turned on. My "dining room" consists of a faux-brick breakfast bar and two stools. The only window at this end of the apartment sits over the sink, and it does little to illuminate the space. A mercy, considering the space.

The wine surprises me. I didn't look at the label—it's the second of the six bottles I picked up at Kroger over the weekend. Buying six bottles at a time gets me a discount and, more importantly, saves me a couple trips. Some part of me argues that it should save me a lot more trips than it does, but the rest of me shuts that little bitch down. The monsters trolling my brain today squash any fear of alcoholism like the ninety-eight-pound weakling it is.

Another sip of the wine—Merlot? Pinot? Who knows. Alone, I don't have to pretend I can distinguish them. Hell, another glass and I won't even be tasting it, but I let myself toy with the idea of getting up to read the label. Kidding myself, of course. I don't care what kind of wine it is; I probably wouldn't remember on my next trip to town anyway. The only reason to get the bottle would be to keep it beside me to make pouring easier. And to put off looking at the mail.

Just do it. It's not like you're going to read it.

It's a big haul today. My phone bill, bank statement, credit card bill. Those I toss into the bowl of coins and used corks. Those I'll open eventually. There's a flyer for carpet cleaning, one for better car insurance, one for a seminar on Creationism and its role in my salvation. What does it say that this flyer is the highlight of my mail so far? I play with the idea of going just to hear about dinosaurs on Noah's Ark but the odds are good that the evening doesn't come with an open bar so the allure is pretty thin for me.

Behind the flyers, my fingers trace the edges of three envelopes. I see them with my fingertips. I know exactly what they'll look like—cheap white number ten envelopes, narrow, black lettering uniformly slanted to the right, smudged and creased where they've been handled by people who don't much care for letter writing, people who read the contents with suspicion before stamping them with the red markings of the Jefferson City Correctional Center stamp.

It's hard to say when they were written. Maybe all three in one day. Maybe it's a week's worth of letters. Does the prison postal system hold mail up? Do they read it carefully? I don't know. I probably never will, since I haven't opened one of these letters in years. With just the most cursory glance, I fan the envelopes out to be sure I'm not overlooking anything, that there's no golden ticket stashed in among their smudgy white sheets. There isn't, of course; there never is. I always check and there never is, so I do with these envelopes what I've done with all the rest that have arrived in the six months I've lived here. I flick them out of my hand over my shoulder, into the hall that leads to the back of the apartment, toward the hall closet. Some of them skitter toward my bedroom. Some of them pile up against the baseboard. Some of them seem to possess a certain self-knowledge and slide themselves under the closet door.

I don't check on them. I don't collect them, not even when I clean. I walk over them; I kick them out of the way. Pretty soon they'll pile up pretty deep. It's February.

My mother writes a lot this time of year.

. . . .

I haven't gotten a card from Jeannie yet. They used to arrive as reliably as dawn. It used to be she would never let a month go by without a card, a letter, a phone call, or all of the above. Especially this time of year. But after this past year, things between us have been different, tender like sore skin that we're trying to toughen up by ignoring it. Still, it's February. We're halfway through the month. To go an entire week—or has it been even longer?—without a peep from her unsettles me. Has she given up on me? Has the horror of it all just become too much?

And then someone knocks at my door. I know with a certainty that I can't explain that this interruption is from Jeannie. A delivery. Flowers, probably. Probably in a sunny little smiley mug with a balloon and a cluster of Gerbera daisies. I take my time getting to the door, wishing for once someone would think to reach out to me with a fruit basket or maybe some of those chocolate-covered strawberries from Edible Arrangements. Someone had sent those to the funeral last year. Weird, I remember their deliciousness more clearly than I remember anything else about that whole month. In this moment, I would give anything for a box of those strawberries. Longing for them while bracing myself for flowers, I pull open the door.

I was right, sort of. Jeannie is the source of the disruption, but she didn't send a deliveryman. There are no flowers, no strawberries. Instead, my cousin herself stands in the doorway, suitcase at her feet.

"Don't even try to close this door, Anna."

I have to laugh. She's so bossy. Jeannie Conroy, my cousin, the savior of my teenage years, the constant lifeguard at the drowning pool of my life. It doesn't even occur to me to resist letting her in or letting her hug me. As many times as we've done this—and we have done this a lot—I'm always surprised at the feel of her. She's tiny, five-three at best, and underneath her soft, wool coat, she feels like a statue. She's bone and muscle or as her mother, Aunt Gretchen, used to say, "There's not an inch of give on her." She's as fit as an Olympian and as cute as a cheerleader.

I'm at the perfect spot in my bottle of wine to acknowledge that nobody on earth ever has or ever will give a better hug. If she'd shown up an hour later, this thought would have brought me to tears. As it is,

I just hang on, resting my cheek on the side of her head, not thinking, just rocking back and forth. I can admit to myself how I felt about not hearing from her—I hated it.

"I knew you weren't going to call." She pulls away and looks up at me. Her eyes shine with tears that balance on her mascara. "I wasn't going to ask permission until we were face to face. So can I come in?" We both know the answer to that so I take her coat and hang it on the hook beside the door.

"Wine?"

"Of course." She stands at the coffee table, hand on her hip, as I fetch another wine glass. I'm glad the bottle I just opened is decent. Jeannie has better taste in just about everything. She peers down the hallway and I know she's noticed the envelopes on the floor. As I pour her a glass, she finishes her survey.

"So, this is your new apartment? It's an absolute shit hole."

I laugh. "Good, that's the look I was going for."

We settle on the couch, her comic look of horror telling me we share an opinion on the furniture. We do the usual catching up—how's the job, how was the trip, we should go shopping, we should have dinner here and there. Jeannie knows the little college town better than I do. She lived and worked here for five years before taking the position at Penn State. She's the reason I got the job in the first place.

It's easy talking with her. It feels so normal, like we chat like this every day. It's warm and loose. Until it's not. We both see the moment it changes; we both know the words that are coming out of her mouth before she ever forms them and we both know how hard the conversation is going to become.

"How are you?"

It's different than the first time she asked me. This time she really wants to know, and it makes me want to down the rest of my wine in one swallow, ditch the glass, and drink right from the bottle. Instead I shrug, knowing that won't fly.

"Tell me."

"Tell you what?"

She braces her elbow on the back of the couch, her hand in her hair, her whole body facing me. I have her undivided attention. "Are you sleeping?"

"Yeah. Pretty well. Yeah." I do, despite my neighbors' attempts to thwart me.

"Good. And you're working. You like the job." She says it as a semi-question and I nod. Then I see her gaze move from my face, over my shoulder. She's looking toward the closet, toward the envelopes.

"Don't," I warn her, and she knows me well enough not to ask. Not that.

"So, Ronnie's insurance—have you gotten anywhere with that?"

"Yep, it's resolved."

"Really?" She brightens and I shake my head.

"Not in my favor." Before she can protest, I hold up my hand. "It was suicide, Jeannie. Nobody pays for suicide. The police report finalized it; the medical examiner backed the findings." She reaches out and squeezes my shoulder. "Hey, I'm lucky I didn't get charged with murder. You know, they always suspect the spouse first."

"Don't even joke about that."

I wasn't. Or maybe I was, I can't tell what emotion I'm projecting these days. I don't even know if there is a word for that emotion. Is there a word for what a person feels when the police question her upon discovering her husband's body hanging in the hall closet? In the fucking hall closet, of all places? What would that word be? *Fear-anguish-rage*? It seems like the kind of word the Japanese would have, or maybe the Swedes.

Whatever it is, I don't have it. But Jeannie knows.

She pushes my hair back behind my ears and it doesn't matter what point in the bottle I have reached, I start to cry. Nothing noisy or gross, just painful cramps in the corners of my mouth that push tears out from behind my lids, my stomach jerking along in rhythm.

"I'd put my head in your lap," I whisper, "but this couch is so disgusting."

And then we're both laughing.

She tells me that it doesn't matter how revolting the sofa is, she's sleeping on it for the foreseeable future. She says it in that tone she uses when she will not allow argument. I really don't want her sleeping here. As ugly as it is, the couch is even more uncomfortable. Plus my plan for the next couple of days (weeks, months) is to remain in that warm and thirsty space between drunk and hungover, until this dark week passes. Until it's time to pick up the envelopes and put them away.

But I don't argue with her. At thirty-four, Jeannie is five years older than I, and when I say she was my savior, that isn't a remnant of teen melodrama. When I was twelve, she was seventeen. She was an adult and I was a gut-shot wreck of a girl, a de facto orphan bleeding to death from the shrapnel of media infamy. I was tall, even then, and too clumsy to handle words like *ward of the state* and *your mother's trial*, so Jeannie took them for me. She threw her tiny, teenage frame in front of me, she opened the door of the so-cool teenage bedroom she was forced to share with her too-young cousin, and if it bothered her, she never, ever let me know.

So even though I don't want her to stay, nothing on earth would make me ask her to leave. Fortunately, I don't have to. My neighbors will take care of that.

We're at the bottom of the bottle of wine when the neighbors' evening commences. Tonight's performance begins with the music—a colon-rattling bass propping up some electronic dance music.

Jeannie jumps in her seat, spinning to face the wall behind her like the music heralded an emerging beast. "What the hell is that?"

"That is the soundtrack of my new life." I don't have to shout, but I'm tempted to. "To be fair, it's a nice change of pace from the howling and the fistfights. If you're really lucky, Katie and Bobby will be in the mood for some rough sex. She likes her hair pulled, he likes her finger in his ass. And they both like to talk about it. A lot. Loudly. Against that wall."

Jeannie's eyes are wide as she turns back to face me. "Have you knocked on the wall? Called the police?"

"Has it been that long since you lived near campus? Maybe I could save myself the trouble and just shove dog shit under my own door."

"Seriously, how long does this last?"

"I don't know. It's usually over when I get up."

"You can sleep through this?"

I nod. "Earplugs."

I see the fight leave her. She would do anything for me, we both know that. If I asked her, she would probably stick her own finger up Bobby's butt. But now she's seen me with her own eyes; I'm not bleeding or starving to death. I haven't slit my wrists. Among my sufficient well-being, the filthiness of the couch, and the promise of a long, loud evening, she finally surrenders and agrees to check in to the Days Inn at the bottom of the hill.

I promise to meet her after work tomorrow and I reassure her that I will be fine.

"Those must be some earplugs."

"Indeed."

When she's gone, I twist the cork off the corkscrew. Next door, Bobby's voice takes on that ugly edge that suggests tonight's main event will involve more fists than fingers. I can hear the girl, Katie, screaming back, and then something glass shatters against the floor. After all these fights, I wonder how and why they even keep anything glass over there.

I didn't lie to Jeannie. I do have earplugs I can count on. I bounce the freed cork in my palm. Here's one. Time to get the other. I reach for another bottle of red.

CHAPTER 2

I wake with a familiar jittery start. My lips feel like they're burning and my teeth hurt. I clench my teeth hard when I'm drunk and it feels like all of my fillings have been rubbed against aluminum foil. I'm wearing only underwear. My shirt is balled up at the foot of the bed and I nearly fall on my face as one foot gets caught in it and the other slides out on a magazine I've dropped. This near pratfall wakes me up faster than I care for.

It's still dark outside. I don't bother setting an alarm anymore. The sugar furnace that is my body blows a pretty shrill whistle when it needs attention, the alcohol burning hot enough to dry up every molecule of water in my system.

The funny thing is, I don't feel that bad. Maybe I'm just so used to feeling this way that it doesn't throw me. Really, if this is the worst I ever wind up feeling for the rest of my life, I can live with it. At least I didn't sleep in the tub again.

But it seems that might have been an option. In the bathroom, I find my jeans and my bra puddled up near the drain and my necklace looped over the stopper. I must have spent a little time in here last night; I must have let my thoughts wander. Probably seeing Jeannie, I tell myself. And today is the day. It's February 17. It's understandable.

. . . .

Cold water, a cold chicken leg, and cold morning air chase off the worst of the lingering horrors as I make my way down the hill toward campus. My head is blessedly clean, scrubbed, and sanitized, with nothing more pressing than keeping my feet stomping one after another down the hill. I stop as I do every morning at that hairpin turn on Everly and see Eastern Allegheny College open up below me and beyond that, the town of Gilead, then head down the hill, across campus, and up to the Jenkins Building.

The operative word is *up*. For a Midwesterner like me, the terrain of southern West Virginia took some getting used to. Everything is on a hill. Everything. These are old mountains; the folks who settled here liked being "a bit hard to reach" and so while Gilead proper might relax in its narrow stretch of bottomland, much of the town's living space is carved into the clay of the mountains. Eastern Allegheny College is no exception.

When I first walked the campus, it took my breath away. Literally. Everything was uphill—"both ways," my guide had joked. Stately brick collegiate buildings bear a distinctive antebellum feel—this used to be Virginia, after all—but these buildings cling to the mountainside. They're embedded, nestled, sometimes as deep as the second floor.

What this means is that most buildings have entrances on multiple floors. *Front door* and *back door* mean different things when one opens up from the central green and the other opens to an expanse of mountains and clouds that could stop your heart with their beauty.

I suppose I'm getting used to it. I don't stop every single time I step outside. Now I just gawk and sigh maybe seven or eight times a day. I split my youth between central Missouri and central Illinois. I spent my married life in Nebraska. Safe to say I am a mountain newbie. A gawker. A convert. Definitely a convert.

This is probably a large part of the reason my hangovers don't kill me. I don't have a car. I sold our car when I left Nebraska—too many bad memories, too many good ones. When I came for the interview, I was assured that the campus shuttle would run me to town whenever I needed. "Besides," the secretary said with a helpful smile, "you can always rent a car at the airport." She failed to mention that the closest airport was in Charleston, two hours away.

So I walk everywhere and yes, it feels like it's uphill most ways, but I like how that feels. I like the changes in my body, the new sturdiness of my legs, the expansion in my lungs.

I think of Ronnie when I walk. My husband would have loved these hills. He would have begged me to put down my book and put on my boots and join him. He would have teased me that flannel was for hiking, not just pajamas, and I probably would have resisted, laughing but unmovable. I would have stayed with my book and let him tell me about his hike.

But now I'm flannel-clad and hiking to work. I try to see the hillsides the way Ronnie would have. It hasn't really snowed yet, which I understand is practically unheard of for these mountains. It's also very bad news for the neighboring ski resorts who are now forced to make their own powder. It's bad news for me, too. From what I'm told, the snow in these mountains is epic, beautiful, changing the mood of campus in one blustery instant to that of a magical retreat. Instead, the lingering darkness and mud-soaking rains have made everyone grumpy and impatient.

Fortunately, flannel and hiking boots are perfectly acceptable attire on campus, even for staff. Fashion and I have always been strangers. I suppose there is some irony in that. I've spent my life among artists— my mother sculpted, my father painted and crafted musical instruments, and my husband wrote poetry. All of them and their friends and colleagues swore an oath to seek beauty in all its forms; beauty tormented them all, chased them, haunted them. And yet not one of them gave a lesser shit how they looked. Or how they dressed their children. Or what their wife wore on their wedding day.

I'm not an artist; I don't see with their eyes or feel pursued by the same hungers. I am, at heart, lazy, and so I naturally ride the path of least resistance, choosing jeans over skirts, long, straight ponytails over stylish cuts. I used to tell Ronnie that the only things I wore on my face were moisturizer and sarcasm. He said he loved it.

I don't dwell on this anymore. I know where those thoughts lead. Those are the thoughts and anxieties of young girls and artists. I know this because that's exactly who I spend my days working with.

The gray mat outside the maintenance door squishes under my boots. It's been soaking up rain on and off for a week but I'm careful to scrub my feet hard over its surface. Walter Voss, the head electrician and general hero of campus, lets me save a few steps and cut through the custodial offices that take up the basement of Jenkins Building, where my office is. Again, with the terrain, the "basement" is only half underground. The other half juts out from the tilted earth not far from the natural-gas station.

I'm not supposed to come in this way. I'm supposed to take the steep cement steps to the left of the maintenance door that lead up to the north entrance on the first floor, just off the staff parking lot. My first week on campus, Walter Voss caught me red-handed—and red-footed. I had tracked mud into his workspace. He stopped me and pointed out the proper entrance for staff. I played dumb—a tactic I'm not proud of utilizing as often as I do—and confessed to being a clueless Midwesterner and newcomer to the campus. I alternated between staring vacantly at him and longingly at the elevator that would take me to my office on the second floor, until he relented and told me to always wipe my feet.

"And keep your trap shut about using that door."

I like this shortcut, and not just for its efficiency. It makes me feel like an insider, like a member of a secret club. As far as I can tell, I'm the only non-maintenance person to use this path. Even Meredith uses the north entrance on the first floor.

Meredith Michener, my supervisor and office mate. Early fifties, strawberry-blond hair that pops up in the craziest directions at the slightest provocation, a fashion sense that even I question—Meredith looks like she walked out of Central Casting's call for "underpaid passion dragon." Her banner reads "Not for profit. I do it for love!"

Really, she has a banner over her desk with those words written in purple glitter.

If I had been on the fence about taking the job (I wasn't) or if I had the sort of qualifications that made employers fight over me (I don't), Meredith Michener would have sealed the deal in my decision. As it was, she wound up being a happy perk of being able to keep a roof over my head.

My title is Student Development Advocate. Meredith is Student Development Coordinator. Our offices are a floor above the English and Fine Arts Departments, whose students we serve. We have the kind of jobs anyone who works in a small private school is familiar with. Funding is limited; miles of red tape are spent for inches of real estate. Recruiting is challenging, so once a student signs up, the administration does all it can to keep them there.

On paper our jobs are coordinating opportunities for employment, external study, scholarships, and internships. In reality, the majority of my day is spent keeping the kids from dropping out of school, freaking out, and generally losing their shit. It's the sort of thing their advisor is technically supposed to handle but they know that if they go through me or Meredith, issues are far less likely to wind up on their student record or be reflected in their grades. We're like an unofficial administrative confessional.

I love my job.

I've been training for it my entire life.

Jeannie hesitated to tell me about the opening. She'd seen it on the newsletter she still receives even though she left EAC for Penn State. She knew I was perfectly qualified for the job—I'd held a similar position at a community college in Chattam, Nebraska. There, the art had been a little less "fine," the paperwork a little heavier, with far more state-funding pressure. But Ronnie had taught there and I had worked there, both of us doing what we could to help young artists beat their paths through the world.

Jeannie thought maybe I should take a new direction in my career, but really, what else did I know? Jeannie and I are both the daughters of professors. Neither of us has ever had a job that wasn't attached to a school in some way. This position specifically requested a familiarity with arts education; who would be more suited than I? Nobody on earth has more experience enduring the drama and anguish of young artists. I know the price art can exact from some souls; I also understand well the difference between the need for drama and the hunger for art. I can tell in one sitting which students pursue the demons and which are pursued.

It's fitting that today is Tuesday, or as the professors dub it, Dooms-day. It's the day students often receive their grades from the previous week as well as realize they are getting penalized for not completing the weekend work.

My first semester working here, Tuesdays meant a long day. Meredith would keep the office open past posted hours. Since we returned from Christmas break, however, she has cut short our availability, sometimes even closing early. She makes up a different reason each week. She claims she hasn't recovered from her holiday merrymaking, that her ears are too full of complaints, that all the stress gives her a rash.

I don't complain, and not because I don't like the work, or am in any hurry to get home, but because when Meredith closes early, she always manages to pull together some sort of delicious treat from the secret stashes she's set up. That chicken leg I grabbed for breakfast won't hold me over for long and I'm hoping that Snack Tuesday will become a tradition.

I don't see her yet but the office is open so I know Meredith has beaten me here. For all I know, she could be hiding somewhere. The mountain of material that fills our workspace defies explanation. It's not just file cabinets and paperwork. It's Rubbermaid tubs and clear plastic snap bins full of god only knows what. Meredith stores yarn, paint cans, even a toaster oven still in the box. Christmas wrap and craft paper are rolled up together behind toolboxes and huge jugs of Elmer's glue.

"Well, we are with the Fine Arts Department," she always says in defense.

I refrain from telling her that's not how art departments work or that it looks more like the craft corner for the criminally insane. I don't have to keep track of it or sort it out. I just have to step around it, so I keep my mouth shut.

Our building was built in the nineteenth century, upgraded not long after that. It retains all the wonderful qualities of old school craftsmanship—oak wainscoting, beveled-glass room dividers, wide-planked hardwood flooring. Unfortunately, it also retains its sixty-plus-year-old heating and cooling system. Even now, mid-February, you could brew tea on the radiator.

I drop my coat on the rack between the door and a bank of file cabinets stacked with cartons of colored folders. I squeeze through an obstacle course of boxes and tubs. Meredith's desk sits in the front of the office, surrounded by the majority of the clutter. My desk is at the far end of the room catty-corner to hers, sectioned off by the frosted-glass half-wall dividers that probably used to be frames in a door. For all I know, the doors are stashed away in here somewhere. As it is, with a little neck-craning, we can see each other when we want to. If we're busy or want privacy, there are plenty of tubs and cabinets to hide behind.

Nine a.m. The bells on the campus chapel ring, Meredith runs in right on cue, waving an insulated carafe of coffee in the air like the head of her enemy. Everything about her reads as motion—her hair, her drapey clothes, the constant flutter of her hands, the eruption of chaos within which she works. She calls to me in a sing-song tone.

"Good morning. It's Tuesday. I'm having my first hot flash of the morning and they're already coming up the stairs. Brace yourself. Midterm exam schedules have been posted."

And just like that, my day is underway, my office is crowded, and the last traces of my hangover are hammered away in the soothing and reassuring and paper-working of Eastern Allegheny College's contribution to the world.

At one o'clock, Meredith tapes a sign on the door alerting the students that even advocates need to eat lunch and that their troubles must keep for thirty minutes. She makes a show of turning the old bolt, locking us inside—or rather, locking the students out—and throwing her back against the door.

"It's a bad time of year for grandmas," she says darkly. "I had three."

"Surprisingly, I am dead-grandma-free so far." It's a weekly tally we keep, a number that shoots up sharply anytime exams are scheduled. What dead grandmas lack in originality, they make up for in sheer volume when it comes to excuses. I glance down at the notes on my blotter. "I have a new one, though—a dead goat. Sounded like a drunk hunter gone mad. I didn't look too closely at the picture. I'm not much for gore."

Studying me, Meredith cocks one brow.

"What?" An old anxiety rumbles deep in my gut—not rising, just reminding me.

Meredith clucks her tongue. "Nothing. It's just that with all your black hair and black clothes, you could pull off a Goth thing. We could add an occult flavor to our counseling."

I put my feet up on my desk and give a thoughtful nod. "True, but do we want to encourage blood sacrifices? I mean, they're already killing their grandmas left and right."

Someone knocks on the door. I laugh at Meredith's expression of rage. The frosted glass on the door only reveals a tall shape.

"Read the sign!" Meredith yells. "It's our lunch break."

"Let me in. It's my lunch break as well."

I roll my eyes at Meredith's look of comically bright surprise. We both recognize the voice. With an exaggerated fluttering of her eyelashes, she clutches her hands over her heart. "I'm rushing to the door as quickly as I can!"

Ellis Trachtenberg graces her with a cool nod as she waves him into the office. He only has eyes for me, which gives Meredith plenty of opportunity to pantomime swooning behind him, fanning herself. I hope it looks like I'm smiling, not laughing.

"I come bearing gifts." He holds up a paper-wrapped book. "Well, a gift."

What can I say? Thanks? You shouldn't have? I don't trust myself to make those words sound sincere, although I mean them, especially the last one. He really shouldn't have brought me a gift. I don't want it.

Ellis Trachtenberg is very, very attractive. Late-forties, tall—six-two, maybe taller. Slender with broad shoulders, dark brown hair graying just-so into that shade that should be trademarked "Naughty Professor." He's even got a large, slightly hooked nose, which is something I've always loved in a man. He's smart, too. Teaches art criticism, theory, history. He's written several academic books, he spearheads the lecture series for the college, and he even has a popular blog on art in the modern world.

Twice divorced, he's something of a rarity in college life—a handsome, available professor who does not sleep with his students. That's the rumor, at least, although I heard some folks in the Bursar's Office suspect he's just so good in bed, he convinces the girls (or boys) to keep their mouths shut. I don't think that's true. For one thing, that's almost impossible to do. For another, Ellis strikes me as an incredibly ethical man, perhaps even moral.

That's just one of the reasons I would never consider dating him. He doesn't come on too strong, but he has been coming on steadily. On the high road. We've met at staff mixers, lectures, student art shows. He likes to ask me questions about art and politics. He leads with his brain and plays down his looks and he acts like he would do the same with any woman he desired—he would choose her for her mind.

It's kind of a shame. If he just wanted to fuck me, I might let that happen. But Ellis Trachtenberg wants to know what I'm thinking; he wants to discuss how I feel, what I want, what I fear. He wants to really see me, in that way he wants to see art. He wants in my head and that is one place I will never let him be. Bed, yes. Head, no.

I've yet to find a socially acceptable way to explain that.

He holds up the package that is obviously a book. "You'll never guess what it is."

Meredith chimes in from across the room. "Did you bring her one of your books?"

"I'm trying to impress her, not bore her to death." His answer is as perfect as his smile—charming, self-effacing, humble, and sincere. It does nothing for me and I can see the thinnest flicker of doubt dart across his expression. For just a moment, he questions himself; he wonders why I don't respond appropriately, why I'm not following the laws of evolution and choosing him as a suitable mate. I think it goes that deep for Ellis Trachtenberg; he believes himself to be on the upswing of the curve of human development and he probably is. Unfortunately for him, I'm bringing up the rear and am content to do so.

He hands me the book and I free it from its plain, brown craftpaper wrapping. A very understated delivery. Nicely done. It's Herbert Mann's *The Eyes of God Turn*, an exploration of the impact of the 1918 flu epidemic on the German Nihilist Art Movement. The book weighs in at almost four hundred pages, a remarkable amount of verbiage for an art movement that lasted less than five years and produced no significant milestones.

"I think you might find this interesting." He starts to lean on my desk but catches himself in a charmingly embarrassed manner. "I saw this and thought of our discussion of Munsch and Brauer. I realize this is a little off field of that, but Mann brings up some challenging ideology. He draws some remarkable parallels that frankly surprised me."

"Wow, great." I thumb through the book as if I might see those parallels laid out for me. I notice he's marked up several passages with blue ink that I would just bet came from a fountain pen. Maybe he should have used a yellow highlighter to drive home the imagery of him pissing on the perimeter of these ideas, to let me know that he saw them first. I don't have the heart to tell him I've already read this book and disagreed with most of it. "It's going right on my to-be-read list."

"I hope it doesn't disappoint."

I'm not in the mood for this anymore. I never was, but I'm especially out of patience now. First of all, it's Tuesday. Tuesdays are hard enough. I soothe frazzled and nervous students. I don't feel like spending my lunch hour shoring up a grown man. And today? Today I have no care to spare. I have a head full of ghosts who need my attention. The conversation ends awkwardly as it dawns on him that I'm not adding any more to it. He mentions something about preparing for a lecture and makes a show of reminding Meredith about an internship at the Corcoran Gallery of Art. He drives the nail into his own exit when he informs her that the Corcoran is in Washington D.C.

"Thanks, I'm pretty sure I know where that is," Meredith says with a lot of teeth.

He gives a manly chuckle and raps his knuckles on her desk and then leaves. Meredith surprises me when I see her flip him off behind his back.

CHAPTER 3

Meredith is heating up something that smells like sausage. I don't hear the microwave running so I'm assuming she's using one of the toaster ovens or hot plates she's got stashed back in her cubbies of madness. I assume she has a refrigerator back there somewhere, too, although I've never seen it. Where else would one keep one's sausage during the workday? I hope she's planning on sharing whatever it is with me for Snack Tuesday because whatever she's making, it smells delicious.

Before I can ask, Karmen Bennett comes in, looking like the rough patch she's been going through is getting rougher. As a student, she focuses mainly on pottery and textiles so it's not unusual for her skin to be tinted with glazes and dyes, and the black eyeliner she slathers on doesn't brighten her face in any way, but those aren't the only things that darken her appearance. I've seen bruises and cuts, scrapes and burns that probably don't all come from art.

I don't speak as she settles herself into the chair across from my desk. It's a production. She carries layers of bags and satchels, lumpy with art supplies and who knows what else. She also dresses like she lives outside—layers and layers of flannel and cotton and scarves and jewelry. It's a look a lot of art students strive for with varying levels of success. Karmen wears it naturally. Once she's contained the landslide of baggage underneath her seat, she tucks one leg underneath her, pulls out a length of fine-gauge copper wire, and starts twisting it around her fingers. I've spent enough time with Karmen to know that she thinks better when her hands are occupied.

I don't rush her. I have a good idea why she's here—the Rising Tide Exhibition cutoff coming up next month—but I've also learned that things turn to shit with some regularity in Karmen's life. I can empathize.

"My second piece didn't happen." Each student is required to submit four pieces to qualify to even make it to the jury for the exhibition. Karmen is working on a series of ceramic sculptures incorporating scrap metal, glass, and fabric. I've seen her work. It's uneven but powerful. Her concept for the submission is strong but won't work without the series.

"The fist?" I think I remember the series in order—each piece represents part of a human body, ranked by their increasing ability to inflict pain. In immature hands, the concept would be melodramatic. Instinct tells me Karmen has earned the experience to bring some depth.

"No, the fist is first. Second is the foot."

"Oh right." I nod. "Kicking, huh? It does hurt."

"I was thinking more like leaving." She winds a length of the wire into a long coil. "Or not leaving."

Karmen is one of the few students from the immediate area. Her records say she still lives with her parents in Elkins, just a few miles away, although I doubt she actually spends much time there. Still, this is home for her, with all the baggage that word brings.

"What happened to it? The foot."

She curls her lip. "Ironically, I kicked it. It shattered. It was flawed."

"Can you fix it?"

She gives me a look I know so very well, the look of an artist talking to a civilian. It's one of the reasons I'm so valued at my job. I supply what other artists and art professors cannot—a complete absence of experience in the act of creation. I offer tiny moments of superiority to people otherwise battered by doubt, the chance to believe in the depths of their soul. "You'll never understand." It does wonders to settle their minds.

It's been said that artists thrive at the intersection of narcissism and self-loathing. My job is to keep them there, safe in the middle, balanced between the blades. I was born to it.

"Unless I want to submit it as a bag of dust with rusted nail heads, I think it's toast." My dumb question has done its work; it's made her admit out loud that the piece is lost and cannot be saved. Her choices now are to make a new one, go in a new direction, or quit. She doesn't want to quit and she knows she's going in the right direction and so she knows what she has to do. It's funny how we can complicate simple decisions. Sometimes all it takes for us to see things the proper way is for someone else to see them wrong.

"What can I do to help?"

She wants to requisition extra hours in the pottery room, something that can be tricky this time of year. I think I can pull it off. Worse comes to worst, I can beg Walter Voss to sneak Karmen in after hours. I would do it for Karmen; something about her makes me want to try a little harder. Something about her tells me that not a lot of people have.

I see her fight to hide a yawn and when she realizes she's been caught, she shakes her head. "I'm working a lot. Extra hours at the library and I took another shift at Ollie's. I need the cash if I'm going to be able to make tuition for next semester. I'm on tonight, four to close, and I'm working a double at the library tomorrow. That's why I had to get in today to see you. I tried to catch you yesterday but you were gone when I got off."

Cobbling together a schedule around college classes and college jobs is never easy. I grew up falling through the cracks of my parents' schedules. I remember my mother saying that people who worked nine-to-five jobs were as exotic to her as unicorns. I am now a unicorn.

The precedent has been set that I do not offer my cell or home number. Some administrators do; most of the advisors do. All of them complain about the nerve and drama of students demanding their attention in the off-hours, waving their loaded voice mailboxes around like badges of honor, like an emotional bankroll of value.

What they never talk about is how infrequently they take those calls; how many of those voice mails they don't answer. To me, it's crueler than not offering my number. When trouble rolls in, nothing escalates the pain like help that won't come.

I'm here now and Karmen knows it. I've come through for her before and even when I can't get her everything she's asked for, I've always tried. She knows that and she's the kind of kid who appreciates it. I recognize a kindred spirit. She begins the complicated process of gathering her belongings when she spies Ellis's book on the corner of my desk.

"Herbert Mann." She turns the book over, scanning the back. "I've heard of this book. Professor Trachtenberg was going on and on about it."

"It must be his passion du jour; he just lent me that."

She considers the book for a moment, her chin tucked down so I can't read her expression. She sets the book down carefully but doesn't manage to get it fully onto the desk. "You going to read it?"

"I already have."

"Good?" She hauls her bags onto her shoulder.

"Overrated."

She snorts a laugh. Not many people associate that word with anything from Ellis Trachtenberg. When she raises her palm to me—a mix of high-five and good-bye—I think she turns a little more abruptly than necessary. Her many bags swing out and catch the book, knocking it to the floor.

"Oops?" She looks back at me and now I snort.

"Leave it."

Karmen smiles and holds out her other hand, palm up. Seated there across an ink stain and a paper cut is a little figure made of copper wire.

She holds it out for me to take. I smile at the simplicity and expressiveness of the little form. I make out crossed legs and folded arms, even a long ponytail coiling down the wire back. It's me—a simple and fluid armature of me that she sculpted with no more effort than I would put into tying my shoelaces.

"I love it," I say, smiling at her through my likeness.

"S'nothing," she says as she heads out the door. I wonder if she understands the depth of her talent.

· · · · · · · · · · · · · · · · · · · ·

It's sausage dip I've been smelling, a creamy bowl of heart attack-inducing goodness that Meredith has been heating up in a freshly emerged Crock-Pot. She tells me we have to wait until four. I don't mind; I'm in no hurry to rush today along. There's a ton of paperwork, as always, phone calls to return, all squeezed in around the diminishing stream of students. Finally, four rolls around and Meredith makes a great show of shutting the office door. No sooner has she thrown the bolt than someone knocks.

I laugh at her stare of disbelief as she hauls the door open once more.

Jeannie peeks her head around the doorframe, sees me, and then smiles a little too brightly at Meredith. "Meredith, how nice to see you. I'm looking for Anna."

"Well, Professor Fitzhugh-Conroy, good to see you, too." Meredith stands aside and lets Jeannie push past her. She talks to my cousin's back. "I'm good. We're all good. The department is good. Busy. We love your cousin. Thank you for sending her to us. The students love her."

"Terrific," Jeannie says, still not listening as she sits in the chair across from me. She is the exact opposite of Karmen Bennett. Tiny, trim, neat, she takes up less than half the space the chair offers. Her posture alone makes the workspace around her seem even more disheveled.

Maybe there is something about this office or this job. Maybe I'm closer to Meredith's mountain of madness than I realized.

"I've been calling your cell all afternoon, Anna."

"I turn it off during office hours." I avoid sounding pious by not telling her the students come first. In my mind, cell phones are for emergencies and since Ronnie's death, I've worked to keep my life emergency-proof.

She keeps her voice low. "So what's the plan?"

I don't have a plan. I didn't know Jeannie would be here. My plan, such as it was, consisted of falling down into a deep, dark, wet hole. She must see this; Jeannie doesn't miss much. She gives me a reassuring nod.

"Meredith?" Her tone borders on saccharine. "I was kind of hoping I could steal my cousin for a little girl-time at Ollie's. Any chance her supervisor is totally awesome and cool and wouldn't mind if she sneaks away a little early?" I add pleading eyes to her request.

"How can I refuse faces like that?" She waves the spoon she's been using to stir the sausage dip, spattering the space around her with greasy bits. "Have a fabulous time. Get the fried pickles. Maybe they'll have some live music tonight."

"Oh god, I hope not," Jeannie groans as I turn off my computer and apply a dusting of order to my desk. "Just what we need, some angsty, talentless wannabe howling about his pain in hopes of getting laid." I laugh as she reaches down and pulls up the Mann book Karmen had knocked off earlier. "Do you need this?" When I just give a vague wave over my desk, she makes an impatient sound and holds the book out to me. "I'm an English professor. This is not an acceptable way to treat a book. Put it somewhere. Don't just leave it on the floor."

Meredith hollers from behind her desk. "Take care of it. That book was a gift!"

I wave my hands over the chaos. "Just put it somewhere. Anywhere." I head for the door and Jeannie follows me out, the smell of sausage wafting behind us.

. . . .

We take Jeannie's car to Ollie's at the bottom of the hill. We don't have to drive. As always, Jeannie wears high, uncomfortable-looking heels but I have no doubt she could and would walk every inch of campus without flinching. She wears her heels like hiking boots; I've even seen her move furniture in them. I'm six inches taller than her and wearing actual hiking boots and I still have to make an effort to keep stride with her through the parking lot.

Ollie's is one of two decent eateries in town. There are chain restaurants on the highway toward Elkins—Applebee's and Chili's and a Cracker Barrel—but Ollie's has a lot more going for it. For one, it's in town. Students can and do literally tumble down the hill from the green to land in the alley behind it. Plus they serve alcohol from a full bar with a decent wine list and a better beer selection. But it's their pepperoni rolls and fried pickles that make them legendary.

Jeannie knows all of this; the staff of EAC spends as much time here as the students. She's the one who told me about pepperoni rolls in the first place. They're a West Virginia favorite—not a calzone, not a sandwich, but a buttery, doughy, spicy ball of deliciousness served everywhere from restaurants to gas stations, each location with its own collection of ardent fans who will fight to claim theirs as the state's finest. I've yet to have a bad one.

"Look at all these craft beers." Jeannie scrutinizes the list. "Jeff would love these." Of course Jeannie's husband is into craft beers. I can see him hunkered down in his basement babying his own batch of hoppy spiced-pumpkin-coriander-honey Belgian pale lager. I must be close because the beer Jeannie orders has a name almost that complicated. I ask for the most regular Sam Adams they have and my cousin laughs.

"As much as you like to drink and you don't like craft beer? Higher alcohol content."

"Do you really think I need a more efficient vehicle for alcohol?" I see Karmen at the bar loading up a tray. She waves to me and says something to our waiter. I hope it's something about making sure the drinks keep coming.

"So tell me who sent you the book." Jeannie leans in over the table.

"First tell me what's the deal with you and Meredith." She tries to play innocent but I shake my head. "I know that 'So nice to see you, too, bitch' tone of yours."

"Oh please, I only vaguely remember her." She leans back to make room for our waiter to set down the beers. "She used to hang out at the faculty functions. Like, all of them. Even the ones that were just for actual faculty. Ellis used to call her 'the cub reporter' because she was always asking questions about everyone and everything. Nosy biddy."

"Ellis Trachtenberg?" She nods until I tell her, "That's who gave me the book."

Jeannie and I have known each other for most of our lives. She's always been polished but I knew her before she had perfected her poise. This means I can see cracks in it that others might miss and I know that that little twitch on the left side of her mouth means she's irritated. And I bet I know why.

Of all of Jeannie's many good qualities, sexual fidelity does not make the list. She's been married to Jeff Conroy twice for a total of nine years and I doubt she's gone one of those years without a side piece. Maybe that's an exaggeration but I wouldn't want to put money on her having strung many faithful years together.

I don't know how much Jeff knows about it; Jeannie dismisses the issue with a regal flick of her hand anytime I ask. I don't care. I'm not married to her. She's always been a loyal and caring friend to me and that's all I've ever worried about. And considering the gene pool from which we sprang and the morality espoused therein, infidelity doesn't even take the bronze. Hell, substance abuse barely gets me a seat at the table.

She gives an exhausted sigh. "Tell me you're not sleeping with him."

In that moment, I am doubly glad I'm not attracted to Ellis Trachtenberg. What would that have been like, to discover Jeannie and I had slept with the same man? Besides being completely against my personal code (Hos before bros? Chicks before dicks?), I don't doubt that it would have pierced me with self-doubt to my very core. I place my cousin in a higher category than myself in every way—she's smarter, prettier, sexier, savvier. To think that any man might also compare my intimate performance against her much more seasoned one? Terrifying.

I shake my head, realizing that answering this question comes with its own perils. If I say the adult equivalent of "Ew, no, gross!" I'm insulting someone she thought enough of to sleep with. Just because that list isn't exclusive doesn't mean it's not an expression of her taste. I decide to stick with my go-to response—playing dumb.

"I don't think he's hitting on me. He just lent me a book."

She levels a "You've got to be kidding" look at me. "He's hitting on you. He's a professor and he gave you a book. It's never just a book."

"Well, even if he decided to hit on me, now that I know about your past with him, I would never consider it."

She raises her glass. "Sisters before misters!"

Even her aphorisms are better than mine.

Karmen waits until we take our celebratory drink before stepping up to the table. "Ms. Ray?" She's different here at Ollie's, less sullen, almost docile. She must really need the tips. "I don't mean to interrupt you, but could I ask a favor?" I nod and she glances at Jeannie with what looks like embarrassment. "Could I borrow that book?"

"Which one?"

"The Herbert Mann book, about the Nihilism movement."

"That Professor Trachtenberg gave me? Sure, but I'll warn you, it's not much of a read."

Karmen sighs. "I know but I need to come up with a topic for next month's paper and I'm thinking that might be an interesting one." As we talk, Jeannie pulls out her phone and busies herself, but I know she's listening. "I thought I'd just check it out," Karmen says. "I mean, the topic. That book isn't in the library."

"Probably because it's not much more than a pretentious four hundred-page hand job." She laughs harder at my joke than it deserves. "Let me guess. This paper is for Professor Trachtenberg's class. You know he's into it; it's a nice way to curry a little favor?"

"Yeah." The admission embarrasses her and I wish I hadn't spelled it out like that. "I'm still in the doghouse with Trachtenberg. I could use a bump."

Either Jeannie is reading something hilarious on her phone or Karmen's words strike a chord with her because I can hear her bitten-back chuckle over the bar's music. No doubt Karmen can as well.

"Yeah, of course," I say. "No problem." Karmen's embarrassment bothers me. "Just run by the office tomorrow."

"Um, is there any way I could get it tonight? Is Mrs. Michener still there? It's just that I may be getting off early tonight and I'll actually have some real time to read it. I could just text my boyfriend to run by and get it before Mrs. Michener leaves. He's, um . . ." She waves over her shoulder toward the bar as if that will explain something. I've never met her boyfriend and the little she's told me about him doesn't suggest he would be helpful in any sort of endeavor, much less a campus favor on a cold afternoon, but that's not for me to decide.

"Sure, just tell him it's in my office. It's—wait." I tap the table to get Jeannie's attention. "Where did you put the book?"

"Huh?" She looks up from her phone with a smile. Nice try.

"The book. Where did you put the book?" She keeps up the wide-eyed stare but this is one area in which she can't compete with me. She doesn't play dumb very well. "The book that Ellis lent me. You picked it up before we left. Where did you put it?"

"Oh, uh, I think, your desk? Or no, maybe that thing with the things on it, the boxes of whatever those blue things were. You know, by the glass partition."

"Mrs. Michener will know," I tell Karmen. "She knows what book you're looking for."

"Thanks, I promise I'll bring it back in one piece." She's walking away and texting her boyfriend before I can say anything else. By remarkable coincidence, whatever Jeannie has been busy with on her phone has conveniently wrapped up at just that moment and she smirks at Karmen's back.

"I guess it doesn't matter how big the school, brown-nosing is everyone's major."

I prefer my beer over her tone and I take a deep drink. "She's a good kid. She could probably use a break. She's pretty talented."

"Yeah, but which talents is she planning on utilizing?" Before I voice my protest, Jeannie holds up her hand in surrender. "I'm just saying she's barking up the wrong tree. Ellis has his faults but he does not sleep with students. She's going to have to get her grades up another way, because that is a line he will not cross."

"Of course not," I say, "he's too busy ethically sleeping with married women." She glares at me. I laugh. "Don't tell me he didn't know you were married, Professor Fitzhugh-Conroy. Lah-tee-dah."

"How many times do I have to tell you? It is my professional name."

I would snort but I've just gulped a large mouthful of beer. As I swallow, it occurs to me that I didn't have any of Meredith's sausage dip, my food hasn't come yet, and all I've eaten today is a cold chicken leg. The waiter catches my eye, noticing my less-than-half-full glass, and gives me the universal gesture of love that asks "Want another?" I nod and he's on it.

This isn't my first visit to Ollie's.

This also isn't my first drink with Jeannie and we know each other well enough to sidestep each other's little aggressions. I can diffuse Jeannie's tendency to lecture and smother; she knows how to maneuver around my early-buzz aggressions. I'll take a few more jabs at what I see as an affectation—Professor Fitzhugh-Conroy is not just pretentious-sounding and difficult to pronounce, it's also kind of funny when you know my cousin's predilection for infidelity. It's a little irritation but Jeannie brings so few with her that the ones I notice stick out. Especially when I'm drinking.

She's forgiven me my jab and is telling me about what transpired between her and Trachtenberg. Okay, this is another thing about Jeannie that does irk me—her tendency to over-discuss her relationship issues, even if said relationship lasted just a weekend. She has a teenager's need to over-analyze every nuance of her interactions with men to the point where I sometimes expect her to pull out a glitter pen and start practicing her married signature.

I'm feeling like a bitch because I'm hungry and that hunger has reached that well-known point where it will either be sated or drunk away with a steady application of booze. I can't really go with option two, or I shouldn't, since I'm in public and I'm with Jeannie. On the other hand, it's February 17. This is a week dedicated to blackout drinking. Jeannie's on a tear of her own, regaling me with issues that doomed her relationship with Trachtenberg, which sound to me like so much high school drama. He was clingy, too serious; he wanted more; he couldn't keep up with her in bed.

All of these issues have one significant similarity—Jeannie is always on the best side of them. Just once I would love to hear her say something like "I think I bored him," or "He wanted someone hotter in bed." But of course she won't. Who would? Even if it were true, nobody likes to tell bad stories about themselves, stories in which they were found to be lacking.

I certainly don't.

Pepperoni rolls arrive along with a basket of fried pickles. So does my next beer and the waiter waits for me to finish the glass in my hand. I swallow and hand it to him.

"Thanks for taking that away," I say solemnly. "I wouldn't want people to think I drink."

CHAPTER 4

Springfield, Illinois
2012
Jeannie Fitzhugh-Conroy, 31 years old
Anna Shuler, 26 years old

"Do you realize that you're twirling your hair?"

"I am not!" Anna jerked her hand away from the piece of ponytail she had wrapped around her index finger. She failed at holding back her grin. "Maybe I'm twirling it a little."

"Oh my god!" Jeannie leaned across the table on her elbows, "Tell me every single thing. Spare no details. Oh my god, tell me it's not Kevin. It's not, is it? I mean if it is, obviously, I'm going to back you up, but oh god, if I have to sit through another one of his short films about the burden of mediocrity chafing his delicate soul, uuugh." She dropped her head back and whispered to the sky. "He is such a pretentious dick!"

When she looked back down, her cousin wasn't smiling.

"Kevin asked me to marry him. I said yes."

Jeannie froze, searching for an impossible solution to unsay her tirade. Anna didn't blink. Fully prepared to throw herself on the knife, Jeannie sighed—and Anna laughed.

"How could you possibly think for even a second that I would marry Kevin? Being a pretentious dick is his best quality!" Jeannie buried her face in her hands as Anna ranted around her laugh. "Do you really think I would marry a guy who made me take a shower before we had sex every single time? He has fourteen hand towels in his bathroom. Fourteen! He refuses to eat cheese of any kind and he insists that Goethe was pronounced 'Geth.' The man collects can openers and you thought I would marry him?"

"You slept with him!" Jeannie protested, grinning. "Be honest. The cheese was the deal breaker, wasn't it?"

Anna nodded solemnly. "It was. I had to draw the line somewhere."

"Well thank god you saw the light." She tapped her wine glass against her cousin's. "Now let's get to the good stuff. Who is he?"

Anna smiled down into her glass. She looked different since Jeannie's visit last February. She looked healthy; she looked happy. She looked like she was in love.

"His name is Ron. Ron Ray."

"Ron Ray?" Jeannie swirled her wine. "Sounds like a super hero. Or a porn star. Or is that the same thing?" When Anna giggled—an honest to god giggle—Jeannie knew this was different. Her cousin wasn't going to pass this one off as a meaningless hookup or dismiss him with her "slightly better than a vibrator" shtick. "What's he like?"

Anna finally looked up from her wine and smiled. "He's nice."

Something loosened in Jeannie's chest, something she'd held clenched for so long. Anna had always preferred difficult men. She called them complex; Jeannie found them troubled at best. Painters, sculptors, musicians—it didn't matter their medium. Anna gravitated toward men who would bully her with their art, talking over her, talking down to her.

Jeannie never understood the attraction or the dynamic. Her cousin would hook up with these men, put up with their shit, but for no apparent reason. She never claimed to be in love. She rarely even approved of their art, secretly judging them with her often more educated viewpoint, but she never let them know. She saved her eye rolls for private discussions with Jeannie and hardly seemed to notice when one man left and another rolled in.

Not once had she described any of them as nice.

And she had certainly never twirled her hair while saying it.

"Go on," Jeannie coaxed. She didn't want to push, but hope bubbled up inside of her. "What does he do for a living?"

"He's a high school English teacher." Anna kept smiling. "I knew you'd like that."

"You know I do." Jeannie wanted to hug Anna, to thank her for not picking another sculptor or director or social-protest graffiti artist. That she'd chosen someone in the same field as Jeannie, well, that touched her. And not to sound like a snob, but that he taught on a lower level than she did made the likelihood of pretentiousness wither. "I can't wait to meet him."

Anna grinned and shifted in her seat, like the idea of all this happiness made her uncomfortable. "Good. He's meeting us here for dinner when he's done at the school. He has to monitor detention this week."

"How cute!" Jeannie knew she gushed and didn't care. Teaching high school, grading papers, monitoring detention—all such gloriously normal and stable ways to spend a day. She could already picture Anna sitting with him in the bleachers, cheering on the varsity basketball team or helping him organize car washes. They could vacation together over summer break.

If nothing else, maybe finally Jeannie wouldn't dread setting an extra place at the table for Anna's date.

She knew she was getting carried away and didn't care. Anna was happy so Jeannie was happy. Then Anna dimmed her daydream.

"He's also a poet. A good one."

Jeannie ran some quick calculations. A poet with a normal full-time job probably trumped an angry welder-slash-bartender or unemployed indie director, right? She thought she hid her concern until Anna's smile slipped.

"What?"

"What?" Jeannie asked, going for innocent. "He sounds great."

Anna didn't fall for it. Jeannie had never hidden her opinions of Anna's choices. "He's actually talented. He's not a pretentious dick. He's a very nice man who happens to be talented, okay? You'll see when you meet him, okay? He's different. He's funny and he's nice and he makes me laugh. And he also writes poetry that is occasionally amazing. Okay?"

"Okay," Jeannie said. "Okay. I will trust you on this. I can't wait to meet him. Really. But you know"—she winked at Anna, trying to lighten the mood—"all poets are nuts. You know that. They are crazier than a bag of bees; it's been scientifically proven."

"Thanks for the warning. I'd hate to bring any kind of mental illness into the family."

Anna finished her wine and reached for the bottle. Jeannie knew this place with her cousin, this familiar territory that could turn into a fight or a cold front if either of them chose to go too far. A sarcastic jab or a well-worded criticism could do it. Each knew the weaknesses in the other's stronghold. They loved each other but sometimes that love felt like mutually assured destruction. Jeannie recognized it; Anna must as well. It was the same dynamic their mothers shared.

The moment passed as it always did. Anna poured them both more wine, punctuating the change of tone. Mental illness didn't make a great conversation starter.

"Have you heard from your mother?" Jeannie resisted the petty urge to start that question with "speaking of which."

"Of course." Anna nodded. "The Natalie Shuler Library of Unopened Letters continues to grow. I wish your mother would stop giving her my address every time I move."

"I gave it to her." Jeannie didn't flinch at Anna's hard stare. "She's your mother, Anna. Not getting mail from her is not going to change that."

"Again, thanks for the great advice."

"Are you ever going to read them? Or are you just going to keep boxing them up and carting them around?" Just because she wanted to avoid a full-on holocaust didn't mean Jeannie could or would resist needling the occasional soft spot. Sometimes the temptation to go too far sang a sweet song.

. . . .

I wake up in the tub.

This is as uncomfortable as it sounds. I took off my pants at some point; they're turned inside out and jammed into the corner behind the door, one hiking boot still trapped in a pant leg. That must have been pretty to see. The fact that I'm freezing accounts for at least half of the jerky shakes that wrack my body. The bath towel I apparently thought would keep me warm and comfortable has done neither. Instead its creases have dug into my hip and ass and feel like they've been grafted to my skin. My bra is unhooked beneath my shirts and when I finally pull myself up into sitting position, I have the sensation of my body collapsing beneath my clothes.

Items clatter at my feet. I try to ignore the sharp spikes of pain that shoot down my neck. I have a bruise at the base of my skull from bracing it on the edge of the tub. I know how much that will hurt in the days to come; I know how long that bruise will last.

My toothbrush is in here with me as well as an open tube of toothpaste that has smeared its contents under the drain plug. At least I had the foresight to bring a plastic tumbler along with me, rather than glass. I've made that mistake before. Glass cups and ceramic tubs do not make good bedfellows. I sniff the plastic tumbler to make sure there is no booze in it—another mistake I've made before—and when I smell nothing, I fill it from the spigot. Drunk Me can be very considerate this way, anticipating my thirst.

The water cramps my stomach and does little to put out the fire in my mouth. My teeth feel loose from being ground so hard and a little voice inside my head warns me that one of these days I'm going to break them and lose them.

I slam another glass. I won't throw up. I never do, not since I stopped drinking whiskey. Now I stick to beer and wine. Like some psychic investigator, Sober Me performs a hands-on examination of Drunk Me's energy field, piecing together the events that brought me to this tub.

Wine. Wine after beer. What's that old saying? Beer then wine, feeling fine. Well, that's bullshit. I don't know what time Jeannie and I got back here. We were in that sober-drunk stage, that level of performance that requires years of functional alcoholism to attain. It rests somewhere in between being able to handle your liquor and being intoxicated so frequently in public that people don't recognize it as drunk anymore. If we had called it a night then, I probably would have woken up in my bed with a light thirst.

As if.

Instead, we came home and opened a bottle of wine. After lots and lots of beers. Not because we don't know when to say when (well, not entirely because of that). No, we decided to open a bottle of wine because it was February 17. That's why Jeannie is here. That's why I'm in the tub. That's why I do stupid things like deciding to check my mailbox before we came up the steps. It's almost like I want to see what's in there.

Did I get letters from Mom? Probably. I don't remember. I don't actually remember getting the mail for that matter but I must have, because I have a piece of it in the tub with me. It's stuck to the back of my knee and is covered with thick splatters of toothpaste, which tells the thirsty Sherlock Holmes in my brain that this is probably what made me decide to sleep in the tub again. The envelope is here, too, badly torn.

It's been forwarded. Fuck, how long is the post office going to honor that forwarding request? Isn't there a statute of limitations on that sort of thing?

It's the newsletter. The Shuler Family Newsletter.

My family. Well, my father's family.

Through the red and blue spattering of toothpaste I see faces smiling back at me, faces that look like mine. "You look like a Shuler," my mom used to say in a way that didn't always feel like a compliment. But I do look like a Shuler. I have their dark hair, ruddy complexion, black eyes. I'm tall like the Shulers and I have their good teeth. I think I look a lot like my uncle. I used to, at least. I haven't seen him in years.

Who keeps me on this list? Who decided that I should get this newsletter and what is their intention? Is it a melancholy reach across a divide that can't be bridged? Is it a passive-aggressive way of reminding me of the other set of genes I carry? Or is it just an oversight? Did someone just forget to delete me from the database and thus subject me to this annual recounting of the loving family, the growing and evolving family I'll never be a part of again?

God, it almost makes me want to drink right now. I would. I could. I have. But I know that doesn't make this any better. Not that I'm ever looking to make things better. I think I'm mostly just looking to keep bad things at a manageable distance. I consider plugging the tub and filling it, soaking in it before I come to my senses. I grab the towel beneath me; it's dry. I didn't soak last night, either. Well, not on the outside at least.

I have to get to work. I sit as cross-legged as I can manage in the narrow tub, run my toothbrush under the spigot and scrape a gob of toothpaste off the side of the tub. That should seem grosser than it does but once the cool mint hits my inflamed mouth, I don't care. I rest my forehead against the faucet and scrub at my teeth. I don't want my eyes to come into focus but of course they do.

"The world may celebrate love on February 14, but we Shulers celebrate the power of love and remembrance on February 17. It's the day we learned that nothing can truly stop a—"

The rest of the headline vanishes under smeared toothpaste. It doesn't matter. I've read that line every year for almost twenty years. I've had almost two decades to absorb the message that nothing, not even death, can keep someone from loving and being loved. Nothing can keep the Shuler clan from loving their son, brother, uncle, David. He's the reason they put their newsletter out in February, rather than in their Christmas cards. He's the reason they send the newsletter out at all, to remind the world that they love their son, that he's still a part of their family.

Unlike me.

Stiff muscles and bruised skull aside, I'm glad I read the newsletter last night. I'm glad I was already many drinks in when I read it; it muffles the bony fist of it under the numbness of a regular hangover. If I had just come home and found that waiting for me? Well, I still would have gotten destroyed, but I would have gotten rage drunk. Or worse, weepy drunk. Every drop of wine would have tasted like tears and loneliness, and I've had enough of that.

It's so quiet in the bathroom. Did Jeannie pass out on my couch? Did my neighbors have a big night? I didn't hear them. That doesn't mean much, but I can't recall any bursts of rage in the fog of my memory. If last night had hurt enough to be a tub night, I would have been looking for anything to divert me from the pain. It's a wonder I haven't gone over there and kicked someone's ass yet.

Of course, this is my first February here.

It's so quiet, distractingly quiet. I cock my head listening for the usual noises. Aside from my neighbors, the apartment complex is not very noisy, but usually in the mornings I can hear traffic on the road in front, birds calling, ambient noise of humans getting their day started. Today I hear nothing. For just a second I wonder if I've gone deaf and then I wonder if that would be a bad thing. But that thought doesn't go anywhere. I hear myself moving inside the tub.

Rising stiffly—I'm really too old to be sleeping anywhere but in a good bed—I lurch out of the tub, out of the bathroom, and move as quietly as possible into my living room. It just feels different. Everything is where it should be, more or less. A wine bottle lies on its side. We had Fritos, apparently—they're spilled across the coffee table. The lamp beside the couch is knocked over but that's not unusual. I always bump it, even when I'm sober. The couch is empty. I hear a soft snore coming from the back of the apartment. Jeannie must have taken my bed.

The overhead light is off but the room is illuminated. Not brightly but brighter than usual. And it's so quiet. It takes me several minutes of staring and wondering before I see what's different.

It's snowing.

I step to the window in the kitchen, wide-eyed. The light off the snow is a luminous gray-blue. It's snowing hard and from the undisturbed drifts over the parking lot below it looks like it's been snowing all night. That's why it's so quiet. A blanket has been thrown over the world.

A quick glance at the clock lets me know that the blanket also muffled my internal alarm clock. It's nine-thirty and I'm late for work. I hate to look away from the snow for even a second, but I run to get dressed. I can't wait to walk in this snow. I can't wait to see the views from the hillsides and from the Jenkins Building.

In less than ten minutes, I bundle up without waking Jeannie and now I'm slogging through the powder. My boots are new and warm, white Snowlions that tie below my knees and are guaranteed to keep me warm down to minus forty. Tights under my jeans and thermal underwear under my shirts, all buried underneath a coat, scarf, hat, and mittens, makes me feel like I'm six again and my mother has bundled me up to go sledding. I feel like my arms should stick out to the sides and I should waddle but I'm a lot taller than I was at six. I'm better at all these clothes. But still, I smile at the feel of it. It's nice to lose myself in a good memory for once.

I fall twice on the way to campus and I don't care. All around me, people are laughing and sliding, trying unsuccessfully to make snowballs with the powder. The flakes are fat and gorgeous, falling like fabric all around me, and I can only catch glimpses of the mountainsides in the distance through the clouds and the snow. This isn't a Midwestern snowstorm. The wind doesn't howl like a tortured soul, like a demon that's coming for you. It's blowing the snow everywhere but the mountains break up its strength, distract it from tearing us all to pieces. The wind seems to play with the snow and even though my eyes are watering and my cheeks are chapped, I can't stop smiling.

I don't even cut through the maintenance room to get to my office. Instead, I haul myself up the concrete steps, kicking off drifts of snow as I go. When I turn the corner to climb up the steps to the front door, the storm pauses. The snow slows for just a moment and I can see out all the way into the valley. I need a bigger word for beautiful. Snowflakes blow into my gaping mouth as the wind picks back up, the snow comes back down, and the view is obscured.

It doesn't matter. I saw it. Everything is better now.

On the second floor, Meredith meets me in the hallway, waving her arms as she does, shooing me back toward the stairs. She yells at me, telling me that my penalty for being an hour late is to take a plastic bag full of books back to the library. She's not mad, I can tell, and she probably would have asked me to take them back even if I'd been on time. She's in house shoes; she's probably stripped off all her outer gear already and doesn't want to put it back on.

I don't even pretend to complain. She doesn't bother to scold me any further, she just shoves the bag into my bundled up arms, and pushes me into the stairwell.

I'm getting better at the snow and only slip once going down the outside stairs but catch myself without even spilling the books. This makes me feel proud, like I'm finally becoming a West Virginian, a mountain-dweller. I wave to Walter Voss, who is coordinating the maintenance crew's shoveling duties. He waves back with his shovel. I suspect it will be a while before they start their work. It would be madness to try to stay ahead of snow like this.

Even here, in the middle of campus with students running and laughing in the snow, silence rules. The snow muffles all but the most extreme sounds—a diesel truck, a high-pitched squeal—and the soft light makes the whole campus look like a dreamscape. I have to push the library doors hard to open them over the black mats that have been put down from the entrance all the way to the circulation desk. Eastern Allegheny College is no stranger to snow. They're prepared to keep the library from being flooded by wet boots.

I shake the snow off the bag. It has piled up on the creases and I scoop what I can off the books that stick out the top. The girl at the desk waves me over, a towel ready to dry off anything that enters. She laughs and tells me not to worry, that she doubts she'll have much work today. It's nice to see I'm not the only one grinning at the weather.

The snow seems to be letting up a bit as I head back to Jenkins. Sounds seem a little clearer—snow blowers and car wheels spinning. I hear a lot of laughter. The sun is trying to break through the heavy clouds and there are intermittent rainbows where it hits the snow just right. I'm going to regret not wearing sunglasses but I don't care. For now the world is gray and blue and white, with bright shots of red brick and green pine. I tip my head back and let the snow fall over my face.

I feel dizzy with the sensation and from looking up into the falling flakes. I shake my head hard, shivering at the snow that slips past my scarf and collar. I could stand here all day.

It's February 18 and the world is completely new.

I laugh when I realize I've stepped off the path and the snow is almost up to my knees. I turn the corner at the student center and the wind gusts up from the valley below, momentarily blinding me with blown snow. I blink it away and stop.

The light is different here. The blue-gray fog is broken, not by brick and spruce but by a sharp, pulsing blue and red. Blue and red. Bright, blinding.

Police lights.

I know what the cop's radio will sound like before I get close enough to hear it. People are talking, gathered in a cluster around the maintenance door at the basement. Sirens sound from over the hill. More cops are showing up. They never come one at a time. They're like starlings; they move in thick, black flocks with lots and lots of noise.

My hangover reemerges with a sour taste in my mouth as I keep trudging closer. Probably a break-in, I tell myself over a voice deep within me whispering something much different. An accident. Someone fell down the stairs or sledded into the building. Someone vandalized the Jenkins Building or someone's car slid off the road and down the embankment. There are plenty of reasons cops would have their lights on. Fewer that they would use their sirens, but I can think of some.

Someone must have been hurt. It must have been an accident. The words roll through my mind as I watch people huddle together, some crying, some hugging, all eyes glued to the maintenance door. College kids are so dramatic. Always weeping. And cops, oh, cops love to turn everything into a fucking scene. I'm shaking my head, willing myself to become annoyed at what is surely an exaggeration of drama for an unimportant event.

A student holds his arm out to stop my planned march through the scene. Cop radios are blaring as two more patrol cars pull up on the parking lot. Everyone's yelling at everyone else to stay back and I really don't have time for this.

"You can't go in there," the kid says, all lit up with the excitement of whatever this bullshit is. "They're closing the whole building. It's a crime scene."

No shit, kid. Anyone could see that. The red and blue flashing lights are a huge giveaway. So is the yellow tape that the cop is stringing from the corner of the building to the edge of the crowd. The urge to lie down and close my eyes is almost more than I can resist and I already know what the kid is going to say happened here. He's dying to tell me. He's dying for me to ask but I already know. I know why they use that tape, why they move so quickly. They don't move like that for vandalism. They don't tape off accident scenes that quickly or into that big of a space. Nope, I know this drill. I know what I'm seeing.

Someone has been murdered.

I've seen it before.

CHAPTER 5

Collins, Illinois
February 1998
Jeannie Fitzhugh, 17 years old
Anna Shuler, 12 years old

This was serious.

Jeannie didn't know exactly what this was but she knew it was serious. At first she thought it was Iggy. Her brother had just gone back to college and Mom and Dad always made a big thing about him not getting in trouble, not forgetting to pay his rent and all that. But this was different. Mom had been on the phone all day. Like, *all* day. And not just one call. Jeannie had heard her more than once say, "She's going to have to call you back."

That meant Jeannie was missing calls and that was so irritating. She was supposed to be meeting Leighanne at the arena for practice. The regionals were coming up, and Mom knew how important those were to her but Jeannie knew this wasn't the time to bitch about it. It wasn't just the phone calls, either. It was the quiet around the phone calls, the way the air felt charged and hushed at the same time, like everything in the house was holding its breath.

Mom and Dad were not fighting in that really deliberate way that meant both of them wanted to freak out on the other one, like when they got lost driving to Montreal last summer. Jeannie and Iggy had sat in the back seat, pressed into silence by the weight of the unshouted words in the front seat. Mom's white lips and Dad's great sighs eventually made Jeannie crack up, and then Mom laughed and all the tension disintegrated.

This wasn't like that.

When she heard her mother raise her voice behind the closed door and hiss "Because she's my sister," Jeannie understood that they were at a whole new level of complicated.

She busied herself in the kitchen making brownies so that she could stay out of the way and keep an ear tuned for what exactly was going on. Aunt Natalie was always good for some serious drama. The door to Dad's office opened and closed a couple of times and Jeannie could hear the door to the crawlspace opening. That's where the suitcases were. Holy cow, how serious was this?

Mom came into the kitchen first, Dad right behind her. He didn't look at her, instead concentrating on putting money inside an envelope. Dad loved organizing things in envelopes. Mom gripped the counter, watching Jeannie stir the brownies that were already mixed. Jeannie didn't care if the brown goo burst into flames, she didn't think she could stop stirring.

"Jeannie, honey, your father and I have to go out of town for a few days. We have to go to Bakerton. To Aunt Natalie's."

Jeannie nodded. "Is she okay? Is it about Uncle David?"

Bull's-eye. Mom's eyes widened and Dad stared at the envelope in his hands so hard it looked like he was trying to make it levitate. Ever since Uncle David left Aunt Natalie last winter, the drama had been building.

"Everyone is fine." Mom-voice. "But something very complicated has happened and . . ." Her voice broke and Jeannie felt her stomach flip-flop. Whatever this was, it was DEFCON 4, for sure. It was serious enough that they were going to leave her alone in the middle of a school week. They were leaving her cash and it didn't look like they were even going to bring up checking in with Mrs. Carnahan across the street. They hadn't even warned her not to have a party.

Jeannie's mom came around the kitchen island and didn't wait for Jeannie to put the gooey spoon down. She hugged her daughter tightly and whispered, "I love you so much."

. . . .

Aunt Natalie had been arrested. Mom told her when she called from Bakerton but she wouldn't say what the crime was. Mom called every day, and every day she sounded a little wearier. The situation went from being "a big misunderstanding" to "a huge mess" to "a very serious situation." On the fourth day, she called to tell Jeannie they were bringing her cousin Anna to stay with them "while this gets sorted out." She asked Jeannie to clean out a few drawers in her room for her young cousin, saying she knew how inconvenient it all was but that it was really important.

When they got back home the next evening, Jeannie was glad she hadn't argued with her mom over this. Her parents looked exhausted; she'd never seen her mom's eyes so red even though she smiled a lot as she petted and fussed over her cousin. Jeannie hadn't seen Anna in over a year. She'd gotten a lot taller—she was almost as tall as Jeannie— and she'd always had that big-eyed look about her. Now, however, as Jeannie's mom took her coat and put down her suitcase, she looked like she had no idea what was happening.

Whatever was going on here, it was a disaster. Dad looked like he'd been hit by a car; Mom looked ten years older. Anna couldn't have looked more like an abandoned puppy. Jeannie, on the other hand, was an honor-roll junior, leading point guard for the Lady Generals, seventeen years old and ready to prove to her parents that she was worth the trust they were placing in her. Jeannie Fitzhugh was a young woman people could count on. She knew just what to do.

"Anna!" Big smile, big hug. She could imagine the long, long days of dour faces and weepy eyes Anna had been lost among. Her mother had been arrested for who knew what—drunk driving? Drugs? Hard to say with Aunt Natalie. And if Uncle David had been involved, that would have just compounded the situation. Well, Jeannie couldn't do anything about that but she could definitely do something about the lost twelve-year-old girl in front of her.

"You've gotten so tall!" She held Anna out at arm's length. "And your hair is so cute!" A total lie. Had nobody thought to brush her cousin's hair? Ever? It didn't matter. Anna's big brown eyes locked onto Jeannie's face, her whole body leaning into the attention being lavished upon her. "C'mon back and see our room. This is the best timing because I just took down all my posters and I'm doing a serious purge. My friend Leighanne and I have been arguing, like, forever over what goes back up. You can be the deciding vote. What are you listening to? Please don't say the Spice Girls. I swear, I'm, like, the only junior who isn't into them."

She chattered brightly, knowing she was talking too much and that probably nobody was hearing a word she said. She also knew it didn't matter. What mattered was the way her cousin's little shoulders relaxed, the way she listened with her whole body, the way she followed her down the hall without hesitation. What mattered was the look in her mother's eyes when Jeannie stepped out of the way to let Anna into the bedroom they would share. Her mom stood at the end of the hallway, hands over her mouth, tears bright in her eyes.

Jeannie winked at her mom, who dropped her hands to mouth the words, "Thank you."

Whatever was going on, it was bad. There probably wasn't anything she could do to make it better, but Jeannie Fitzhugh decided that night that the one thing she could do was keep it from getting worse for her young cousin, Anna Shuler.

. . . .

It wasn't going to be easy. Since they'd usually only seen each other on vacations during the summer, Jeannie forgot that Anna had been home-schooled by her parents and her parents were weird. Throw in being an only child and Anna was pretty much Jeannie's opposite in every way. But just like doing box-jumps and making one hundred free throws in a row, Jeannie took her on as a project.

Music seemed like a good place to start. Jewel, of course, and No Doubt, Matchbox Twenty. Fiona Apple and The Verve Pipe seemed a little dark for her sad-eyed cousin, so she decided to keep it light. When Anna told her she listened to someone named Pete Seeger and Édith Piaf, Jeannie was thrown. When she found that her cousin didn't recognize a picture of Homer Simpson and had never seen *Titanic* or even *Seinfeld*, Jeannie decided to try another tact.

Sitting on the edge of the bed, after looking down into the ugly clothes piled up in her cousin's suitcase, Jeannie untangled a lock of Anna's hair from her copper necklace. "Do you even *like* Édith What-ever? Or that Pete guy?"

Anna nodded quickly. "It's real music. Not pop." The answer sounded rehearsed, as if she were taking a test.

"Oh, not pop, huh?" She leaned in to whisper. "Do you know why it's called pop?" Anna shook her head. "Because it's popular. And it's popular because it's good. Have you ever heard any of it? Like Pink? Chumbawamba? Sugar Ray? None of it?" Anna kept shaking her head, looking for all the world like Jeannie was offering her a drug that was both incredibly dangerous and impossibly tempting. Jeannie squeezed her hand. "Oh my god, you have got so much listening to do. We are going to have so much fun! Do you want to watch *Daria*?"

It was a lot to throw at a kid on her first day and Jeannie saw most of it bouncing off of Anna's glassy eyes. The first real success came from the junk food pantry and Jeannie finally left Anna curled up in the papasan chair with a can of Diet Coke and a bag of Cheetos. That she opted to read a biography of some guy named Max Ernst instead of watching *Friends* would just be written off to fatigue.

Mom and Dad were back behind the closed doors of Dad's office so Jeannie cleaned up the kitchen and did a little homework. As bad as this no doubt was, it felt nice to be able to help in some way; it felt nice to not be the youngest in the house who had to be cared for rather than counted on. By eleven, the office door was still closed. It looked like she would be the one getting Anna to bed.

Anna had already put herself to bed. She lay curled up on the tiniest sliver of the queen-sized bed, barely covering herself with the edge of the blanket. That was sweet—she didn't want to take up any room. The wave of tenderness that welled up surprised Jeannie. God, Anna was so young. How much would it suck to have to leave your house? To live with relatives while your mom was in jail? Feeling very much like her own mother, Jeannie pulled the covers more fully over Anna, tucked her in, and climbed in carefully on the other side of the bed.

. . . .

Mom found Anna in the tub. The bedside clock read one-nineteen when Jeannie opened her eyes, hearing noises in the hallway. Mom was guiding a closed-eyed Anna back into bed, tucking her in just as Jeannie had done earlier. Anna mumbled in her sleep, resisting until the covers were tucked up under her chin. Her breathing evened out as Jeannie sat up in bed.

"Go back to sleep," Mom whispered, and Jeannie nodded and settled back down. When she heard her mom head back to the kitchen instead of her bedroom, however, Jeannie couldn't stay put. Slipping out as carefully as possible, she followed her.

Mom sat at the dining room table, a green gallon bottle of Gallo Chablis in front of her, drinking from one of Grandma's good wine glasses. Another wine glass sat empty at the empty seat beside her. Dad had obviously called it a night.

"Go back to bed."

"Mom." Jeannie sat in the seat her father had vacated. "Tell me what is going on."

Her mother closed her eyes, swaying slightly in her seat. She looked a little tipsy. Judging from how much was left in the bottle, Jeannie thought she should have looked a lot drunker. Maybe that's what had happened to Dad.

"Jeannie, oh Jeannie, it's bad. It's very bad. I don't want you to know what this is." She reached out and squeezed her daughter's hands. "Just be good to Anna."

"I will, Mom. I promise I'll take care of her, but I do kind of need to know what happened. I mean, what if I'm, like, 'Oh let's watch this show about coke dealers and it turns out Aunt Natalie was arrested for coke? Tell me what I'm protecting her from. And what if she asks when she's going to see her mom again? How long is Aunt Natalie going to be in jail?"

"It wasn't coke. And she's going to be in jail for a long time." Her mom bent over the table and Jeannie could see a tear hanging off her chin, ready to drop to the table. The breath she finally pulled in caught and tore through her and Jeannie squeezed her hand more tightly. This was scaring the crap out of her but she couldn't let her mother be alone in this. And this was obviously much, much worse than coke.

She was almost afraid to whisper the words.

"Did she kill someone?"

Mom nodded.

"Uncle David?"

Mom nodded again, her face pinched tight against the sobs that made her chest heave.

"Oh my god, oh my god." Putting this into words made her thoughts jumble and jump. This was so much worse than anything else. Poor Anna. There had to be a way out of this—this didn't happen in their family. "Oh my god. What happened? Was it self-defense? Did he come back and start fighting or something?" Her mom kept shaking her head, eyes shut tight, and Jeannie couldn't stop peppering her with questions. Uncle David had run off almost a year ago, and then he just showed up and Aunt Natalie killed him? There had to be some kind of sense to this. "How do they know she did it? Did she confess? Can they prove it?"

The sob she'd been holding back broke out of her mother's mouth as a moan. She squeezed her daughter's hand tightly enough to hurt. The look she leveled at Jeannie made the already horrible night worse.

"That's all you need to know. You need to take care of Anna because she has a very, very hard road ahead of her. You just need to know that I love you and Anna needs you."

"Mom, tell me." She couldn't explain why but she needed to know everything. She needed to be entrusted with this. She was old enough.

Her mother said nothing. Instead she reached into the back pocket of her jeans and pulled out a page of newspaper that looked more ragged than it should. It was dated a week ago. Jeannie scowled at the headline and then at the large black-and-white photo of her cousin in the middle of the page. Then she looked more closely at the picture, trying to make sense of what she read in the caption below it.

She pressed the page to the table, her hands covering the story, trying to make it go away. If she knew she wasn't old enough to handle this, what on earth was Anna supposed to do with it?

CHAPTER 6

I don't know what to do.

I want to go back to my office but I don't know what the police are going to do. I don't know if they're going to shut down the whole building. I don't know if heading back to my office, my workday, will look odd or out of place when there is a dead body in the basement. I don't know who's dead and I don't care, but I can't let anyone know that I don't care.

I don't know what to do but I know what not to do. I know not to draw attention to myself. I know how important it is to behave appropriately in situations like this because, believe it or not, there is a protocol of proper behavior for this scene. Nobody knows it before they've been here; the cops know it and they don't like to divulge that information beforehand. They issue no pamphlets like "Hey! There's a body! What do I do now?"

As I watch the clusters of uniforms—black and green; the state police have arrived—I see a great deal of useless milling around. Rubbernecking. It's safe to say that I have more experience in a scene like this than anyone else present, and I still don't know what to do.

Radios squawk and lights flash from within the open basement doorway. Pictures. Lots of flash pictures will be taken for what will be a scrapbook of the worst day of someone's life. Death is messy. Even if the act is tidy, the official recognition of the deed is messy. Cops and technicians and EMTs and reporters and insurance adjustors run pell-mell over the site of human dispatch, not just unconcerned that they're leaving a mess that someone else will have to clean up, but as if they feel entitled, nay, obligated, to smear their mark on the scene.

Cops and paramedics and even firefighters are here, hitching their pants up, sipping coffee, making jokes among themselves that they'll tell themselves are "gallows humor." They'll tell themselves that the job demands a certain callousness, that otherwise it would kill them. They tell themselves that they are world-weary, a last defense to keep the madness of murder from the sheeplike civilians gathered around gawking at the horror.

Most of them are fucking morons who wouldn't know horror if it fisted them. Most of them wouldn't last a minute in a real emergency and almost none of them have the first clue what they're doing there, besides basking in the excitement. Most of them are unnecessary at best. But not all of them.

I can see them. I can see the ones who are working. I remember them; I know the look. The ones who are paying attention, who will worry about the details. Maybe because it reflects on their job performance, maybe because they want justice, maybe they just don't like puzzles.

Then I realize that I don't have a dog in this fight. What's that line? Not my circus, not my monkeys? I'm not attached to this scene. I won't be questioned. This isn't my house. This is no one I love. I have absolutely nothing to add to the discussion of what has taken place. Like the moment the snow cleared and I saw the vista before me, this makes me feel better. It unplugs me from the dark current that has stopped my boots in their tracks.

I turn to head up the stairs to the left, where all the snow has been trampled away by the parade of emergency responders. They've packed the powder down and made it slick so I have to hang on to the railing and watch my step. Halfway up, I turn for a last glance over the circus below me, the one in which I have no monkeys.

One person isn't looking toward the basement or at their phone or into their coffee. One person—a Gilead cop about my age—isn't looking down. She's looking up. At me. She's watching me leave the crime scene.

I probably have more experience at crime scenes than anyone on campus and I just broke the cardinal rule. I just drew attention to myself.

"Well, fuck you, little sister," I mutter as I resume my climb. Let the newbies watch the spectacle. I've seen it.

A crowd is gathered at the top of the steps at the end of the sidewalk from the north door. It's like the cheap seats for the show below, people who want to know what's happening but don't want to fully commit to the event. Good for you, I think, as I cut through their whispering midst. Keep your distance. With any luck, you won't ever have to have a front row seat.

A glance out over the valley gives me nothing; a heavy, snow-blown cloud hangs over the treetops and I can't see anything. It's okay. I don't feel like being out here anymore anyway.

The hall to my office is quiet. Everyone is probably gathered around on one of the tiers, watching the action. I push open the office door and there's Meredith at her desk, phone under her chin, gesturing to a pile of paper like whoever she's talking to can see what she's pointing at. She looks up when I enter, points her fingers at the receiver like a gun, and pantomimes shooting whoever is on the other end. The familiarity of the gesture, as well as its inappropriateness under the circumstances, makes me laugh.

She's correcting the spelling of a student's name—once, twice—and then nearly screams out the letters in correct order. To be fair, the name is a mouthful—Ionuscorfu—but Meredith will not be swayed. It's that internship at the Corcoran Gallery that Ellis had mentioned. Meredith is relentless when it comes to connecting students and opportunities. I hope whoever is on the other end gets on board with her plan quickly or they're going to have a very bad day.

By the time she slams the phone down in victory, my boots are off and I'm jumping over the puddle of melted snow around them. Unlike my boss, I didn't think to bring house shoes and if my socks get wet, this day will blow even worse than it already promises to.

She grins at me from the divider. "How do you like your first snow-storm?"

"There's someone dead in the basement." I probably could have approached that more delicately but it's out there now. Meredith looks at me like I'm speaking in code. "Didn't you hear the sirens?"

"I heard them." She glances out the window, the meaning of my words dawning on her. "I thought it was an accident. The usual car-sliding-over-an-embankment sort of thing. Someone is dead? Who? Where?"

"The boiler room." I'm not the one who answers. It's Lyle Dunfee, from the Adjunct's Office, sticking his head in the door. "It was found by one of the maintenance guys. They've got the whole scene sealed off and told us all to stay in our offices until the police have a chance to interview us. All of us." His eyes glow with that same excitement of the kids gathered around the yellow tape. Why does this turn so many people on?

"Thanks, Lyle." Meredith all but shoos the little man out of our office, dismissing him and his ghoulish enthusiasm. We hear him spreading the news to everyone he passes on the way to his office. This is big news.

Meredith's scowl has none of the veiled titillation I've seen. "That's awful. I wonder who it was. Probably gas." She's speaking to herself more than to me. "That boiler is a thousand years old. It's a wonder it hasn't killed us all." She gives me a weary smile and then turns back toward her desk. "Oh well, I'm not dead. Neither are you. Neither is this paperwork, so we might as well get back to it."

I'm relieved at her business-as-usual attitude and am fully prepared to get back to the mountain of forms awaiting my attention when she steps around to face me again.

"You don't think it's suicide, do you?"

I don't move.

"It's just, you know, this time of year. It's so dark and the holidays are over. So many kids go to such a dark place this time of year." She sighs and leans her shoulder against the partition. "Am I being morbid? I'm being morbid."

I can't nod or shake my head.

She doesn't seem to notice that I've turned to stone. "I know. I know. I am being morbid, but I have to warn you. I don't know what it was like in Nebraska, but this time of year you really have to keep an eye on these kids. This time of year, when it's so dark and they're drinking and they're breaking up with each other and they're not passing their classes and who knows what else is going wrong, some of these kids can really drop off the edge fast." She sighs. "Let's hope that's not it. I'd hate for that to be your first snowstorm memory."

I never told Meredith about Ron. All she knows of my past is that my husband died "after a prolonged illness." It was an illness, a dark sickness that drove him to that closet. She's wrong about these kids. It's not the darkness. It's not the holidays. The demon that drives them to kill themselves is an addiction—an addiction to destruction that they have to fight their whole lives, however short they might be.

But if it's suicide, the thought rolls in unbidden, then the police won't question anyone. They'll take their pictures, file their reports, and be gone. The relief I feel at that thought bumps against my guilt at feeling it.

I don't pay attention to anything but my desk for a while. Paperwork gets a bad rap but at times like this, there is no substitute more sublime than the bureaucratic paper dance that keeps the money coming into school and keeps the kids from leaving it. I read grant proposals and juried exhibition rules and scholarship cut-off dates with the part of my brain that feels like working. The rest of me ignores the sounds of sirens and radios and people marching through the hallway until a particular radio squawk is too close to ignore.

There's a cop in the office. I act like I don't notice him and it pleases me that Meredith holds up her hand to silence him while she finishes up on the phone. He's white, like all the cops I saw downstairs. Like all the cops I saw in Nebraska. Funny that I'd think of that right now. I guess I'm trying to find ways to classify them, to distinguish them from the cops in attendance at the various crime scenes I've visited in my life. So far, no luck.

This one is chubby and the bulky utility belt only sets off his gut and thick thighs. His heavy jacket keeps catching on his gun as he fans it against his body, trying to find some relief from the heat in the office. His radio is loud enough to be heard from space and he keeps touching it, as if he can compel one of the endless relays to be directed to him. There's a snow clump melting on his hat and I'm much more interested in watching it slide to the floor than in anything he might have to say.

When Meredith doesn't wrap up her phone call in a timely enough manner for him, he huffs, hitches up his belt, and finally notices me through the dividers. Clearly, he's no detective. He nods at me as he heads toward me, the "Ma'am" he throws my way sounding like he stole it from a cowboy movie. He stands at the corner of my desk and I see that he can't be twenty-five years old. He is a kid. I should probably stop heaping so much hostility on him. Probably.

He pulls out a notebook. "Ma'am, I'd like to ask you some questions pertaining to the incident that occurred on the premises earlier this morning."

Jesus, do they send them to school for this kind of shit? "Pertaining to the incident"? I'd bet everything I own that this kid would struggle to spell *pertaining*. He probably has incendiary opinions on NASCAR. If I asked him, he'd tell me he doesn't trust the French but for the life of him couldn't honestly tell me why. His dream vacation is Myrtle Beach or maybe Daytona and he thinks Africa is a country.

He thinks everyone that works at the college is a snob. In this case, I guess he's right. The much-ignored sane part of my brain suggests that I might be projecting on this poor guy, that my silent disapproval and snap judgment might be more the result of my own fear bias than any actual shortcomings on his part. I also realize I sound just like my mother. He's not helping, however, with his foot-to-foot shifting and endless readjusting of his overloaded belt.

After he's found the proper page in the notebook he's been rifling through, but before I'm forced to pretend to be polite, Meredith finishes her call and whooshes our way with her usual fanfare. Hair, arms, random edges of sweater all flapping and signaling that we should not start whatever this is without her.

"A thousand apologies. Important call. Desperate student and all that. I'm here. I'm all yours, Officer . . . ?" She squints at the breast of his jacket, what I would consider a universally understood gesture requesting one to reveal one's nametag. He just blinks at her. She'll just have to make do with addressing him as "Officer." For surely that is what he is. There is no world in which this man is a detective.

He refers to his notebook. "Ma'am, I'd like to ask you some questions pertaining to the incident that occurred on the premises earlier this morning."

Ah, a word-for-word repeat. A script. Yet another in a long list of reasons to be glad nobody I love is dead at that scene. If someone were murdered, and that murderer is in this building, and this cop is responsible for collecting the evidence to capture said murderer, Justice can go ahead and take a spa day. It won't be called to duty any time soon.

Meredith settles at the edge of my desk, her attention fully on Officer Chubby. "In the basement, right? I heard the sirens."

"Ladies, this is just a preliminary examination of persons on the scene at the—"

"Was it suicide?" Meredith interjects.

"I'm not at liberty to discuss the—"

"Oh, is it a crime scene?"

"At this juncture, ma'am, we cannot—"

"Of course, you can't tell us anything." Meredith nods to me. "If it's a crime scene, they have to establish the whereabouts of anyone normally on the premises. I watch a lot of true-crime shows."

This puffs up the already puffy Officer Chubby, restoring his place as lawful authority, not some civilian hanger-on. "Ma'am, I know television makes this all look like a lot of fun, with lots of excitement. The reality is most of police work is just that—work. Hard work."

"Oh, I'm sure." Meredith nods a lot, her pale red curls flopping around her face. "They make it look easy. One hour, crime solved. You guys have to actually do the hard work, right? To solve the crime?"

He gives her a humble-brag shrug, tugs on his belt, and does that full-face sniff. What is it with macho guys and that sniff? I can't believe Meredith is getting dazzled by this dollar-store cop-talk knock-off.

"So it is a crime scene?"

"Anytime there is an unnatural or unusual death, protocol says we—"

"Sure, sure, notify next of kin, collect evidence, determine COD, all that." She's nodding and I'm getting a little hypnotized by the bounce of one lively curl that juts out over her ear. I watch it spring around when she turns back to me. "COD, that's *cause of death*. Cop talk."

I lean back in my chair, content to watch her hair flounce and frizz as she responds to the cop's questions with animation. She's dying to answer him, he's enjoying the focus. She gives him our names and department and doesn't seem to judge him at all when she has to spell both of our names twice. My name is Anna Ray. She has to spell it twice. Slowly.

But in a minute, I go from half listening to watching in surprise. Yes, Meredith is jumping in to answer his questions with enthusiasm and, yes, Officer Chubby appears fully invested in his World-Weary

Beat Cop character. So invested, as a matter of fact, that he doesn't realize that Meredith is interrogating him.

In ten minutes of lively back and forth, we learn that the dead body is an adult male. From the condition of the body and evidence on the scene, suicide has been ruled out; an accident seems unlikely, leaving homicide in the lead. He learns our names, titles, and what time we got to work. It doesn't seem like a fair exchange of information, but Officer Chubby doesn't notice. Instead he lets Meredith fawn over him, shaking her head and clucking her tongue at the brave and thankless work he and his fellow officers have before them. Another unnecessary hitch of his belt, another Gary Cooper nod, and of course another manly sniff, and Officer Chubby thanks us for our cooperation and wishes us good day.

Once he's gone, Meredith turns those wide eyes on me. "Wow, it looks like we missed a lot this morning. Can you believe that? A murder?"

"I'm still trying to wrap my head around what just happened here. You totally pumped that guy for information. I thought he was going to show you police records."

She waves me off. "Oh that. He was dying to talk about it."

"He was here to get information. Now we probably know more than he does. He's going to go back to the station, look at his notes, and go 'Hey . . . ' You're a master interrogator."

She scowls at me. "Never underestimate my ability to find stuff out, but really, let's not oversell this. You saw that guy. I've eaten sandwiches that could outwit him. I just wanted to know what was going on and I didn't want to wait for Lyle Dunfee to tell us. I hate when he has the skinny on campus gossip." She grimaces. "I guess this isn't really campus gossip, is it? I mean, someone is dead. You don't think it's Walter Voss, do you? Oh, wouldn't that be awful?"

"I don't think so. I saw him on the way to the library." That seems like a hundred years ago. My estimation of this day has plunged and soared so many times since waking up in the tub I'm getting the bends. And I haven't even had any breakfast yet. I mention this last bit to

Meredith, confident she'll have something delicious stashed in her many cubbies.

"I love it!" She jumps off the desk, her trailing sweater creating a small paper avalanche. "Appetite in the face of death, a celebration of life in the face of mortality."

"And I'm hungover."

She frowns her disapproval. "Oh, yeah. Ollie's. Did you have fun?" She heads back to her end of the office and starts shifting and pulling at boxes and tubs. "I forgot Professor Fitzhugh-Conroy was your cousin. That goes a long way toward explaining how you came all the way here from Nebraska." She disappears, bending over behind her desk. "I thought maybe you'd just had enough of wide-open spaces."

I've followed her to her desk. I figure if I'm going to beg breakfast out of her, it's too much to ask her to deliver. There, I learn one of her secrets.

"You do have a refrigerator tucked away in here."

"Of course I do." She pulls out a Pyrex bowl with a blue lid and slams the fridge with her knee. "I have two of them. You don't think I'd risk salmonella poisoning and leave sausage dip out at room temperature. Is it salmonella you get from pork?"

"Trichinosis," I say as she pulls off the lid. "Is that the sausage dip from yesterday?"

"Too gross for morning?"

"Are you kidding?"

"I figured as much. You strike me as an unhealthy eater." She pulls out a tall, purple Rubbermaid tub from beside a filing cabinet. Within it, I see plastic utensils, packages of paper plates, paper towels, even pot holders. She chooses a long-handled spoon and starts stirring the cold dip. "A few minutes in the microwave and this will be perfect."

She hands me the bowl. I know where the microwave is, sort of. It takes me a minute to scan the wall unit that blocks the southern window. Only Meredith, I think, would block southern exposure to store mountains of boxes and crates of god only knew what. I find the white microwave partially disguised under bumper stickers declaring "Stop Bitching! Start a Revolution!" and "Women who behave rarely make history." I have to push the Greenpeace logo to open the door. In four minutes, my hangover will be that much further away.

"Your cousin was very popular here."

It takes me a minute to remember what we were talking about, so focused am I on the smell of warming sausage. "Oh yeah, Jeannie. She's always popular. She's easy to like."

"She was a well-respected professor. Tough. The kids put a lot of weight on her opinion. Maybe a little too much sometimes." She sets out paper plates and pulls a bag of Tostitos Scoops from her desk drawer. "What's she doing back here? She's not leaving Penn State, is she? That's quite a step up."

"No, she just came in for a visit. She has a graduate student covering her for the week." I'd rather not get into the real reason Jeannie is here now, this week. I don't want to bring up the discussion of anniversaries.

"She picked a bad week to come through the mountains. She'll be lucky to get home this month with this snow. Speaking of which . . ." She joins me beside the microwave, crouching at my feet to pull out a squat cardboard box decoupaged with pictures of Paris. "You're going to need these." From within the box, she pulls out a pair of maroon corduroy house shoes.

She sets them beside my feet, guiding me into them as I'm pulling hot dip from the microwave. I almost protest until I feel how cozy they are.

"You're welcome."

"Wow." I set the dip down and let her spoon out a gob onto my plate. "Student advocacy, diner, and haberdashery. How do you do it?"

"They belong to my son. I got them for him for Christmas one year but he left them when he moved to Nashville. Said they were for old men." Her smile is sad when she pulls a framed photograph from the corner of her desk to show me. I'm really glad I have a mouthful of chips and dip when she holds it in front of me. She nods as my eyes widen. "I know, right? So handsome. That's my beautiful boy, Derek. Hard to believe he was ever a little boy."

I take my time swallowing my mouthful, grateful I don't have to make an immediate comment on the man-child in the picture. Maybe it's because I've never had kids of my own, maybe it's because of the type of people I was born among, but I've never been good at lying about pictures of people's kids. Meredith's son towers over her in the photo but not in any manly, athletic way. He looks like a pasty ogre with bad skin and worse facial hair and a surly smirk that reveals at least two crooked teeth. As socially awkward as I am, however, even I know the wisdom of keeping my big mouth shut on the matter. In her eyes, he is an Adonis.

So I nod. And keep chewing. She puts the photo back but keeps it turned toward us. I have to say something so I focus on the background of the picture. "Was that taken at Ollie's?"

"It was. Derek went to EAC for three years, studied English and music. He would play guitar at Ollie's on their open mic night." She actually blushes with pride at the memory. "Despite your cousin's opinion to the contrary, many talented students do play at Ollie's. Derek is so gifted. Everyone says so."

"Does he still play?"

"Well." She turns the picture back so it faces her. Her finger lingers over his face. "He moved to Nashville. You know the story. It's a tough business. Not everyone is tough enough. That eternal struggle between art and commerce." I know that struggle all too well. I'm never more reminded of it than in late February, and I really wish I could think of something to change the subject. I bite loudly into a chip.

Lyle Dunfee from the Adjunct's Office comes to my rescue when he sticks his head in the door again, just as breathless as he was earlier. "Offices are closing at eleven. Classes are cancelled due to the death." Before we can respond, he whirls away, reveling in his newest duty of delivering the news. He doesn't get far. I hear his phone beep and then I hear him gasp in the hall. He actually gasps.

"No press!" he shouts. I don't know why he shouts it or to whom he is shouting, but he shouts it like CNN is bearing down on him. "We just got an e-mail from the President's Office. Do not speak to the press." Another beep, another gasp, and then what sounds like a combination moan and sob. Meredith cocks her eyebrow in comic concern. Lyle's dramatics are nothing new.

"Should we bother reading our e-mail?" she asks me. "Or should we just let Lyle perform them for us?"

I scoop up more sausage onto my Tostitos. "To be fair, it's probably devastating him that he can't talk with the press. I'm sure he had a statement prepared."

We hear more voices in the hall, more gasps of shock. That must be some e-mail. Meredith clicks her computer to life and opens her inbox. She scans the screen for a moment, clicking through e-mails, and then shrugs. "It just says we're closing early due to a tragedy. We're cooperating with the investigation, blah blah blah." Click. Click. "Refrain from speculating. Blah blah blah. Information will be disseminated as the investigation continues . . . troubled times . . . statements to the press are discouraged, blah blah blah. I don't see anything especially shocking. Except, you know, the fact that there's a dead body downstairs."

"Well, the dead body is just the beginning," I say around a mouthful of food. "Now the real excitement starts. Now the professional mourners kick in. Who wants a funeral dirge when we can have the extended dead dance remix?"

Meredith looks at me with an odd expression on her face and I think maybe I'm showing too much callousness. Maybe I shouldn't make my familiarity with this sort of thing so obvious. Before I can deflect her attention, Lyle throws himself against our doorframe, clutching his phone to his chest, biting his lip. I have my own opinion on whether or not he is biting back tears or biting his lip hard enough to raise them. I'm going to ignore them either way.

"You did not hear this from me." He glances around furtively, as if we don't know he's already told everyone on the floor. We also know that he is dying to tell us and god help anyone who tries to take credit for breaking whatever this news is. "They've identified the body."

The last word disappears in a breathy sob as Lyle grinds his pale knuckle against his lips. Here we go, step two of the Great Grief Showcase: I Knew Him Better Than You. Whoever is being carted off to the morgue is now becoming best friends with dozens of people who wouldn't have lent them cab fare a week ago. Upon hearing the victim's name, Lyle and his kind will suddenly remember months, years, decades they had spent bonding and growing with the deceased, cherishing them and sharing intimacies. Not because they actually give a shit about them but because that intimacy will bump them up higher on the grieving pecking order. Their tears will hurt more, their lives will matter more because a bigger hole has been torn into it by this untimely, tragic death.

I am too familiar with the massive wave of bullshit bearing down on me and I know I'm not polite enough to fake my way through this conversation so I turn in my seat and pretend to do something with the bottom of my shoe. Whatever kicks Lyle is going to get from his grief parade, he's not going to get them from me.

Meredith does what I cannot and will not do. She leans in, her face a mask of concern. "Who is it, Lyle?"

"It's . . . oh my god, I can't believe it. I can't even . . ."

Oh for fuck's sake, Lyle, spit it out. Then you can hurry home and update your Facebook profile with pictures of the unlucky sap.

"It was Ellis."

Just the first name. He's going to make us ask for the last name. I'm hiding my eye roll as the name sinks in.

Ellis Trachtenberg.

CHAPTER 7

And just like that, I feel guilty.

It's such an easy emotion to fall into, a wide splash of unpleasant that covers your soul from top to bottom with none of the relief of believing you've been wronged. It's a feel-bad you believe you deserve and it clings to you like napalm.

In a split second, I feel guilty for the mean things I've been thinking about Lyle. People are whispering and crying in the hallway and I feel guilty for my gut reaction, which is to dismiss them as drama queens and hangers-on. They knew Ellis. Everyone in this building has worked at this small college longer than I have, a lot longer in most cases, and they knew Ellis Trachtenberg. They counted him among their friends and now he's gone forever.

Death guilt works like one of those ethics experiments that use hidden cameras on unsuspecting people. They're left in a room all alone, unsupervised, unaware. A bowl of candy is left on the table, or maybe a file or an unmarked button. Do they eat the candy? Open the file? Push the button? They're not told of any consequences. They entered the room in the middle of their day, in the middle of their lives, their minds and hearts preoccupied with the busyness of their own wants and needs.

Maybe they eat the candy, maybe they ignore the file. Regardless, the experiment ends; the moderator comes into the room, judging them on a test they had no idea they were taking. In a heartbeat, they are thieves or cowards or rule breakers or sheep. Branded. The test is over. No do-overs.

That's what death does. It rips someone out of the stream of your life, the life you're living with varying levels of success and selfishness, and holds that raw absence against you like a measuring stick. Were you kind to them? Did you make their life better? Did you ever think of them, put them first, go out of your way to love them a little more? Did you only think of yourself? Are you sure? Or do you hear the echoes of every less-than-kind thing you ever said, every gentle encouragement you ever withheld out of pettiness, fatigue, or apathy?

Too late now. Test over.

And unless you're a psychopath or a saint, you probably failed.

You earn a *G* for guilt.

"Are you okay, Anna?"

Meredith puts her hand on mine, leaning close to me. I'm just sitting here, frozen. I almost say something before I remember I've got a mouthful of Tostitos and dip that have turned to warm putty on my tongue. I nod and swallow, trying to remember how to sit in a chair and be normal. "Yeah, yeah," I manage to say. "So awful, oh my god. How awful." The words roll out on their own as my mind runs its own litany.

No dog in this fight.

No skin in this game.

Not my monkeys.

Over and over, faster than a blink, reassurances based on flesh and animals swirl around my head, drawing me away from the gravitational pull of death. I can't judge these people, these decent people being pulled into a wave of mourning that will grow as they feed it. It's a basic human reaction; to be enthralled by the sharp ache of grief at a life snuffed out is as inevitable as death itself. Ellis Trachtenberg is probably the first murder victim any of them have ever known.

"Are we sure about this, Lyle?"

And then there's Meredith. There should always be a Meredith. Someone who keeps their cool, remains human and compassionate and feels no compulsion to grieve more than any other. I suppose it's a level of maturity, although I haven't seen enough of it in my life to know if it's a common step. Meredith's eyes aren't red but her face is somber. She's still holding my hand and I can feel a slight tremor in her grip.

Lyle is not faring so well. His cheeks glow with a rosiness that contradicts the anguish he's trying to project. He looks up from the phone he has been hammering at with his thumbs to challenge Meredith's question with a look of hurt outrage.

"Well, Shanea from the President's Office said she heard the police talking in his office. She's right there in the same room as Bev, his secretary, and I don't think she would have just made that up. It's kind of a messed-up thing to lie about, don't you think?"

As I suspected, Lyle has claimed this story as his own, lashing out at anyone who dares challenge his narrative or its source. Meredith gives me a look that tells me she understands this too and thinks about as highly of it as I do. She squeezes my hand and lets it go.

"I just think we should be respectful and be careful about spreading any information we haven't received officially. God forbid word gets back to his family before the police have had a chance to talk with them. They don't need to hear rumors."

"Especially if it's not him." Desiree Jackson, Lyle's office mate, leans in behind Lyle. A small crowd has gathered around Lyle, the event crier, who has unfortunately chosen to camp out in our doorway. "Nothing like hearing about your own death when you're just running late."

"Is he running late?" Lyle asks like the question offends him. "Ellis is never late. In all the years he has worked at this school, he has never been late. That's not his way. He takes his classes very seriously. He would not—"

"Nobody is questioning his devotion," Meredith says, and I think again how lucky the world is to have Merediths who can tactfully shut down scenes like this. "We just don't want to jump to any conclusions. Has anyone tried to call him?"

"He's not in his office," Desiree says. "Shanea told us that."

Lyle scowls at her. "He's not in his office because he's dead in our building."

"Has anyone tried his cell?" Meredith's voice has that tone it takes when she's tired of dumbing things down. "Maybe the snow held him up. Lyle, why don't you call his cell?"

Lyle's mouth opens and closes a few times, then he focuses on his phone. I can see him scrambling to save face. He can't very well play Dead Man's Grieving Best Friend if he admits he doesn't even have the man's phone number.

Meredith saves him from his lie but sacrifices me. "Don't you have his number, Anna?"

There is probably some pathology I suffer from that makes me think that cramming something in my mouth will save me from answering questions I don't want to answer. My first impulse is usually alcohol but in its absence, Tostitos and dip seem a fitting substitute. I'm seriously tempted to just shove a mitt-full of chips into my mouth even as I know that won't work. Instead, I go with my other standby.

"Uh, I don't think so."

"Yes, you do," Meredith says, surprised at the stupidity of my answer. "You did."

"I did." Of course I did. Ellis typed it into my phone the second night I met him at a staff mixer. Meredith had been there and had teased me about it the next day. Playing dumb is harder when you have smart people playing beside you. But I try. "I don't have my phone."

"You don't have your phone?" Lyle's tone is a vocal eye roll. I suspect Lyle eats, sleeps, and showers with his phone.

"I don't." I pat my pockets, prepared to lie until I realize I don't have to. I really don't have my phone. I don't have my purse, my wallet, not even my lip balm. I'd been so dazzled by the snow and so thick-headed from my hangover that I'd just charged out of the apartment with nothing in my hands but my mittens. I don't even know if I have my keys. Shit.

"I have his number on my desk," Desiree says, and I'm pretty sure Lyle is close to not speaking to her anymore. "Let's call him."

"And say what?" Lyle snaps. "'Are you dead?' 'Who did it?'"

"Enough!" Meredith bangs her hands on the desk. "Desiree, please go try Ellis's number. Let us know if he answers. Either way, we're all then going to go home and enjoy this lovely snow day. We need to pray for whoever it was that died in our building and maybe try to keep in mind that someone has died. Someone we probably know." She stares at Lyle and Desiree, who both looked chastened. "Okay?"

Like sulking teenagers, the two turn away from our door. A moment later we hear Lyle chastising whoever else is out in the hall, repeating Meredith's orders almost word for word. She shakes her head as the noise from the hallway fades.

"Unbelievable," she says. "We work with children. Not the students. The students are almost adults. We work with children." Then she sighs, resting her chin in her hand. "I hope it isn't Ellis. I mean, I wish it wasn't anyone, but I hope it isn't Ellis. He has so much of his life ahead of him. It would be such a loss for the school and the students."

She sounds sincere, none of that gleeful titillation masked as grief. It strikes me again how very grown up Meredith is and how few people like this I've known in my life. Her genuine sadness awakens a dull throb deep within me, an ember of grief banked in layers of cynicism and self-protection. In the dark heat that blooms from it, I think of Ronnie. His face rises unbidden in my memory, not with any of the anger or anguish I've attached to it this past year, but the way I saw him when we were in love, when he lit me up and took my breath away and made me happy.

I almost say something. I almost bring that memory to life by letting it slip out my lips, but I catch myself. Bringing that up, talking about my dead husband when Ellis Trachtenberg may be lying dead in an ambulance, murdered, could appear as manipulative as Lyle's attention-grabbing scenes. Today, this moment, this horror that has occurred so close to us is not about us. It's not about Ronnie. It's not my grief. It's not Meredith's. We're free from the burden of immediate pain. That's for someone else to bear. Some unlucky soul has to lean into that knife. There's no need to borrow that agony. We all get our chance.

"I should go," I say.

CHAPTER 8

Collins, Illinois
February 1998
Anna Shuler, 12 years old

Transcript: assessment session 1, AS #426911-S - juvenile. Marsteller
Rep: Bakerton, MO, PD—Case Ref C7-2690X

JDM: Hi, Anna, I'm Dr. Marsteller.

Patient: Hello.

JDM: Are you comfortable? Good. Anna, do you understand why you're here?

Patient: Aunt Gretchen said I'm supposed to talk to you.

JDM: Do you know why?

Patient: You're with the police.

JDM: Hmm, sort of. I work with the police but I'm not a police officer. I'm a counselor. Do you know what that means?

Patient: That people tell you their problems and you tell them what's wrong with them.

JDM: Well, you're partly right. People do tell me their problems, but then we talk about ways to make them better. To make them easier to deal with. Sometimes all it takes is talking about a problem to make things feel a lot better.

Patient: Oh.

JDM: Your Aunt Gretchen thought that maybe talking to me would make all of this a little easier for you to handle. You know, maybe we could talk about some things that you don't feel comfortable talking about with the people in your family.

Patient: The police want me to talk to you, too.

JDM: The police want to make sure you're okay. You've been through a lot these past couple of weeks. They mentioned how smart you are and how grown up you've been through all of this.

Patient: They think I'm lying about what happened. They think there's something I didn't tell them, that I . . .

JDM: That you what?

JDM: Anna, what do you think the police want you to say? It's okay if you tell me. Anna?

JDM: Are you angry with the police? Because they arrested your mother? Do you understand why they arrested your mother?

JDM: Anna?

JDM: It's going to be a long hour if we just sit here not talking to each other.

JDM: Anna?

JDM: Anna?

· · · · · · · · · · · · · · · · · · ·

Jeannie's mother was going to kill her. She was late picking up Anna from the counselor. Jeannie drummed her hands on the steering wheel, waiting for the light to change. She wasn't that late, not really. Fifteen minutes? Twenty? Anna wasn't that little a kid. Yeah, she was only twelve, but she was really grown up. Jeannie didn't understand why Mom and Dad freaked out about just letting Anna walk down to the library after her appointment. It was only, like, a half a block away. It wasn't like she'd be sitting alone at an airport or a bus station. But no, Jeannie had to pick her up at the counselor's office.

Mom and Dad were worried about her, Jeannie knew. Really freaked out by the whole thing, which was totally understandable since she herself nearly passed out when Mom showed her that newspaper article. God, what a mess. Jeannie felt a sick tumbling in her stomach every time she thought about it. Stuff like this wasn't supposed to happen in the real world. This was the kind of stuff that showed up in movies and those gross true-crime TV shows.

Aunt Natalie had killed Uncle David. Aunt Natalie. Tiny little Aunt Natalie with all that pale blond hair, all those bangles and beaded necklaces and clunky wooden clogs. One time, an old rattrap truck rattled past their house and Dad had winked at Jeannie and said, "Sounds like Aunt Natalie." She was always just this crazy mess of a woman, kind of cool but always so weird. She had opinions on everything and Mom spent most of their time together sighing and telling her to chill out. And Uncle David, god, he was such a drag. Always so pissed off about everything.

But as weird as they were, who murders people?

"My aunt is a murderer." Jeannie tried the words on, seeing how it felt to say them aloud. She could only do this when she was alone in the car, which wasn't often. "My aunt killed my uncle. There is a murderer in my family."

The family shame. That's what they would have called it on TV. On TV it would be the secret that would haunt Jeannie, that she would keep to herself but that other people would somehow sense about her. It would cast a shadow on her, make her mysterious, maybe a little dangerous. Jeannie hadn't told Leighanne yet; she'd just hinted that something really serious was going on in her family that she couldn't talk about. Leighanne wanted to know what it was but also didn't want to act like it was any big deal. Leighanne was already kind of jealous over all the attention Jeannie was getting for regionals, so she would probably try to play it all off like the whole thing was no big deal, but there was no way anyone could think this wasn't a big deal.

The light finally changed and Jeannie made the turn onto Emerson Avenue, where the counselor's office was. Anna sat out front, on a bench, her book bag between her legs. God, Jeannie thought, how is a little kid like that supposed to deal with this? Jeannie felt ashamed at her earlier musings. This wasn't a TV show; this wasn't about attention. It didn't make anyone look cool. It was as far from cool as anyone could possibly get.

There was a space open a few doors up from where Anna sat but, pulling up alongside it, Jeannie doubted her parallel parking abilities.

It would take forever and it wasn't like they were staying. She pulled ahead to the loading zone at the corner. As she put on her flashers, she looked in the rearview mirror. A man was on the bench, too, talking with Anna. At first she'd thought he was just waiting there for the bus, but now that she really looked at him, Jeannie could see he was talking with her cousin.

Jeannie slammed the car door. "Anna!" If this guy was some kind of creeper, Jeannie would bust him out, big-time. Jeannie had no problem at all with the idea of going into one of the offices on this street and calling the police. Anna was just a little kid; grown men shouldn't be talking with her.

Anna stood up when she heard her name, pulling her backpack up to her chest. Jeannie marched forward, her eyes on the guy, ready to give him hell if he made trouble. He was old, like in his forties, and paunchy like the guys who hung out at the American Legion watching when the girls' basketball team did wind sprints in the parking lot. She wasn't scared of him. She had her basketball shoes on and she had no doubt she could both kick him in the balls and run with Anna if need be.

Then he smiled at her. She hesitated.

"You must be Jeannie, right? The famous cousin? Running a little late, huh?"

Anna didn't say anything, just hugged her bag to her body. Jeannie stepped closer, slower now but ready to jump in between him and Anna if she needed to. He didn't look at all worried.

"You were late getting here and I didn't want to leave Anna just sitting by herself. She doesn't really know the town, does she?"

Oh shit, busted. "Drills ran late. And there was traffic by the mall. I didn't want to speed." Jeannie knew she was talking too fast. Would this guy rat her out to her parents? She didn't want to lose the car this week. Time to turn on the charm. Smile. "Are you Dr. Marsteller?" He accepted her handshake.

"So"—he kept shaking her hand—"tough times for your family. How are things? How are you dealing with all of this? Happy to have your cousin living with you?"

"Of course, oh my god, I love Anna. It's like I finally have a little sister."

"How much do you know about what happened? The murder?"

Jeannie didn't want to be rude but this handshake was lasting way too long. She pulled her hand back gently at first. Then she saw Anna's face. Her cousin's eyes were huge and dark; she looked like she'd been slapped, staring at Jeannie with what looked like an accusation. Jeannie jerked her hand away from the man's grasp.

"He's not Dr. Marsteller." Anna's cheeks burned red. "He's a reporter."

The man didn't lose that oily smile. "Can you tell me how you're dealing, knowing your aunt is a murderer? Has it made it tough at school?"

"Oh my god." Jeannie jerked Anna closer to her, pushing her in front of her toward the car. She kept glancing over her shoulder as the man shouted after them.

"Did you see her do it, Anna? Did you see what she used?"

"Don't listen to him."

"Or is she covering for you, Anna?" He was following them.

"Get in the car."

He pounded on the window beside Anna's head as Jeannie hurried to start the car.

"When did he die, Anna?"

"Ignore him."

"How long was the body in the house?"

Jeannie floored it, shooting the car through the intersection, not even worrying that the light was red. Horns blared and tires screeched somewhere behind them. The only sound Jeannie Fitzhugh heard was the muffled, panicked breaths of her cousin.

. . . .

She pulled into the Dairy Barn. She didn't want ice cream and she didn't want Anna to think she was trying to pacify her like a baby but Jeannie's hands were shaking so bad she wasn't sure she could control the car. Plus, even though Mom wouldn't be home until after six and Dad was out at meetings all afternoon, she couldn't take Anna home in her current state. Her parents would lose their minds if they found out that a reporter had chased them and that he'd gotten to Anna because she had been late picking her up.

Beside her, Anna trembled so hard Jeannie could see it. She looked like she was getting ready to spring through the windshield. Her fingers dug into the straps of the backpack that she clutched to her chest like a shield. She didn't look left or right, just stared straight ahead.

"Anna?"

Jeannie had heard people talk about shooting daggers with their eyes but when Anna spun on her, it was the first time she'd really understood it. She half expected a punch to sail her way.

"I don't want to talk about it."

"Okay. Do you want to talk about a Reese's Blaster?" Anna kept glaring. "It's a milkshake where they grind up Reese's Cups and put in caramel sauce. It'll totally make you sick and it's totally worth it." As she spoke, the fire faded from her cousin's eyes. Her posture relaxed, transforming her back into the little girl she was supposed to be rather than the angry animal she had been a moment ago. "Do you want chocolate or vanilla?" Anna only blinked. "Let's get chocolate. Let's get the big ones."

She rolled the window down to give their order to the carhop. When the girl had gone, Jeannie rolled it back up and turned up the heat. She made a show of fidgeting around beneath the seat for her purse, pulling out money, giving Anna time to pull herself together.

When she straightened back up, Anna sat just as she had before, staring at Jeannie, only now her eyes were soft and huge. Jeannie understood that look. Anna trusted her, was begging her for something she didn't know how to ask for.

Everyone wanted Anna to talk. She hadn't talked to anyone. She hadn't cried, she hadn't told anyone anything about the day her mother was arrested. The police, Mom and Dad, the counselor, now even the newspapers—everyone wanted Anna to talk about this horrible thing that had happened in the middle of her world, to give everyone the details they couldn't figure out themselves. There were things that only Anna and her mother knew and everyone wanted Anna to tell what those things were.

Anna trusted Jeannie. Even though they really didn't know each other that well and they didn't have much in common, Jeannie could see in her cousin's face that she trusted her. She wanted Jeannie to tell her what to do. She wanted Jeannie to make everything okay, to make anything okay.

If Jeannie told her cousin to talk, she probably would. Anna trusted her. Jeannie was probably the only thing she did trust at this point. Jeannie had to take care of this. She had to do what was right.

"Everybody wants you to talk about it. Everyone thinks it can help. Maybe it can. I don't know."

Anna clutched her backpack more tightly.

"But you don't have to." She laid her head back against the seat. "You don't ever have to tell me if you don't want. You can if you want, you can tell me anything, but you don't have to."

Anna said nothing. Jeannie reached across the seat and pushed back a lock of hair that had come loose from Anna's ponytail. She tucked it behind her cousin's ear and kept her hand beside her face.

"No matter what you do, just remember that this isn't you. All of this, it isn't you. It's something that happened to you but it isn't who you are. I know who you are. You're my cousin, Anna. This is something that happened. It's not who you are."

Anna let go of the backpack. It slid between her legs down to the floor of the car. Her shoulders slumped and she leaned her cheek into Jeannie's palm. Then she started to cry.

CHAPTER 9

Nobody leaves.

There's no reason to stay. Offices are closed; classes are cancelled. They're predicting more snow this afternoon so traveling won't get any easier for a while. There are a hundred reasons we should all be bundling up and shutting out the lights and making our way home to our loved ones and significant others. I should be preparing to regret not getting down to Kroger to pick up six more bottles since, by my estimation, I only have two remaining significant others from my last shopping trip.

I could be home, snowed in with Jeannie, stocked up with no place to go and no one expecting us, requiring no motor skills finer than working the corkscrew to ride out the darkest nights of the year. We could coat ourselves in Cheetos dust and body grease, splash a cheap Merlot on the door like lamb's blood on the lintel as the Unholy Spirit of February blows over the land looking for souls to slaughter.

The dark allure of this image pulls at me with a force even I know is unhealthy. If Meredith were to pull out anything stronger than coffee at this moment, my mind could easily drop into a Swedish art film, complete with hooded figures, screaming birds, and hollow-eyed children.

I want to go to that place. Finally. I can feel the draw of going that far down that hole. That I'm given the chance due to the death—no, the murder—of someone I knew, a man who flirted with me, whom Jeannie slept with, and all the sexual baggage those facts bring with them, good lord, I'm looking at a scorched earth-scene that makes Wagner's darkest work look like a rom-com. I can almost hear Johann Goethe suggesting that maybe I lighten up a bit.

This makes me laugh. I catch it before it becomes a full-on snort chortle, but Meredith hears it anyway. She cocks a friendly eyebrow, wanting to be in on the joke, but I spare her that. The funniest thing about my thoughts at this moment is how unfunny they are.

I don't know why everyone else is sticking around but I'm here so I don't have to go down that hole. As badly as I want to, that's how badly I don't want to, and I don't force myself to justify my logic. I know with decades of certainty that that hole will keep. That pain stays fresh no matter how long I make it wait. Out in the hallway Desiree shushes Lyle, who has laughed abruptly. They whisper to each other, both struggling against that contagious giggling that always breaks out in grim situations. I wish they wouldn't muffle it. I want to hear Lyle's throaty guffaw and Desiree's high-pitched cackle.

I want to keep these corduroy slippers on and keep on eating Meredith's delicious sausage dip until I burst. I want there to be a reason to just stay put; to stay in this sudden limbo where we're not working, we're not leaving, we're not doing anything really but actively not doing the things we're supposed to be doing. I wouldn't even mind seeing Officer Chubby huffing through the building, sniffing and scratching.

Meredith makes no move to leave either. She rolls her chair over to the shelf on the other side of her desk and returns a moment later with a package wrapped in a plastic grocery bag.

"I was saving these for something special." From the bag, she pulls out a flat, white box tied with a red ribbon. I can smell the chocolate as she lifts the lid. "If we take anything away from what's happened today it should be that every day is special."

Twenty-four dark squares fill the box. I read the little card on the lid.

"Hand-made artisanal chocolates; sea-salt caramels, organic lavender, organic ginger."

"My three favorite flavors in the world." Meredith gazes at the chocolates. "A gift from my son for Christmas. Ever since he was a little boy, he always paid attention to what I loved. He's always known how to make me smile." She gives a sad laugh. "I wish I could have stayed with him in Nashville longer." She pushes the box toward me.

"Are you sure?" I ask, hoping the answer is yes. "These look expensive."

"They are expensive. I've been saving them."

"Why would you save these? How could you save them? How could you resist?"

She gives me a look that's hard to read, a strange mixture of happy and sad. "I like to save things for special occasions. I like to make things last." She waves at the piles of chaos behind her. "I'm obviously very good at hanging on to things."

I laugh but resist grabbing a chocolate. "But these are yours. Your son picked them out specially for you. You don't have to share them."

"I want to." She pushes the box closer and I don't resist any longer. "I want you to eat these candies with me. I want us to enjoy them together. Today. It's a sad day. Someone has lost everything today." She picks up a dark square and examines it. "Someone's heart is going to be broken when they hear the news. Someone is going to wonder if they'll ever recover from this."

"Oh my god," I mutter around the chocolate. Rich, bitter chocolate crumbles around salty, gooey caramel that erupts like ecstasy on my tongue. To be honest, even if it had tasted like cat litter I would have reacted the same way. I don't want to follow Meredith's melancholy train of thought. The candy makes it easy to change the subject. Meredith moans around the candy in her mouth.

"Caramel," I say around the fingers I'm licking just in case I missed a sliver of chocolate.

"Abender," she mumbles and points to the center row. Lavender. As I reach for another, I've never been happier that Meredith is a hoarder. I toast her with chocolate-coated ginger.

"To your son. He's a good man."

"Yes, he is. He's my finest creation. And if you will pardon a mother's vanity, I think he is the best thing to ever come out of Eastern Allegheny College."

We both sigh over our treats. Meredith opens her carafe and pours coffee into her mug. She fishes another mug off an S-hook I hadn't noticed on the shelf behind her and fills a cup for me. "I have cream," she says, motioning to the refrigerator. "And Splenda. I have sugar, too. And Sweet'N Low." She spins her chair around and runs her fingers over a row of narrow plastic bins. "I think I still have some agave syrup up here, too somewhere."

I laugh. "Of course you do. You probably have a small barista tied up in one of those baskets." I take the cup and tap it against hers. "Black is fine. Perfect. Thank you."

"My pleasure." She settles back in her chair, nodding her permission to take another chocolate. The odds are excellent this box does not survive our session. I *mmm* through another caramel and don't even flinch when Meredith starts talking again.

"So what about you? Are you close with your dad?"

I know this territory well enough not to react.

"He died when I was young."

"Oh I'm sorry." Meredith is the rare type of person who makes that sound sincere. "How old were you?"

"Eleven."

She makes a *tsk* sound. "That is young. That's a hard age." I'm preparing my answer for the traditional follow-up question but Meredith spares me the lie of how he died. Instead she goes with, "What about your mom? Are you two close? Do you have brothers and sisters?"

"No," I say, glad to have an answer for the last question that may or may not answer the first two. "I'm an only child. I'm one of those weirdos." I give the smile that has convinced therapists and teachers for decades.

"Hey, don't say that." She wags her finger at me. "I only had one child. There's nothing wrong with only children. They're special. As I always say to Derek, 'I got it right with you. I didn't need to keep trying.'"

She toasts me with her mug and I take a long time for my sip, very glad at that moment to be drinking coffee, something bitter and stimulating enough to keep me from letting something fall out of my mouth about how much words like that mean to a kid.

"Isn't it sad," she says over her cup, "that it takes something as horrible as death to make us stop and take the time to get to know the people around us? This is our second semester together and this is the first time you've told me about your father."

"It's not the kind of thing to lead with, you know? It was a long time ago."

"Were you lonely? As an only child?"

My thankfulness at being here is rapidly losing ground to my desire to go home to Jeannie and climb into a bottle as it becomes clear that Meredith plans to keep this conversation in the somber zone. "No, I had Jeannie. We grew up together. I don't know what it's like to have a real sister, but I can't imagine it could be anything closer than what we had."

"That's nice. That's one thing I worried about with Derek. Was he lonely? Would another sibling have made him more social? He's so isolated. He's so intense. He broods."

I look at the ungainly man-child in the photo. It seems we have something in common.

I'm about ready to start brooding myself. I hate to leave this chocolate behind, but if Destiny demands that I spend my day on these kinds of thoughts, it's best I prepare accordingly. I'm wondering how much effort it will take to get all the way back home, get my wallet, and get down to Kroger and back. Two bottles of wine simply won't cut it. Then again, I reason, Jeannie is here. She knew Ellis; she'll want to talk about it. She'll worry about leaving me alone to go to a dark place. She'll pick up more wine.

Sometimes it's just that basic for me.

"Did you and your husband try to have children?"

The question surprises me out of my consumption-strategy daydream. Meredith has never asked me personal questions like this. She's never struck me as the type to jam a conversational crowbar like that into another person and I'm so surprised by it that I almost answer. I almost start talking. I almost tell her in one awful, wordy, brutally sober monologue about Ronnie and what he was and what I am and why there couldn't possibly be a worse time in all the world for someone to kill Ellis Trachtenberg.

Two things spare us this conversation. The first is that in my surprise, I inhale a sliver of candied ginger. Not enough to close off my esophagus, just enough to lodge a fiber of the caustic root on my epiglottis so that I immediately start hacking. Meredith shoves a napkin at me and slides my coffee cup within reach. She looks for all the world like she's preparing to give me the Heimlich maneuver. I flutter my hands in front of me, both waving her off and fanning out the flames I feel blasting up my throat and out over my face.

"I'm okay," I gasp, riding out the rhythm of my throat spasm. "Ginger."

"I'm so sorry." She pushes my coffee into my hand. "Drink. Take a drink. I'm so sorry. I didn't mean to take you by surprise." She waits for me to take a sip of my coffee, keep it down, try another. I nod at her with relief when I believe I will survive. I'm thinking the rawness in my throat was worth it for the distraction it caused, but then she starts again.

"It's just, you know, I can't help but think about things like that when I hear about someone dying suddenly." God damn it, she's going to keep going there. "I know your husband was sick, but did you want children? Did you try? It's absolutely none of my business."

You got that right.

"I have no right in the world to ask, do I?"

You do not.

"But we're just like that, aren't we?"

Who? Me? No.

"Women, I mean. I guess maybe we just look at the world a little differently. We look at life differently. Maybe because we can give it, we look differently at anyone taking it away."

I am seriously considering jamming another piece of ginger deep into my throat, maybe even into hers. She's not looking at me, which might explain why this woman I have considered my friend for months now has suddenly morphed into this stranger espousing this biological bullshit. I can hear my mother in my head losing her mind over this sort of gender-stereotyping, howling about imprisoning ourselves in our ovaries and dismissing our rightful intellect in the name of hormonal flow.

Surely if Meredith looked at me, if she looked into my eyes, she would see my mother dancing in my brain, raging and shaking her fist, demanding that her daughter not be lumped into such maudlin, parochial, regressive categories. Surely she would see her outrage, the arguments she had implanted so deeply within me, that no woman's reality and reasoning be conscripted or predicted by something as primitive as a procreational urge.

Surely if Meredith looked at me at that moment, she would see my mother. She would have to, because she certainly wouldn't be seeing me, because I am gone. In that moment, I am wholly and totally gone, absent, away. In that moment, I am hiding behind my mother's rage, protected by the only shield she ever offered me, the most powerful force ever to blow through my young life.

I haven't spoken to my mother in almost two decades and I can still feel the blast of that heat blow through me, leveling me.

Apparently this apocalypse of mine has gone unnoticed by Meredith because she's still talking to herself in that soft voice. "Life is so fragile. It's so worth fighting for. You never realize how much it means to you until you see it taken away from someone else. Then you know, then you really know what is worth fighting for."

I have no idea what she's talking about at this point. I'm suddenly aware of how hot I've become. I'm wearing tights and thermal underwear under my clothes, the windows are closed to keep the snow out. I'm drinking hot coffee, and coughing up ginger, and scrambling for an escape from this conversation when the most unlikely savior walks in.

A cop.

The cop who watched me walk away from the crime scene.

She's got another cop with her, which should make me sit up and be cautious—this is a lot of police officers to come through an office in one day—but I'm so desperate to not hear what Meredith is talking about that I once again do the wrong thing. I've been here before; I've been in the focus of the police gaze before and I know better than to act rashly, but for the life of me I cannot get my shit together.

"Hi," I say to the waiting officers. My voice squeaks from the rawness of my throat. I've kicked back the chair several inches without even realizing it and now I'm sitting at an awkward angle to both Meredith and the door, facing neither. I tell myself in a hurry that I'm not acting as weird as I think I am, but judging from the look Meredith is giving me, I'm probably wrong.

"Can we help you, officers?" Meredith sounds like an adult. I think I should shift my chair but can't decide if I should turn it back toward my boss or around to face the cops. Everything feels complicated.

"Hi." The cop smiles, looking relaxed. "I'm Detective Hinton, this is Officer Neighborgall."

"Oh, Detective Hinton!" Meredith's face lights up. "You were one of the officers who helped us collect toys for the Christmas drive. You put in so many hours. It was such a success. How nice to see you again."

"I'm looking to speak with Anna Ray. And Meredith Michener."

Now I wish I had turned my chair all the way around to face the door.

"You found us," Meredith says with enthusiasm. She says it with a smile, like she didn't hear the period in that statement. Or maybe like she did. They want to speak to me. And then they want to speak to Meredith. In that order of importance. "What can we do for you?"

"We'd like to ask you a couple of questions about what happened in the building." No stilted cop talk here. Hinton has actual questions that will require more than just our names and titles to answer. It's then that I hear the voices in the hallway. Other cops are standing in other doorways; other radios squawk, but much more quietly now. They are looking for information. They are looking for something specific and they are looking for it here.

Meredith must recognize the change in tenor. Officer Chubby is nowhere to be found. She waves her hand, inviting the cops into the office. "We're all yours."

They step into the room together, Hinton one step ahead of her partner. It doesn't escape me that they stand close enough to effectively block the door without being obvious about it. I wonder if that's intentional or just from years of habit. Hinton's gaze on me isn't steely or aggressive but it never wavers.

"Is there somewhere we can talk, Mrs. Ray?"

"Right here is fine." I hope I sound helpful.

Officer Neighborgall takes off his hat and shakes melted snow off of it and into a garbage can by the door. He's smiling. "Well, I'll tell you, it'll save us a lot of time if we can split it up."

I notice his use of pronouns—split *it* up, not split *us* up. I can see their dynamic. Hinton is younger than her partner, with a wide, smooth face that doesn't look like it's been marked by too many smiles. She doesn't look cold, just serious and calm. Neighborgall, on the other hand, is ruddy and whiskery, his salt-and-pepper mustache needs a trim and his cheeks look chapped. His eyes wrinkle when he smiles and I suspect his accent is a bit of an affectation. I'd wager he's the one who steps forward when dealing with the good-old-boy types who refuse to acknowledge Hinton's rank.

He strikes me as a tap dancer and a bullshitter. I wonder if he resents being paired with Hinton or if she resents being paired with him. I realize I'm thinking way too much about this and that everyone in the room is waiting for me to say something.

"My desk is back there." I point past the divider. "Will that work? Private enough?"

I want to make her say it, put her on the spot. Am I being questioned privately? Or is splitting us up just a time-saver?

"That'll be fine," Hinton says with a nod toward my desk.

I push myself out of the chair, meeting Meredith's eye as I do. We stare at each other for just a second. Her eyes widen with a look that says this particular excitement is a surprise. At least I think that's what it says. She might just be wondering why I'm staring at her. My gaze flickers to the chocolate.

"Do you mind?"

"What?" Clearly her thoughts were somewhere else. "Of course. Please, take some more. Take a couple."

I do. The last two caramels and a lavender. The urge to shove something in my mouth is strong right now. I'm not ready to risk another ginger, but caramel will keep me nicely busy.

Hinton watches me pick out the chocolates, watches me pick up my mug, watches me nudge the chair out of the way. Nothing aggressive about it, I tell myself. Does she think it's weird that I'm stopping for snacks? She's waiting to follow me to my desk. What else is she going to watch? Neighborgall's eyes are wrinkled like he's smiling but his mustache hides his lips.

I calm down as I head for my desk, recognizing my own stupid knee-jerk reactions. There's been a murder. This is a small town. The body was found in the basement of our building. Of course the cops are going to talk to everyone more than once. They're in other offices right now, aren't they? You're not that special, Anna. Nobody is looking at you. I think about Jeannie's need to be the star of every story she tells, how she feels all eyes and hearts and groins are focused on her. I wonder if this is a psychology unique to our gene pool.

I set coffee and chocolates down on a file of grant applications and drop into my chair. Hinton pulls out a notebook and motions toward the chair opposite me.

"Do you mind if I sit?"

"Of course, go ahead."

She mutters her thanks and tries to get comfortable in the chair, tugging on her jacket and adjusting her belt. I've never sat in that chair. It doesn't look uncomfortable but nobody ever seems able to settle in it. In some ways, that makes it a perfect office chair. Nobody should want to stay in it.

Her radio squawks and in the chatter, I hear Hinton's name. She pulls the handset off the clip on her jacket. "This is Hinton. Tell Brody it's a go on that. We're finishing up in Jenkins. Tell the captain we won't be long." More chatter and she silences it.

They won't be long. That's a good sign. I inform my body that it's okay to relax, that we require neither fight nor flight in the foreseeable future. Hinton opens her notebook but doesn't bother with the pen.

"Can you tell me what you know about what happened in the basement?"

"Someone died. I saw you all taping off the scene when I came back from the library." She nods and waits for me to keep talking. "Everything else is just rumors."

"What are the rumors?"

"That Ellis Trachtenberg was killed."

"Do you know Professor Trachtenberg?"

"Is it true?" Just because I'm relaxed doesn't mean I feel like doing all the talking.

She considers me for a second and then nods. "It is. Sometimes I don't know why we bother trying to keep a lid on things. I guess there are no secrets at a small college. We haven't informed his family yet so I would appreciate it if you kept that to yourself." She gives a resigned hand wave toward the hallway where we can hear people going back and forth. "You know, inasmuch as is possible."

"Sure, I know."

Another look at her notebook and we're back to it. "How well did you know Professor Trachtenberg?"

Shrug. "Not that well. Work friends."

She's not taking notes. "How would you describe your relationship?"

"I just did. Work friends."

Still no notes. "When is the last time you spoke with Mr. Trachtenberg?"

It takes me a minute to believe the timeline. It feels like years. "Yesterday. He came by the office. It was at lunchtime."

"What for?"

Detective Hinton has a nice voice. It's soft without being weak, cool without being dismissive. Her manner projects a comfortable amount of interest without triggering a sense of being grilled. Unless of course you've been grilled before.

I know this part. I know this balance. Leaving gaps in the conversation, hoping the other person will feel compelled to fill them. A string of simple questions that feel innocuous until you remember that this isn't small talk; this isn't a cocktail party and the person asking you the questions isn't networking or flirting or killing time. They're looking for something and that something is not necessarily in your words.

The absolute worst thing to do—besides blurt out a confession, of course—is to switch to an obviously defensive stance. Don't stonewall but don't volunteer.

I have to remind myself that I don't need to stonewall or volunteer. This isn't my show. I have nothing to add.

"He dropped off a book about an obscure art movement he was teaching." I toss a careless glance to a pile of textbooks heaped on a nearby filing cabinet. I don't know if the Mann book is there; I just want to make it clear that this is a college office. Books come and go.

"What was the name of that book?" I tell her and she writes it down. "And after that?"

"After that, he left. Said he was working on a lecture."

"No, I mean when did you talk to him after that?"

"I didn't."

Her finger twitches on her notebook. "You didn't talk to Ellis Trachtenberg at any time after that? No messages, nothing?" When I shake my head, she nods. "Where were you last night, Mrs. Ray?"

Something small and sharp in the pit of my stomach tells me I might have relaxed too soon. "I had dinner with my cousin last night. We went to Ollie's."

"Your cousin's name?"

I spell Jeannie's name for her, leaving out the Fitzhugh, leaving out that she used to teach here. I have to catch myself from offering too much information, managing to supply just her name and the fact that she's visiting. No more. I tell myself that if this is something they need to know, they can learn it themselves.

"How late were you out?"

Here's where it starts to fall apart. Here's where it can all go wrong because here's where I don't know what the truth is. I'm not about to tell Detective Hinton that I was hammered last night and woke up half-naked in the bathtub reading a family newsletter.

"I don't know. It was late. We sat around drinking for a while. You know, just catching up. Once we get started, we tend to talk on and on." Something I'm trying very hard not to do just now.

She smiles as she glances over her notes. "Yeah, my sister and I are the same way. Is your cousin staying with you, Mrs. Ray, in your apartment at Everly Place?"

Nice switchback, I think. Friendly little mention of her sister followed by letting me know she already has my address. The police haven't been on scene for five hours and they've already noted my address.

"It's Ms. Ray, Detective, and the answer is yes and no." I match her friendly tone, keep it light. I give no sign that I've noticed her access to my information. "She's staying with me but she's also keeping a room at the Days Inn. My apartment's a dump."

"I know." She laughs softly. "I used to live in those apartments years ago. They were a dump then, too. Those are usually for students. Why do you live there? If you don't mind my asking."

It's a little late to worry about what I mind, don't you think? "I moved here right after I took the job. There wasn't much time to search for a place before the semester started. My plan was to just stay long enough to find a nicer place but then, you know, work started and bills started and it was just easier to stay put."

"Yeah." She nods, tapping her fingers along the edge of her notebook. "It's easy to get stuck, isn't it? You make plans and you have the best intentions and then life just creeps in on you. You can't get anything done. You can't make things happen. It's frustrating."

Before I can finish my 'What are you going to do?' shrug, she changes course.

"Are you married, Ms. Ray?"

"Widowed." The word sounds so strange. I still can't make it fit. It's a word for women whose men went to war. It's a word for women with bulky sweaters who knit and dust knick-knacks. Put the right color in front of it and it's for a different type of woman altogether.

"Were you dating Ellis Trachtenberg?"

"No."

"Did you want to?"

"No." I think maybe I should have questioned that question, asked her what the hell she meant by that. My rapid answer suggests forethought, preparation for this line of questioning. Fuck it, I'm tired of this line of questioning. I'm tired of this day. I have no dog in this fight. I shouldn't have to think this hard to tell the truth.

"Can you think of any reason someone would kill Ellis Trachtenberg?"

"No. From what I knew of him, he was a good man."

"But you didn't want to go out with him."

Really? We're doing this? I am only partially successful in keeping the anger out of my tone. "No, Detective. I didn't want to go out with him. I don't want to go out with anyone. My husband hasn't been dead a year."

She nods again and puts her notebook away. She rises and thanks me for my time and gives me her card but I'm not listening. I'm hearing my words echo in my head. My husband hasn't been dead a year? That's not right.

As of this morning, he's been dead a year and a day.

CHAPTER 10

Whatever compelled me to remain here has left. I'm going to find no shelter from my thoughts here anymore so I rise to follow Detective Hinton out of the office, but she holds up her hand to slow me down.

Meredith and Officer Neighborgall are still talking. There's nothing unusual about that—Meredith can make a conversation last. What is unusual, or at least worth noting, to my mind, is that, whatever they're discussing, Detective Hinton considers it private. Maybe that's just standard procedure, keeping witness statements discrete, but I don't much care for police procedure, standard or not.

We wait a few seconds, not much more than a minute, when we both see the body language in front of us change. Neighborgall shakes his head and Meredith laughs and everyone can tell that the interview is over. Hinton drops her hand and, like an obedient child in the crosswalk, I follow her into Meredith's space.

"So you tell Jodi to call me whenever she's ready to start painting and I'll be there." Meredith bumps her fist on the desk for emphasis.

Neighborgall shakes his head before replacing his hat. "I'll tell her, but you know Jodi. She does her own thing her way and what I say makes absolutely no difference."

Meredith laughs. "It's a good husband who recognizes that."

She's still laughing as she pours herself some more coffee. She doesn't see Neighborgall and Hinton share that silent pause-and-nod so common to partners.

"Thank you both for your time." Detective Hinton nods to each of us. "You have our cards. If you think of anything you might have forgotten to tell us, anything at all that you think might be relevant to the investigation, call us anytime."

"Of course," Meredith says. "And of course if you have any more questions, don't hesitate to ask us anything else. We're always here."

Hinton gives her a small smile. "Aren't the offices closing?"

Meredith laughs again, like this is great fun for her. "Oh, that's right! Well don't worry. We're not going to leave town or anything. Especially in this weather. We're due another foot, they're saying. Looks like we're going to get a whole winter's worth of snow this week."

Neighborgall adjusts his belt. "Well, you be safe out there. Don't drive if you don't have to. They're clearing the roads now but who knows how it will get later."

"Loud and clear, Kenny," Meredith says. So it's Kenny for her. She tones down the cheer. "And good luck with this. I can't believe this happened. If there's anything we can do to help, please let us know. We all liked Professor Trachtenberg so very much."

"We'll do our best." He opens the door and waves Detective Hinton through first. "We really appreciate your time, ladies." Hinton just nods. Neighborgall is in charge of the niceties.

He pulls the door shut behind them and we hear radios squawking and footsteps. I lean toward the glass, wanting to hear if they say anything, but Meredith interrupts my spying.

"Whew! Two police visits in one day. What did they ask you?"

"Nothing, really." Nothing I feel like thinking about. "If I knew him, did I know any reason why someone would hurt him. I was pretty much useless to them." I grab my coat from the rack and slip it on. I hear my keys jingle in my pocket. Thank god.

Meredith watches me wrestle with my zipper. "I guess they have to talk to everyone. Can you imagine trying to solve a crime?" I give up on the zipper and start sorting out my wet-mitten situation. She watches me like I'm interesting. "I mean, we see it on TV and we know how it's going to go. Suspects are introduced and we can start narrowing it down, but what do the police do in real life? How do they narrow down an entire campus of people? And that's not including the people Ellis knew outside of school. How do you narrow down a person's entire life to find the one person who hated them enough to kill him?"

I shrug and slip my hat on. "I have no idea. I'm glad I don't have to do it." She makes a little *hmm* sound, like she's wondering what I'll say next. I don't keep her in suspense. "Well, I guess that's all we can do today. I guess the offices will still be closed tomorrow, right? So I guess I'll see you Friday."

She's smiling at me. "Are you forgetting something?"

There's a question. She has no idea the things I plan on forgetting for the next forty-eight hours, but it's a safe guess that's not what she means.

She nods toward my feet.

"Shit." I'm still wearing the house shoes she lent me. Meredith laughs as I peel off my mittens and hat. I'm already hot and I haven't even zipped my jacket yet. A mitten gets tangled in my sleeve when I try to shed everything at once and I don't see that Meredith has come around the desk to help me. She pulls the jacket free of my arms and takes the mitten from my fist. Before I can reach for my boots she grabs my shoulders and holds me at arm's length.

"Are you okay?"

"Yeah, I'm fine." I stop just short of shaking her off. "It's just my mind is somewhere else. And these slippers are really comfortable." I smile and she smiles but we are wearing two different expressions.

She rubs my arms and I can't decide if I hate the feeling or really love it. "It's okay to be upset, Anna. It's okay to feel bad." I decide to hate the gesture and to get away from it but she holds on, leaning in close. I imagine all of the students she has soothed with this voice. "I know you and Ellis were friends. You were even maybe on the verge of being something more?" She asks the question like she already knows the answer, which clearly she does not. I shake my head and she nods.

"I know. I know. I teased you about it and I know you're still conflicted. You've lost your husband and it's hard when time moves on and—"

"What? No." I free myself from her but, pinned between her and the coat rack, I don't have anywhere to go. "I wasn't conflicted. There was nothing to be conflicted about. There was nothing going on with Ellis Trachtenberg. Wait, did you tell the cop there was?"

"No, Anna." She gives me room, holding up her hands. "Your name didn't come up in the questions. Why would it? I didn't mean to upset you. I'm sorry."

Now I feel like an ass. Now I wish I'd just gone ahead and left in the slippers. Cold feet would be preferable to this little scene I'm causing. Fortunately Meredith is no stranger to eruptions of drama and she's gone back to her mother hen countenance. She talks over my apology as she heads back to her desk.

"It's been a horrible day. This is a horrible thing. Nobody knows how to behave when something like this happens. How would we?"

Is she kidding? I could write a fucking book. Of anyone, I should know how to behave, and yet I keep screwing it up. I'm shoving my feet into my boots when Meredith jingles her keys.

"Ride home?"

"No, that's okay. I like the snow."

"You sure? How about a grocery run?" I look up at that and she nods. "Uh-huh. You weren't prepared for the snow, were you? You learn that lesson fast around here. Always keep a stockpile handy." She waves to the mountain behind her. "A skill you can plainly see that I've mastered."

"Shit," I say again, patting my pockets. "I left without my purse this morning." From my back pocket I pull out two wadded-up twenties. That's enough for a couple bottles, I figure, if I lower my already low standards. Beggars can't be choosers.

"I'll spot you," Meredith said, shrugging into her coat and collecting her purse. Before I can argue, she's turned off the lights and is waiting to lock the door behind me. "Trust me," she says, "I'll sleep better knowing you're not snowed into your apartment living on mustard packets and old tater tots."

. . . .

Kroger is not quite the bedlam I feared it would be. Meredith warns me that I'll be out of luck if I'm looking for bread or milk. I laugh as I leave her to wait in the car. I'm not even sure I'd know where to look for either of those anymore.

She only had thirty dollars on her, which she insisted I take. I didn't want to. It's not that I feel uncomfortable borrowing cash; I have the money in my wallet at home. It will be nothing to pay her back. It's that I know Meredith expects to see actual groceries purchased on this trip. She's driving me here as a favor to me to be sure I'm not snowed in without food. There's no polite way to tell her that I don't want food, that I think I have food. Sure, it's probably all frozen pizzas and a buffet of chips, but it's food. What I want is wine. What I want is to wake up well on the other side of this anniversary.

What I absolutely don't want, however, is to trigger any sort of alarm in Meredith.

So I get a buggy and head for the wine aisle. I'm calculating how many bottles I can carry at the bottom of those plastic grocery bags without it being obviously the largest part of the bulk. Three. I feel safe with three. Then I wander. Club Crackers sound good. Some cream cheese.

Package of salami. I feel like I'm back in college, high as a kite, bouncing around a convenience store at the whim of my taste buds.

I could live on this much food for a month. Then I see the produce section on the other side of the deli counter. Meredith will feel assured if she sees produce. A bundle of celery and a bag of clementines to fill out the top of the bags will do nicely. I check myself out so I can bag the groceries to properly camouflage the wine. I'm almost thirty years old and I'm hiding my booze.

Back at the car, I fit the bags behind the passenger seat. Meredith acts like she's not looking at my haul but then gives herself away. "Clementines. I love them."

I knew she would.

. . . .

It's snowing again and the higher we climb toward my apartment complex, the more neglected the roads. Meredith doesn't flinch; her heavy Subaru four-wheel drive handles the snow without a slip. At the turn-off to the parking lot on Everly Road, a snowbank lines the road where the state crews plowed. Nobody has shoveled the lot yet. A few tracks have broken the crest of the plowed snow. There's no way to tell if they run through the actual entrance or not.

"I'll get out here," I say, reaching behind me for the bags.

"Don't be ridiculous."

Before I can complain or reassure her or whatever it might take to get Meredith to let me out, she maneuvers her car along the tracks, over the snow, and rolls easily into the lot. "I've been driving in this stuff for forty years," she says with a grin. "A little pile of snow like that isn't going to stop me."

"Well, I appreciate it. You didn't have to—"

Meredith shuts off the engine. Surely she's not planning on coming in.

She nods, answering a question I didn't ask. "I'm coming with you." She holds up a hand to stop my protest. "I am coming in with you. I'm going to make sure you're okay. I'm going to see where you live. You're going to talk to me and I'm going to talk to you, just like two human beings who know each other. You know, like maybe we're friends."

"Meredith . . ."

"I don't want to hear it. You're upset. I don't leave my friends alone when they're upset."

Well, fuck.

I've got bigger problems heading my way over the next few nights so I decide not to waste any energy on this one. Meredith wants to make sure I'm okay. She's going to want to sit down, make a little small talk, reassure herself that there's no hangman's noose waiting for me inside my foyer. I know how to handle this. It's just like reassuring Jeannie.

Speak of the devil.

We're at the bottom of the steps when a car door slams.

"Anna?" Jeannie marches through the snow, bundled up like she just left a fashion show in the Swiss Alps. Furry après-ski boots cover snug wool pants; a fluffy down jacket manages to be both puffy and formfitting. Even her hat is adorable and stylish, seemingly designed to accommodate her equally fluffy ponytail. "Where have you been?"

All the style in the world can't hide that expression on her face. Jeannie is pissed.

"Hi, Professor." Meredith waves a gloved hand. She doesn't seem to read my cousin's mood at all. "Have any trouble getting around in the snow?"

How can I describe the look Jeannie turns on her? If we were in high school, that would probably be called a mean-girl look. It would probably end with Meredith getting banished from the cool kids' table in the cafeteria, resigning her to a walk of shame to the nerd corner. But this isn't high school and, with me comprising the entirety of Jeannie's clique, she doesn't wield a lot of clout. Caught as I am in the web of

Meredith's concern, I think there is a real possibility I may get mother-henned to death today.

Jeannie examines the grocery bags in my hands and notices that Meredith carries nothing but her purse. "I have some things to bring up. It's going to take more than one trip."

"I'll help!" Meredith is all smiles and I wonder if she's enjoying whatever is happening here. They trudge off to Jeannie's car as I head up the steps, glad to get the wine unpacked without Meredith examining my alcohol-to-food ratio.

Jeannie wasn't kidding about having some stuff. She and Meredith return in a moment with tote bags and a suitcase and head out for another trip. I see food in some of the tote bags. Jeannie doesn't mess around when it comes to laying out a spread and as I unpack foil-wrapped containers, I think maybe I need food more than I'm admitting. I peel back the foil of a gorgeous green salad full of orange slices and almonds that looks like it holds more nutrition than I've consumed in months.

When they return with the second load, Meredith puts down two huge jugs of water. Jeannie sets a cardboard box down at the foot of the kitchen counter and holds out her hand.

"Keys."

I hand them over without delay and without knowing why. Before I can ask she's out the door again.

Meredith starts unpacking one of the tote bags. "Boy, your cousin doesn't mess around does she? Or travel light?"

"She worries about me."

She pats my shoulder. "That seems to be going around."

I pry back the lid of a container and discover cinnamon rolls waiting to be baked. I could weep with joy at the smell of them. The door slams and Jeannie tosses my keys onto the counter.

She has my mail.

We share a look as she tosses it onto the coffee table. She knows what's in the stack. She knows what I'll do with most of it. Fortunately, she also senses my desire to keep all of this from Meredith. My boss doesn't seem to notice any of this; she's busy unpacking and commenting on all the delectables Jeannie has delivered.

"You pulled all of this together from a hotel room?" Meredith marvels, holding up a plate of stuffed dates dusted with powdered sugar.

Normally this sort of comment would please Jeannie, prompting her to shrug off the praise with a modest dismissal, as if everyone were capable of this level of culinary wizardry. Instead, she answers with a curt, "Yeah. People cater. You can buy food to go."

That's when I know she's really pissed.

An old fear ignites in my gut. I've always been afraid of Jeannie's anger. It brings into sharp relief the balance of power between us: I need Jeannie. She does not need me. She has a life and a family and absolutely nothing to hide from anyone. She has never turned that anger on me, not in all the years we have been close, but still the presence of her temper freezes me, nails me to the floor, and makes me want to apologize for anything, for everything.

I turn to face her, my hands at my side, open and exposed. Part of me almost hopes this is it, this is the time she turns that wrath on me and finally delivers the death blow. Part of me is tired of waiting for it. Part of me has been expecting it most of my life.

She steps past Meredith, who is looking for a place to put a package of yeast rolls. The kitchen hardly has room for one person; with three, we are far too close. When Meredith bumps into Jeannie and starts to ask about a gourmet salad dressing, Jeannie's voice drops to a hiss. "Could you give us a second?"

Meredith tries to play the jolly card, holding up the bottle of dressing. Jeannie snatches it out of her hand and slams it on the counter.

"A second, please?"

Jeannie sounds just like her mother. Meredith's eyes go wide and she backs out of the kitchen but she's faking her fear. She gives me the look kids give another kid getting sent to the principal's office, a look that says "Ooh, you're gonna get it now!" But again, this isn't high school. This isn't a principal and if I get expelled from Jeannie's life, I have lost everything.

Jeannie stares up at me. With no heels, she is six inches shorter than I am. The flush of anger on her face and the tightness of her expression bring out wrinkles around her eyes and mouth that I've never noticed before. It's strange. I never think of Jeannie aging.

"Are you going to tell me what is going on?" She's whispering. I don't know if it's to keep Meredith from hearing or to keep herself from screaming at me. I don't know what she wants to hear. I shake my head. "I have been calling you all day."

"I forgot my phone."

"You forgot your phone? Today?" She steps in closer, pointing a finger up at me. "You don't forget your phone today. Not today. Not this week. Don't pretend you don't know what I'm talking about."

"I'm sorry."

She doesn't want to hear that. "I called your office phone. I got your voice mail three times. Three times." Her finger is getting very close to my face. "And then, after I got all this food, I went to campus to pick you up. In this snow, I drove all over Gilead to get all of this. I drove up to campus in all this snow to get you, and do you know what I found? Do you, Anna?"

I close my eyes.

"I saw the police, Anna. I saw ambulances and police cars. I saw crime scene tape. All of it centered on your building. Where you work. I came looking for you and I found a crime scene. Today. Today of all days."

I open my eyes when I hear her voice break.

"Do you know where my mind went? Do you know what that looked like to me, Anna?" The hand pointing at me trembles and then rubs her wet eyes. "Do you have any idea how scared I was?"

"I'm sorry."

She finally exhales, shaking her head, and then pulls me in for a tight hug. I keep apologizing, feeling her tremble against me. I don't know why she always forgives me. I don't know why she keeps putting up with my shit. I really don't.

Of course, she recovers first.

"And I knew you'd have nothing to eat because, god forbid you should actually look at a weather forecast." She steps away and starts folding an empty tote bag.

Relief makes my voice breathy. "I got groceries."

She raises an eyebrow. "Let me guess. Slim Jims and Lucky Charms. But no milk."

"No, I got—" I think of the salami and cream cheese. "Actually that's pretty close."

She laughs an *uh-huh* and we move around each other, putting food away. Meredith reminds us of her presence.

"Everything okay in there?" She's settled on the couch, pretending to leaf through an old magazine.

"We're fine!" Jeannie answers for me, shooting me a "What is she doing here?" look. I shrug and try to dodge Jeannie as she heads for my cabinet. She takes the Club Crackers from my hands. "Go. Go sit down. Let me put this stuff away. I've got to heat up the enchiladas. Go entertain your guest."

"Anything I can do to help?" Meredith gets up and heads our way.

"Yeah," Jeannie says and fires a pack of toilet paper over the bar at her. "Put this in the bathroom. Please." Meredith fumbles the catch and the package bounces toward me. I step around the bar to scoop it up, embarrassed.

Meredith takes the toilet paper from me with a knowing look. "I've got it." She keeps her voice low. "You go talk to your cousin."

"I'm sorry. She's just worried."

"I know. I know." She gives me a motherly pat and heads down the hall toward my bathroom. I wait until she closes the door behind her.

"God, Jeannie, that was kind of rude."

"What? She asked if she could help. Open the wine."

I grab one of my smuggled bottles and start digging through the clutter for the corkscrew. The toilet flushes and Meredith laughs in the hallway.

"Not much of a housekeeper, are you, Anna?"

I look over my shoulder, fully prepared to apologize for my bathroom, and I freeze.

"Put those down."

"Oh, I don't mind," Meredith says, scooping up my mother's letters. "I'll just get these off the floor and—"

"Put them down!"

I don't mean to scream but she's on her knees, scooping up letters with one hand. With the other, she's reaching for the closet door. I realize I'm holding the corkscrew like a knife.

"Please, Meredith. Put them down."

Her eyes are wide, afraid. "Okay," she says softly. "Okay." Very slowly, she puts the envelopes back on the floor and rises to her feet. Jeannie is silent behind me. There is no dignified way to redeem this situation so I don't even try. I turn back to my wine and jab the corkscrew in deep. Jeannie goes back to covering a pan in foil, Meredith makes her way to the counter. I can't leave things like this.

"We've got this covered, Meredith. Would you like a glass of wine?" I calm down, feeling safe again with Jeannie in the kitchen. I don't want Meredith to stick around, but she did drive me home and she did lend me money and she did express genuine concern at my well-being. It wouldn't kill me to act like a grown up for a little while.

"Thank you, but no. I don't drink." I admire her ability to say that without a trace of sanctimony. She's bent down by the kitchen bar, looking into the box Jeannie hauled up. I see twelve bottles of wine. God bless you, Jeannie. She closes the flaps and wipes her hands on her pants. "Oh well, it looks like you're stocked up. That should keep you for the spring thaw."

Jeannie laughs.

Meredith's hands flutter in that way she has. She looks nervous and I feel bad. I want to say something to put her at ease but I want the wine more. I'm pouring Jeannie's glass when Meredith steps in closer to me, her voice soft.

"I hope it's okay, but"—her hands flutter toward the purse hanging off her shoulder—"I found your cell phone. You must have left it in the bathroom. I hope it's okay that I picked it up. It's just that I know you said you didn't have it and I thought that maybe—"

"It's okay, Meredith."

She's got her advocate voice on. "I don't want you to think that I'm messing with anything that belongs to you or that I'm violating your space."

"It's okay, Meredith. Really. It's okay. Put the phone anywhere."

She only looks partially reassured. She looks at me like she's trying to figure out if there is something really wrong with me. God knows, I'm familiar with that look. She nods and pulls the phone out of her pocket. "I just thought you should know you have messages."

Jeannie sighs an impatient sigh, her back to us. I know Meredith is trying to be helpful. I really should be nicer. I wave my hand toward the counter. "Please, I'll listen to them later. Just put it down."

But Meredith doesn't. She turns to face me at an odd angle, leaning over the counter so her back is to Jeannie. She holds up the phone between us and taps the screen. She keeps her voice low.

"You have a message," she says again. "One you might want to hear?"

I am not in the mood for this but even less in the mood to argue. I snatch the phone from her, swipe it to life and put the message on speaker so I can concentrate on filling my own glass. I expect to hear Jeannie's voice, demanding to know why I'm not picking up the damn phone on this day, of all days. I'll delete it after the first "God damn it, Anna." Shouldn't take long. Instead I hear a man speak, his tone soft and well-modulated.

"Hello, Anna, it's Ellis. Um, Trachtenberg." He clears his throat, which I can barely hear over the sharp breath I suck in. Meredith's eyes are wide, her hands clamped over her mouth. Her face flushes red right up to her strawberry-blond hairline. Jeannie slams the oven shut as the message plays on.

"I was wondering if we could talk. I was hoping"—he sighs—"I was hoping we could talk. I have something for you, something I'd like you to have." I hear background noise and then the unmistakable creak of an office chair. He sounds like he's talking to himself and I can't help but wonder who the hell leaves a message like this. I'm tempted to yell "Get to the point!" but even I behave better than that. When I'm sober. Which I really wish I weren't at this moment.

"You know what?" Ellis is still talking. "I'm just going to come by your office. It's late but maybe you're still there. If you're not, I'll just leave it for you. Or I'll get it to you tomorrow. It's supposed to snow tonight." I can hear the smile in his voice. "Gilead is absolutely gorgeous in the snow. Maybe you'll let me take you on a walk to some of the better views from above campus. Okay, wow, I'm going on and on, aren't I?" There's that charming laugh again. "I'll wrap this up and try to do this face to face. If you get this, call me. I'll be in my office all night. I've got a lot of work but I would really like to give you something. Tonight, if possible. Or tomorrow. Whatever works for you."

He pauses and sighs. "Goodnight, Anna. I'm thinking of you. I hope you're well."

The call ends and a woman's voice comes on, instructing me to press one to hear the message again—as if that would ever be an option—seven to delete, nine to skip. I'm reaching to push seven when Meredith grabs the phone away from me.

"You can't delete that!" Her face is very red.

Jeannie snorts and reaches for her wine. "Oh please," she says. I hadn't realized she'd come so close. "That's a standard Ellis message. He loves being mysterious. Trust me, you can delete it. He'll leave more."

Meredith looks like she might faint. It takes her a few gasped sounds before she can make the words. "How can you say that? My god, how can you talk about him like that?"

Jeannie rolls her eyes. I want to stop her before she says anything else but my thoughts won't fall into place.

"Come on." She looks at me like I've lost my mind, which is entirely possible. "What are you going to do? Transcribe it and put it in your hope chest? He's probably got another book for you or a poem, something dark and spare about the symbolic purity of snow."

I hold up my hand to stop her but Meredith speaks first.

"You are a horrible person."

"Hey!" I snap, but Meredith won't be stopped.

"You have always been a horrible person and now you're just proving it."

I don't know what she expects Jeannie to say but I'd bet she isn't expecting a laugh. Jeannie can pack more derision and dismissal into one laugh than any five people could ever hope to achieve as a team. She cocks her hip, waggling her wine glass like a prop, and I know how withering her tone will be before she speaks.

"Hey, Meredith? I don't know what kind of romantic fantasies you may be constructing vicariously through my cousin, but I think I know Ellis a little better than you and—"

"He's dead." I say it quickly.

"Yeah," Jeannie nods, smiling, not hearing me but assuming I'm backing her play. "Ellis Trachtenberg is a bore who thinks he can talk his way—"

"He's dead, Jeannie." She pauses, hearing me. "Ellis was killed last night. That's what the crime scene was. That's why the police were there."

She almost spills her wine when she sets it down, gripping the counter hard. "Oh my god," she whispers once and then again. "What happened?"

Some of the redness has left Meredith's face and her tone isn't warm, but it is less caustic. "Someone killed him in the basement of Jenkins. Last night. It must have been late."

"How was he killed?"

"I don't know. The police didn't say." Meredith shakes her head and then stares at Jeannie. "What did you think had happened? When you went by the school, looking for Anna, and saw the police?"

Jeannie ignores her question. She stares at me. "He was killed last night? Yesterday?" I don't answer. "Did they arrest anybody?"

"Not when we were there," I say. "They were asking us questions. All of us." I say it before she can ask. I don't think she would ask anything in front of Meredith. I don't think she will say anything about the horrible coincidence of the date of Ellis's murder.

Meredith waves my phone in front of me. "Did you tell the police about this call? Did you tell them you talked to Ellis?"

"I just got the message. You heard it when I did."

"Because you forgot your phone." Meredith says it like an almost-question, like a doubt, and now I can feel my cheeks burning. If someone walked in on us at that moment, we'd look like a trio of sunburned broads or maybe a communal hot flash.

"Yeah, Meredith, I forgot my phone." My voice rises. "I forgot it. I walked out without it and I didn't get my messages. Guilty as charged."

Jeannie puts her hand on my arm, distracting me from whatever is coming over me long enough to see tears in Meredith's eyes. She looks like I just slapped her.

"I'm not accusing you of anything, Anna. My god, you can't think that I think you had anything to do with something this horrible, can you?" She stands, looking a little unsteady. "This has just been a terrible day. I'm really sorry if I've upset you. I'm going to go. But you really need to tell the police about this message. You may be the last person Ellis talked to."

"Besides whoever killed him," Jeannie says.

"Obviously." Meredith looks exasperated. She pulls her purse higher onto her shoulder and starts backing away toward the door. "I'm going to go. It's been a long, hard day. I'm going to leave you two alone to do whatever it is you all need to do."

Jeannie and I say nothing as she leaves.

CHAPTER 11

After Meredith leaves, I can't tell if I feel more awkward or less. It's not the first time my boss has made me aware of just how bad I am at being a person. Emotions flow through her naturally and logically; they tend to fall off of me like scabs. Sometimes I feel like watching her and learning from her. This is not one of those times. Jeannie is here with a case of wine. It's snowing again and the day is not going to get any brighter, literally or metaphorically.

Meredith was worried about me. She was upset about Ellis and she seemed to be having a hard time forgiving Jeannie for her innocent but snarky remarks about the dead man. She looked tired and she could probably smell those delicious enchiladas Jeannie put in the oven. I should have invited her to eat with us. I should have apologized for being so weird. At the very least, I should have given her her thirty dollars back, but I didn't. I let her leave in an unsettled state.

And now that she's gone, I relax.

I'll make things better with Meredith later. This isn't the time for that. My job and my boss will keep. The letters on my floor and coffee table will keep. Later, I'll scoop them up and put them in the box that's waiting for them in the closet. Later, I'll take care of everything later, but not now. Now Jeannie is here. February 17 is behind me and we're going to make sure it stays there for another year.

This is what we do.

We eat. Chips and guacamole, enchiladas, ice cream. We drink bottles of red and open a bottle of Baileys but because of all the food, I don't drop off that cliff of oblivion. Instead I float on this warm ocean of carbohydrates. We play backgammon and rummy; we watch two episodes of *Judge Judy*. Jeannie beats every contestant on *Wheel of Fortune* and I shut her down during *Jeopardy!*.

Jeannie pulls out her phone and a little bullet speaker and starts DJ-ing blasts from our past. We bounce from Britney Spears to Korn to Eminem to Queens of the Stone Age—songs we both know all the words to, songs we've both been drunk on. Songs that came after the worst of my childhood.

We sing songs we sang when I was in high school and she was in college, and when I was in college and she was in grad school. We sing songs we sang together in bars and in cars and on double dates. We howl through "Nookie" and roll through "Country Grammar" without a bump or a worry. We interrupt each other with mentions of guys we slept with or didn't sleep with or wanted to sleep with or shouldn't have slept with. We shout names and bars and drinks at each other and respond with eye-rolls or shrieks or groans.

Jeannie drives this bus but I copilot right beside her. We know this road and we don't veer out of our lane. We don't look too far back; we never, ever mention certain names. We bring up no humiliations or heartbreaks. We keep our melancholy superficial. We recite stupid pieces of poetry that for some reason we both know. There's no Keats or Wordsworth; these are hokey poems about racehorses and dead dogs and kittens at St. Peter's gate.

Neither of us mentions it, but we know we sound just like our mothers. I remember hearing them, sitting on porches and lawn chairs, or slouched around dinner tables or on sofas late at night, early in the morning, drunk on white wine or vodka or maybe even high.

Their voices would change as they talked, losing form and control as they morphed from mothers and professors and artists and wives back into their original form—the Lewis girls, Gretchen and Natalie, pretty, blond sisters from eastern Kansas, dealing with the fallout from their own fucked up parents. They would turn to each other in times of crisis—when Grandpa Boo died, when Uncle Jeff lost yet another job, when my dad got arrested for something I wasn't allowed to know about. They'd put their kids to bed and banish their husbands to golf courses and TV rooms. They would establish the rules of truce with the opening of the first bottle and then they would get sailor drunk, laughing and singing and letting the other see in them the girl they used to be.

I always loved hearing them and only now do I understand what they were really doing. They were calling ghosts. They understood that there are unholy nights when malevolent spirits roam the earth. These aren't traditional demons; they answer to no priest. They're terrors and griefs and losses and they can drag a soul to hell faster than any claw-footed beast. There's no point pretending they're not there. No, the thing to do when the demons come for you is to call up the lesser demons of your own, hide in plain sight among the silly, frilly, ridiculous demons of your shared stupidity, letting the clamor of them drown out the banshee howls, letting the hilarious frenzy of them beat the bushes, fill the shadows, and clog the abysses so nobody falls into them.

You don't defeat your demons. That's pop-psychology bullshit. You outwait them. You talk over them. You bore them with your silliness when they roar up at their most powerful. You find someone you can trust, someone you can count on not to call them down by name, and you ignore those motherfuckers until their time is up, until the bus that brought them in rolls up to take them back to the bleachers of hell where all they can do is catcall and threaten.

It's probably not healthy and it sure doesn't solve anything but some things can't be solved. Some things just have to be endured. Jeannie knows that. Our mothers knew that. We come from a long line of endurers.

The snow is on our side, insulating us and isolating us. The light stays low and blue, never reaching night blackness, never becoming true daylight. Sounds stay lower than our singing—we hear snowplows and cars sliding, salt trucks grinding along, and the occasional scrape of a shovel somewhere on the grounds. My neighbors cede the floor. I'm the noisemaker tonight. Today. Day and night tumble together, marked only by piles of corks, wadded up napkins, and dirty plates. We wake up at one point and have cinnamon rolls, but I don't know if they're dessert or breakfast.

The only slip off our carefully charted path is a small one and I'm not sure who makes it. Ellis Trachtenberg comes up. Just a mention of him as a man—so it must have been Jeannie who brought that up—and by the time it's out in the conversational herd, thoughts of his death trail behind it like a smell. Jeannie, always better than I at all things soothing and healing, addresses the issue with simplicity.

"Shitty timing."

That's all she says about that and pulls a bag of tater tots from the freezer. Slammed appliance doors punctuate the statement, clattering cookie sheets clear the air. No talk of the odds, no calling down the demon that wants this to be a pattern—February 17, the day of dead men. I ignore the pernicious whisper: *One is a tragedy. Two, a coincidence. Third time's a charm? No, sweetheart, that's a curse. That's a curse. That's a curse.*

That whisper would deafen me if Jeannie didn't pick that moment to blast "Tommy Gets His Tonsils Out" and in seconds we're howling along with The Replacements and eating French onion dip with our fingers.

I'm pretty sure this is breakfast.

I never pass out but I do sleep a soft, thirsty sleep that makes me feel puffy and fuzzy when I wake up. Jeannie's in the bed beside me, the *Cosmo* Bedside Astrologer stuck to her cheek. I forgot we'd been reading that. Jeannie had been highlighting important passages in it the way we used to do in high school. I forget that part too until I find the pink highlighter has scrawled some cryptic message onto my pillowcase while we slept.

A half-empty package of Twizzlers fall off my lap as I sit up, trying to figure out why I'm awake. My phone. I hear it ringing. It's been ringing for a while. I wonder why my answering machine doesn't kick on before I realize it's my cell phone that's resting dangerously near a puddle of water that's splashed from a now empty glass by my bed.

"Hello?"

I don't hesitate to answer it. I'm too sleepy to worry and too saturated with the safety of Jeannie's presence.

"Finally." Meredith. "I was starting to worry about you. You didn't check your e-mail."

"Not yet." Good lord. "What's up?"

"Well, we're open today. You're late for work."

"I thought the offices were closed today." I realize my mistake as I say it. Today is Friday; I missed Thursday. I'm dreading the knowing questions from Meredith about how one misses an entire day but they don't come. Instead, her tone is odd, loud, distracted.

"Yeah, yeah, I thought as much. You're on your way?"

I can't tell if she's speaking to me. "Uh, yeah?"

She whispers into the phone. "You are home, right? At your apartment?"

"Yeah." Why is she whispering? Is she still talking to me?

"Alrighty!" Loud voice again. "Shake a leg, sister. See you in a bit."

The call ends and Jeannie flings the magazine off the bed.

"Why does she talk so loud?" Jeannie buries her head under the pillow. "I could hear her. How can you be late for work? You said the offices were closed."

I don't bother explaining, knowing the answer will dawn on her like it did for me. I hear her "Oh yeah" as I drag myself to the bathroom. She follows me, nudging me out of the way to brush her teeth, stepping past me to pee while I tie back my hair. It's nice in kind of a gross way, sharing my bathroom with Jeannie like we used to.

"You don't have to get up," I say. "I'm going in to work. You can sleep."

She wants to come down to campus with me. Funeral arrangements for Ellis will be posted somewhere; people will be making plans. She wants to see her old coworkers; she knows better than to count on me to get the plans correct. Plus I get the feeling that she doesn't want to end our little bender. We have to be sober—or work on getting there; we're in uncertain territory right now—but she seems to feel the same glow I feel. We didn't fight at all last night. We didn't needle or provoke. We laughed and cried and ate and sang and we're both happily stuffed and hungover from it. We don't want it to end.

She drives me to campus. The roads are clear and salted for now although more snow hangs dark in the clouds. She parks illegally and follows me into Jenkins through the north door on the first floor. We hear people in the hallway as we head for the stairwell. This is Ellis's floor. His coworkers mill around and a sense of limbo pervades the floor. Jeannie hesitates, drawn to her former coworkers, drawn to the center of attention, but then she pushes open the stairwell door and waves me through. She's not done with me yet.

My floor isn't a bastion of productivity either. Lyle and Desiree hold court at the little kitchenette and both greet us with a perky hello. I can't tell if they're speaking louder than usual or if it's my hangover. I get my answer at the door to the office.

Detective Hinton rises when I walk through the door. She's been waiting for me. Judging by the worried smile on Meredith's face, she's been waiting a while. Nobody looks happy about it.

"Mrs. Ray, good morning."

She pushes back her jacket as she stands. I don't know if it's intentional but the move shows me her handcuffs.

"We need to talk."

CHAPTER 12

"Let's go to my office."

I wave a hand toward my end of the room. Meredith looks pale; Jeannie holds her mouth in a tight, white line. Officer Neighborgall steps out from the corner he's been standing in, looking even more bristly and red-faced than when we first met. Hinton gives me a cool nod and walks ahead of me toward my desk.

Me? I'm relaxed. Weirdly so. Maybe it's a hangover, maybe it's a testimony to the power of a solid base of nutritious food, but I don't feel any stab of anxiety. Today is February 20. I have three hundred and sixty-two days before I plan on being afraid again.

Jeannie and I follow the detective until Neighborgall clears his throat behind us. Hinton looks back at us.

"We should speak privately, Mrs. Ray."

"It's Ms. Ray, Detective," I remind her again. "Or you can just call me Anna. This is my cousin Jeannie. It's okay with me if she sits in with us, if it's all the same to you. Unless this is something official. Is this something official?"

Hinton studies me for a moment, then her eyes flicker over Jeannie. "Not yet."

"Great, after you."

I can feel Jeannie tense beside me. I can almost hear her thinking that she wishes she'd worn heels and something more intimidating than the snow boots and leggings. Her instinct, as always, is to jump in front of me and handle any difficulty. Funny though, for all the problems she has handled for me, Jeannie has never been there when the police have shown up. Not last year, not eighteen years ago. This is one of the few areas in which I am the expert.

I sit down at my desk. Jeannie moves a pile of books and papers off a low stool and sits beside me. Only Jeannie, I think, could make such a lowly perch look important. Detective Hinton takes her time settling in on the uncomfortable office chair. She doesn't make many adjustments; she's apparently not concerned with comfort right now. Her attention is on her notebook. And on me.

She asks me again if I spoke with Ellis the night he was murdered. They must have checked his phone. I pull mine out and tell her about the message.

"You didn't mention it on Wednesday."

"I didn't know about it. I didn't check my messages until after we spoke."

"On Wednesday."

"On Wednesday."

She stares at me. "Today's Friday." I nod at that irrefutable fact, not volunteering anything. What am I going to say? That it's not Friday? "Why didn't you let us know?"

I don't bother answering. Instead I replay the message on speaker. Jeannie sighs at the sound of Ellis's voice but Hinton shows no reaction. I end the call.

"Do you have any idea what he wanted to give you, Ms. Ray? What he wanted to talk about?" I shake my head. "Was there any indication that he had come back to your office at any point after you spoke with him at lunchtime? Had he left you any note or messages on your desk? Anything you can recall?"

I wave my hands over the chaos on my desk. "I didn't notice anything."

Hinton pretends to glance at her notes. "You were late to work that morning. You didn't go to your desk when you arrived. Instead you took some books back to the library and when you returned, the uniforms were on site taping off the crime scene."

She looks at me expectantly, as if this is something I might challenge her on. I hear Jeannie breathing sharply through her nose, instinctively reacting to her tone, sensing bait in a trap but I know better. There's nothing there. I'm hiding nothing and she hasn't asked me if I am. This is bush league questioning and frankly I expected better of Hinton.

"Right."

"So you never really got a chance to look around your office to see if anything was different, if anything had been left for you. The police were moving through the building, people were upset. You could have missed something. The way you missed the voice mail message."

I hear the faintest click of Jeannie's tongue letting me know her estimation of Detective Hinton's standing is sinking as quickly as mine. I wouldn't have taken the detective to be the kind of cop who makes icebergs out of ice cubes hoping to sink someone's little ship. Or at least I thought she might be the kind of cop to be a little better at it. This is her angle?

"Of course," she says with gentleness, "you had a lot on your mind. February seventeenth. It's a bad day for you, isn't it?"

My estimation of her skills elevates with unfortunate speed.

I realize another reason I'm so relaxed. I've been expecting this. I'm always expecting the police. I'm always expecting to be questioned.

She looks toward her notes. "February seventeenth is the day your husband died. Am I right? Suicide? That must have been hard."

I fall into a stillness I have spent a lifetime mastering. I wonder how much she knows about that date, how much she knows about hard deaths. She'll get nothing from me.

"Did Professor Trachtenberg know about your husband's death?"

"No."

"No? You didn't talk about it with him?"

"No."

"Why not?"

"Why would I?"

She shifts in the chair and I'm having trouble reading her expression. She's not like the cops in Nebraska, whose wide, pale faces broadcast their shifting opinions like billboards—pity, horror, suspicion, cynicism. She's not like the cops in Missouri—fat and freckled, panicked and horrified and pretending that I couldn't see or hear them. No, Detective Hinton isn't looking at me like that. She looks thoughtful. She looks calm and patient and I have to remind myself that I'm not lying to her.

"Ms. Ray, Professor Trachtenberg had a gift for you in his pocket when we found him. It had your name on it. Do you know what he was bringing you?" I shake my head. Hinton pulls a photograph out of her inside pocket and slides it across the desk. It's a dark color photograph of a small potted plant wrapped in paper and tied with twine. I squint to make out the details.

"It's rosemary, Ms. Ray. Is there any significance to rosemary for you?"

I shake my head again. There's the obvious, of course, and it's so obvious and so much what I would have expected of Ellis. A part of me I should be ashamed of feels grateful that I didn't have to endure receiving this gift. I wonder if I would have been able to suppress my contempt at such a saccharine gesture from someone trying to get into my pants via my grief. I want to think better of him, to hope there is a more esoteric meaning to this, but Jeannie says it aloud.

"Rosemary for remembrance." She speaks to Hinton. "It's from Shakespeare."

"I know," Hinton says. "Hamlet. Ophelia talking with her brother, Laertes. I went to college, too." She ignores Jeannie's smirk and pulls the photo closer to her. "This suggests that Professor Trachtenberg did know about your husband's death. It suggests that he was trying to comfort you, reach out to you. The message on your phone supports that idea. We know he was pursuing a relationship with you."

"I told you there was no relationship. We weren't seeing each other."

"But he was pursuing it." She lets that sit there for a moment. "We've spoken with several people who were aware of his interest in you. He discussed getting to know you, being interested in your opinion on a number of topics. He even asked certain staff members about possibly arranging events where you might be together."

I'm uncomfortable talking about this in front of Jeannie. I'm embarrassed and awkward, as if this information has morphed into some weird confession discovered in a teenage diary I never would have kept but that is written in my handwriting nonetheless. As if Trachtenberg's misguided interest were somehow my fault.

Jeannie's shoulder brushes against mine. She's leaned in close. "If Anna says there was no relationship, there was no relationship, regardless of what Ellis might have wanted."

"That might be true," Hinton says, "but the fact is, people were aware of his feelings for you, Ms. Ray. And Professor Trachtenberg was a man who attracted a lot of attention. He had a great deal of influence on campus and a lot of people vied for his attention, personally and professionally. Someone might have been aware of his attention on you. They might have been jealous or resentful of it."

"Jealous enough to kill him?" This seems impossible to me.

She nods. "The nature of the scene suggests rage."

Jeannie is warm beside me. "How was he killed?"

"I can't tell you that. It's part of the investigation." She looks from Jeannie to me. "I can tell you that there were very distinctive details at the scene. Not accidental. Deliberate. Specific."

We stare at her. What are we supposed to say to that? Is she waiting for us to reveal our knowledge of these details? For us to suddenly slip up and say something like, "Oh, you mean the bloody clown nose and Murano glass letter opener?" She must decide that's not coming, because she follows up with something much worse.

"Your husband was an English professor, wasn't he?"

"He taught composition at a community college." I begin to wish I had blurted out that clown nose remark.

"His suicide was quite dramatic. I read the report from the Chattam Police Department." Jeannie squeezes my arm. Hinton just keeps on talking with that soft, nice voice of hers. "According to the report, he hung himself in your home. He also took a large combination of medications which he washed down with alcohol and, according to the autopsy, managed to cut deeply into both wrists before kicking the chair away to hang himself."

"Boxes." The word squeaks out of my closing throat. "He kicked away boxes to hang himself. In my closet. In our closet. Our hall closet." My arm burns where Jeannie squeezes too hard and I'm glad for the point of pain. It helps me focus. It helps me kick out of that ugly eddy that wants to pull me down. I clear my throat, recovered. "He was serious about killing himself. It was no cry for help. Ronnie wanted to die."

Hinton tilts her head. "Is that a comfort?"

"No. Maybe." I've never asked myself that. It feels like something I will think about now that it's out there. "I don't know."

She doesn't give me time to think about it. Instead she slides another piece of paper across the desk. "This is a consent form, granting us permission to examine your phone for evidence. We'll record Professor Trachtenberg's message as well as access your social media and e-mail accounts."

I don't touch the paper. "Why?"

"You were the last person Ellis Trachtenberg called before he died. You must have had several contacts in common. We're searching for any sign of hostility, threat, anger from the people around him."

"You're searching for it on my phone?"

"Yes. We need the message. It's evidence."

Jeannie continues to squeeze my arm. "Don't you need a search warrant for that?"

"Not if Ms. Ray gives us consent." Hinton's tone stays level and pleasant. "If you don't consent to turn over the phone, we will get a search warrant. In the meantime, an officer will be assigned to stay with you at all times to be sure no evidence is destroyed until we return with the search warrant—which we will have no trouble getting. We will still take your phone. We will still download the contents. The difference is you may not get your phone back until tomorrow or Sunday or maybe even Monday."

I don't care about my phone. The only person I would ever call is sitting beside me. Still, my hands don't want to take that piece of paper. "I don't really have any social media. I mean, I have Facebook and LinkedIn but I don't even know if I'm logged in on my phone. I'm not even sure I know the passwords for them."

Hinton nods. "It's okay. We can take care of that."

She pushes the paper closer to me and I pick up my pen. I wonder how many thousands of drops of ink have been spilled putting my name on police documents. I can feel Jeannie's disapproval at my signing. She probably thinks I should make this harder, I should resist, I should examine my rights in this situation, but I know that's futile. The police have a mission. A dead body gives them permission to do pretty much anything they want. Warrants and investigations and interrogations are all fingers that make up the fist that they can use with any level of strength justice deems fitting.

Fuck them. Take my phone. Read my e-mails. Someone might as well.

I sign the form, put my phone on top of it, and push them both back to Hinton. She puts the phone in an evidence bag and tucks it into one of her many pockets.

"Is there anything else?" I ask with suicidal pluck.

There is. Of course.

"We found your fingerprints at the scene. Can you explain why?"

Gee, you'd think she would have led with that. "I go through the basement."

"That door is for maintenance only."

"Walter Voss told me I could. I cut through as a shortcut. He told me it was okay as long as I didn't tell anyone. That door isn't locked during the day."

"You are the only non-maintenance worker whose fingerprints we found."

"Maybe Walter Voss has a crush on me, too." It's the wrong thing to say and I know it but I don't care. Maybe I do care. Maybe I want to irritate the very calm Detective Hinton, who can't seem to make up her mind if she's going to treat me like a suspect or not.

"How do you know those are Anna's fingerprints?" Jeannie's voice is sharp.

"They're on file with the school. Digital scans on the day Ms. Ray consented to a background check as terms of her employment as per policy implemented for new hires after 2012. Do you remember agreeing to the terms of your employment, Ms. Ray?"

I do. Barely. I remember mountains of paperwork for employment coming in on the heels of mountains of paperwork for insurance and interment and indemnity. Who knows what I agreed to?

"Can you tell me what you might have touched in the maintenance room?"

"The door? The elevator button, maybe the door to the stairs." I try to think. I come through the basement in the morning, half awake, sometimes half sober. Did I ever stop to scrape mud off my shoes? Get something from my purse? Blow my nose? Did I ever do any of those things while supporting myself against a shelf? Did my hands brush a wrench or a hammer or a Colt 45 or whatever the hell might have killed Ellis? Can anyone fully account for where their hands have been? "I don't know. I don't pay attention. I wipe my feet and head upstairs."

She nods and I wait for her to pull out a photo of a flamethrower or a bear trap or some other bizarre device that could have left "distinctive" wounds on Ellis and that had somehow passed through my hands. Instead, she flips a page in her notebook.

"You said Professor Trachtenberg brought you a book on Tuesday. Herbert Mann, *The Eyes of God Turn*." Her finger twitches against her notebook. I've seen that before. "Do you still have that book?"

I fumble. "Yes? I think. Somewhere." I work to trace my steps back in my mind.

"That girl borrowed it," Jeannie says. "Right? That's the book about the art movement you said was so bad, isn't it? That waitress asked you about it."

"Oh, yeah, Karmen. She was supposed to pick it up. Or send her boyfriend to get it."

Hinton is watching me look around for the book. "Did she? Or he? Get the book?"

"I don't know." I can't say why but the idea of the book missing bothers me. I didn't care for the book or the gesture from Ellis but I appreciate the idea of it in an abstract way. I like that books are given to a person from a person. I like it with a distant formality that makes me worry more about the book than about the dead man who gave it to me. It's easier for me to worry about a book. I stand up and start scanning surfaces around my desk. ·

"I don't see it." I'm talking to myself. "Wait, Meredith would know. Meredith would have to have been here if he picked it up. I was gone by then."

"Where were you?" Hinton asks softly, as if she doesn't want to distract me from my rambling but my focus has returned. I don't see the book. Worry is now futile.

"We were at Ollie's. Jeannie and I. I left work early. That's where I saw Karmen."

"Karmen?"

"The girl who asked for the book." I return to my seat. Whatever spell Hinton had cast over me is broken now and I have the strange feeling of having just woken up. "She's a student who works at Ollie's. And at the library."

"Karmen Bennett?" Hinton's voice stays level but that finger twitches again.

"Yes. She's a third-year student. Talented." A protective surge rises within me at Hinton's interest in Karmen. "She wanted the book to write a paper."

Jeannie chimes in. "For extra credit. She said she wanted to curry favor with Ellis." I shoot Jeannie a look that is just shy of a glare and she looks surprised. "That's what she said. She said she was low on favor with Ellis and hoped the paper would help."

Hinton lowers her notebook to her lap and I wonder if she's aware of her twitchy finger. "Do you have an address for Ms. Bennett?"

"Her parents live over in Elkins but I don't think she stays there much. I think she lives mostly with her boyfriend."

"His name?"

I shake my head. My interest in Karmen is purely academic. I know her personal life is turbulent and I've made a point of keeping my distance from it. I don't feel the need to share any of this with the detective. Hinton must sense this—or she already has her answer and doesn't really need it from me—and closes her notebook.

"Thank you for your time, Ms. Ray." She rises and pats her pocket. "I'll call you as soon as we're finished with your phone."

"Do you have Anna's home number?" Jeannie asks.

"We do."

Of course they do. I nod. They have my employment file, my fingerprints, my background check. Now they have my phone. Hinton is almost out the door when she stops, turning around like an old TV detective. She even starts with:

"One more thing. That book that the professor gave you. Is it a common book? Are there a lot of copies of it around campus?"

"No, I doubt it." I almost say my usual disparaging things about the book and the movement it entails but I don't. That abstract guilt comes over me. I don't worry about speaking ill of the dead but I can't bring myself to speak ill of the dead man's book.

Hinton nods. "I'll ask Mrs. Michener if anyone picked up the book. If you see Karmen Bennett around, have her call me."

"Sure," I say. I think we all know I'm lying.

CHAPTER 13

Meredith doesn't know where the book is.

"The last I saw it was when Anna and her cousin were leaving. Professor Fitzhugh-Conroy picked up the book and Anna told her to put it somewhere. Then they left."

Hinton turns to Jeannie. "You had it? Where did you put it?"

Jeannie glances around and points to a file cabinet opposite my desk, piled high with blue shelf boxes. "There, I think. There were magazines there, too, I think."

"Is it there now?"

She steps closer and shakes her head. "I don't see it."

"Nobody came to pick it up?" Hinton asks Meredith.

"Not while I was here, but I wasn't in the office all the time." She waits while Hinton turns her notebook over in her hands, probably waiting to see if the detective will write any of this down, but the pen stays capped. "I took some files downstairs, some applications that needed to be signed and some brochures I'd been asked to get."

At Hinton's urging she starts listing a dozen or so names in both the English and Fine Arts Departments. Ellis's name is on that list. Hinton doesn't interrupt her at the mention of his name but waits until she's certain she's given the complete list.

"So you did speak with Professor Trachtenberg Tuesday night."

"I did." She sounds surprised, as if it just occurred to her that this might be of interest to the police. "There's nothing unusual about that. I speak with—I spoke with—Professor Trachtenberg often. He is the head of the department; he has a lot of influence on his students and their plans. We often discussed opportunities and programs that might benefit the students. He liked to be kept informed about any personal issues they might have."

Hinton and Neighborgall stand quietly, letting Meredith talk. I want to shut her up. I want to warn her about nervous chatter, that it's catnip to investigators and that nothing digs a hole faster than a babbling mouth, but Meredith becomes indignant, as only the innocent can.

"So yes, yes, I spoke with Professor Trachtenberg that afternoon but I'm sure I wasn't the last person to do so. There were still plenty of people in their offices."

She finally takes a breath, her argument made. Hinton doesn't jump right in. Her voice stays soft and cool, as if she's just shooting the breeze.

"Did you talk about Ms. Ray with him?"

"Anna? No. Why would I?" Meredith says. "I don't think so. Well, he asked if she liked the book. I said she did. I think that was it."

Hinton nods. "That book. Yeah, you don't know where it is? You didn't see anyone come in to pick it up?"

Meredith waves her hands over the piles of confusion that make up our workspace. "Nobody picked it up from me. Nobody came in asking for it, but I don't lock the door when I go downstairs. There's nothing in here to steal." She laughs. "Nothing anyone could find at least."

"So you didn't see Karmen Bennett come in to get the book? Or her boyfriend?"

Meredith shakes her head. "I've never met him. I don't think he goes to school here. So to answer your question, no. I didn't see anyone come in for the book, but that doesn't mean someone didn't get it. I'm sorry I can't be more helpful."

Hinton reassures her and thanks us. She taps her jacket where my phone must be hiding and promises to call me when they're done with it. Neighborgall holds the door for his partner. A habitual gentleman.

When the door is closed and the residual energy of the police has scattered, Meredith falls back in her chair and sighs. "What is so interesting about that book?" I'm wondering the same thing when Jeannie posits her own opinion.

"I think they're more interested in that girl, the waitress, who wanted the book."

"That's ridiculous," I say, still prickly and protective over Karmen, still touchy about that book, still not letting myself think about the fact that I'm ranking these in importance over the death of a coworker. "They can't think Karmen had anything to do with Ellis's death. Why would they? What could possibly be her motive?"

I see Meredith frown. "Well, I'm not saying it's a motive but they are definitely interested in her because of her difficulties last year. You know she lost her scholarship, right?" I don't. I didn't know she ever had one but I know she's struggled financially. Meredith nods. "I can't imagine it's anything she likes to talk about. Professor Trachtenberg failed her in two classes; he claimed she was too high to do the work and that she shouldn't be in school if she was just going to party her way through it. He has—I mean, he had a bit of reputation for that. It cost her her scholarship."

"That's what the cops were asking you about?"

Meredith purses her lips. "I thought they were here to talk with you."

"Yeah, Hinton was," I say, "but I saw you and Neighborgall chatting nicely in the meantime."

What is it about the presence of police that makes every subsequent conversation sound like an interrogation? Meredith must sense the escalation because she lets go of the arms of her chair and crumples a bit in her seat.

"He had a list of students he wanted to ask me about."

"What about them?"

She sighs and looks straight at me, focusing on my face in a way that is less about me, more about not addressing Jeannie. "I don't think we should discuss it."

"I think we should."

Jeannie leans against a file cabinet. "Don't let me stop you."

Meredith's hands frame the arms of her chair, like she's resisting the urge to grip them. Her tone is forced-friendly. "I appreciate your permission, Professor. And before you ask, yes, your name came up, too. Kenny"—she corrects herself—"Officer Neighborgall had a list of students who might be angry at Professor Trachtenberg or at the staff in general. Students who had failed out, who had lost their financial aid because of bad grades, who maybe didn't get the referrals and recommendations they needed to get whatever was their greatest heart's desire, that sort of thing."

"Why did Jeannie's name come up?"

"If I may be blunt, your cousin is a great deal like Ellis Trachtenberg in that she never hesitated to come down hard on a student."

"Am I supposed to be offended by that?" Jeannie asks. If her eyebrows get any higher, they're going to vanish into her hairline. "I don't think being compared to Ellis is an insult."

"I'm not saying it is," Meredith says in a tone that screams that's exactly what she's saying. "It's just that you and Professor Trachtenberg probably cost more students their education than all of the other faculty combined."

Oh, those are fighting words and Jeannie stands up to take them on. "I didn't cost students their education. I'm not here to hand them a diploma for showing up. This is an institution of higher education. Knowledge is something you work for. I don't hand out trophies for participation and neither does Ellis. Neither should any of the faculty." Her voice rises as she marches toward Meredith's desk. This has the feeling of an old argument because Jeannie sounds well-prepared. She rests her hands on the desk, ignoring the piles of paper, and leans toward my boss's face.

"I know you enjoy sitting here and comforting the students when their feelings are hurt. You like enrolling them in those little contests and getting their work into those adorable local art shows and anthologies and I'm sure the students think you're better than Grandma at Christmas." Jeannie's voice takes on that nasty edge I know so well. "But I'm here to educate them. I'm here to make sure they learn. And if they don't do the work, they don't get the grade. They fail. People fail, Meredith. In real life, people fail and they lose. And that's life. And it's not my job to make them feel okay about it. That's not why I'm here."

"You're not here anymore."

"No." Jeannie laughs and straightens up. "No, now I'm at Penn State, where this kind of argument doesn't have to happen, where students and faculty agree to treat higher education like the revered institution it is, not like a sleep-away camp."

This is the closest I've seen my boss come to losing her temper and for just a second I wonder if she's going to smack Jeannie in the face with the box of Glad freezer bags that's sitting on the corner of her desk. Instead, she exhales, leaning farther back in her chair. She shrugs in a gesture of surrender and takes the high road. Well played, I think. Jeannie is itching for a fight and I know how well she can fight. Nothing takes the glory out of a victory like passive surrender.

I decide not to think about the fact that in insulting Meredith, she's also insulting my job. Jeannie takes education seriously. It's not an affectation. She demands a lot of herself and a lot of her students just as her mother, an English professor, demanded a lot of her. Considering some of the other traits and conditions we've dredged out of our gene pool, the demand for high academic standards doesn't seem all that bad.

But I didn't know she had failed that many students.

Meredith seems keen to make peace, although I give her credit for doing so with a twist. "To be fair, Professor Trachtenberg held the students to a higher standard than you did. He was quite a bit harsher than you were." Before the comparison can be judged badly, she redeems it. "You at least gave the students a chance to make up the work. You seemed to judge them on their academic performance. Professor Trachtenberg had a tendency to take it a little too far."

Jeannie nods, accepting the peace. "True. He always did get a little too bent about students getting high. My feeling was always that I didn't care what state they were in as long as they did the work. He never could abide any kind of substance abuse."

I almost snort at that. He hated substance abuse and wanted to go out with me? That would have been interesting. The little dust-up between Meredith and Jeannie ends with an awkward quiet that my boss covers with noisy paper shuffling. Meredith starts to say something about valuing students when the office door pops open once more.

"Am I interrupting?" It's Charlie Ziglar, Ellis's TA, looking like he's spent the last three days sleeping at his desk.

"Hey, Zig." Meredith smiles and waves him in. "How are you holding up?"

The slope of his shoulders and the stains on his shirt agree with his heavy sigh. "It's been a long week. Everything is up in the air. Everything is a mess and on top of it all, every kid in school is having a complete meltdown." He hands Meredith a thick file folder. "Here's the amended schedule for the time being. Classes are going to resume on Monday; we're working to cover all of Ellis's classes. We're still working to find the best way to make that happen." He speaks as if he's said these sentences a hundred times already. Meredith just nods and smiles and lets him ramble.

"We got it, Zig. Don't you worry." She puts the folder to the side. "We won't let anyone freak out on you. We'll get through this."

She sounds so certain, so grown up, that even I fight the urge to choke up. Zig doesn't stand a chance. Fat tears rise up in his eyes, spilling over when he nods. He stands there, big hands hanging down at his sides like he's forgotten what they're for.

Meredith speaks softly. "Has there been any word about arrangements?"

That's what transforms his silent tears to a choked sob. He shakes his head and shoves his hands into his pockets. "They can't make any arrangements until the investigation is over. They need his . . . They can't release him until the case is closed. God." The big hands come back out and cover his wet face. He looks like an enormous, heartbroken toddler who needs a nap and a hug. Jeannie steps up from behind him and rubs his shoulder.

He accepts the touch, nodding behind his hands and scrubbing the tears out of his red-rimmed eyes. He wipes his palms on his wrinkled shirt like he's sick of finding them damp. It takes a long time for tears to dry up. When he looks over his shoulder to find his comforter, his eyes widen.

"Oh, oh. Hi." He tugs at the tails of his shirt as he turns to face Jeannie. "Professor Fitzhugh-Conroy. Hi. I didn't know you were here."

Jeannie smiles and continues to rub his arm. "Hi, Zig. Good to see you."

"You, too." He says it quickly, automatically, and then fumbles. "Did you . . . are you here for . . . ? How long are you here? We don't know when the funeral is. Have you been downstairs? I didn't know you were in. Nobody said anything. I mean, it's been, you know, but—"

Jeannie cuts off his disastrous train of chatter with a hand squeeze and a step back. "Actually I came in for another reason and it was just really bad timing."

"Yeah." He stares at her. "Yeah it is."

It's a strange thing to say and Jeannie just leaves it there as she backs away from him, closer to me. Zig nods and wipes his hands again on his shirt, mumbling something about getting back to work. He offers a mangled invitation to Jeannie to stop by and say hello. I've heard worse invitations in my life but not many. He tosses a grateful smile to Meredith and hustles out of the office.

"It must be a mess downstairs," Jeannie says, shaking her head.

"It's going to be a mess for a while," Meredith agrees. "Ellis Trachtenberg is going to be tough to replace. He really was one of a kind." We stand there in the awkward silence that's becoming the norm for this office until Meredith taps the edge of the file folder against her desk with a sharp rap. "Unfortunately, that mess means we have a lot of work to do." When Jeannie and I just stand there, Meredith drops the folder with a loud slap. She speaks slowly and clearly, like she's speaking to children. "I'm afraid that means it's time for us to get back to work. Professor? If you don't mind, I really need Anna to get back to her desk. To work. Yes?"

"What? Oh yes. Of course." Jeannie snaps to, pulling on her coat and grabbing her enormous purse. "I have a ton of work to do. I'll call you later."

Out of nowhere, the urge to make her stay blows in. I almost grab her hand. "Are you going to stop by downstairs? See your old stomping grounds?"

"No," Jeannie says, pulling out her phone and swiping it to life. "I have to check in with my TA. I haven't even talked to Jeff since I've been here." She glances up from her scrolling to smile at me. She whispers. "I'll see you after work."

I nod and hold the door for her. I feel stupid because I watch her walk all the way down the hall, her face down in her phone. I want her to turn around and wave or something. I don't know what I want but I don't want to see her go. It's stupid because I'm going to see her again soon. She's not leaving town; she's just leaving my office. But still I watch her.

"I hope she can stick around for the funeral." I say it out loud but not really to Meredith.

"That might be a while." My boss seems to have lost the urge to get back to work now that Jeannie's gone, because she's still stretched back in her chair. "This investigation might take some time. It's a horrible crime." I nod and head toward my desk but Meredith isn't done. "I've heard some of the details of the crime scene. Off the record, of course, but you know how it is. People can't keep a secret, especially a grisly one."

I hate that word—grisly. "Well, Hinton strikes me as pretty sharp. Maybe they'll catch a break. I'm sure Ellis's family would like to have this all behind them."

"Your cousin will probably have to get back to work before then though. I suppose that's for the best."

"What does that mean?"

"Nothing." She smiles at me. "Just that I'm sure Professor Fitzhugh-Conroy is busy."

Meredith isn't trying very hard to sell that lie. "That's not what you meant." Her innocent gasp doesn't work either. "Why would it be for the best if Jeannie isn't here for the funeral? What is it with you and Jeannie? She's not the first professor to get snotty with you."

That innocence turns to indignation. "I get along with the other professors very well, thank you very much. I don't consider 'snotty' to be an especially desired quality in a professional, particularly in an educator."

I refrain from bringing up the instances I've seen of professors and TAs being short with my boss. Meredith works passionately for her students but I've seen that passion exasperate others in the department whose visions don't jibe with hers. But Jeannie is the first person I've seen elicit any real anger.

"You don't like Jeannie. Why not? Everybody likes Jeannie."

She turns back to her paperwork. "You might be surprised to learn the truth about that." It's such a pissy thing to say and so unlike Meredith. I'm not in the mood for whatever this is. I turn to head back to my desk when I hear her sigh.

"Anna, I'm sorry. I shouldn't have said that. That was petty and immature. God, I sounded like Lyle."

I lean against the divider, arms folded. "Why don't you like Jeannie?"

"I do like Jeannie. I do, inasmuch as I know her. To be honest, we didn't interact that much, but I know the students respected her. That's what really matters."

"And?"

She chooses her words carefully. "It's just awkward that she's here now. With what just happened. With the funeral coming up. I mean, all things considered, you've got to agree, right? Professor Fitzhugh-Conroy here for Ellis's funeral? That's going to be awkward. You saw Zig's reaction and he's so nice, he wouldn't say boo to a fart."

Zig did seem uncomfortable when he saw Jeannie. He seemed shocked. "Why would that be awkward? Because they dated?"

"Is that what she told you? That they dated?" She seems uncomfortable with what she's saying but it's my face that's turning red. I don't want to hear what I think she's going to say. "Maybe they dated briefly at the beginning but, Anna, your cousin didn't take it well when Ellis broke it off. If there was even anything to break off. It was not pretty. She caused a couple of scenes around campus that were, well, unprofessional. She didn't tell you any of this?"

I don't say anything but I can feel my cheeks burning. Of course she didn't tell me and of course it was bound to happen. Just because I think Jeannie is perfect doesn't mean she never fails. I can't be the only one in the family with less-than-illustrious moments and, all things considered, handling a breakup badly isn't an abomination. But still, she never told me anything about it. She never even hinted at it. I'm embarrassed for her and embarrassed for me. I can feel myself channeling that embarrassment into anger toward Meredith.

She must see it in my face, because she says, "You know what?" She shakes her head. "I shouldn't have said that. I don't know why I did. It's mostly gossip. There are always two sides to every story and you know how gossip spreads. Well, I'm proving it right now, aren't I? It spreads by stupid people like me repeating stories they heard somewhere else and not even thinking about how those words might hurt."

Meredith should give a course in how to deliver a proper apology. All my anger flees, my cheeks cool off, and I feel bad for my readiness to ratchet things up at such short notice. "It's okay," I say and I mean it. Meredith is kooky and frantic but she's not a gossip and she's been good to me. I decide to let us both off the hook. "This is just a shitty situation. I think we should all give ourselves a 'get out of jail free' card for bad behavior until spring."

She smiles. "Now that's a good plan! I'll write up a memo. Until then, however, we have work to do. We have two dozen Literature majors looking for summer programs that they can't afford and an art exhibition coming up that has just lost one of its main judges."

I groan and head back to my desk. Despite Jeannie's derogatory reference to "adorable local art shows," the Rising Tide Exhibition is a serious undertaking with a strong reputation and Ellis Trachtenberg played a big role in getting it there. His absence might hurt the show and the funding, which will trickle down as bad news for the student artists.

Even dead, he's screwing Karmen Bennett. It irks me that he killed her scholarship for such a sanctimonious reason. I know drugs are illegal and detrimental to education and all the other saintly proclamations we're all supposed to make against chemical addictions, but maybe she needed the drugs. Did he ever consider that? Maybe her life was such an uninterrupted shit storm that the drugs kept the worst of the pain at bay. Did he look down at her and tell her that she was just hiding from the pain? That when she straightened up, those problems would still be there? Did she then flip him off and tell him that they'd be there whether or not she was high, that they weren't going away, and so why the hell wouldn't she take her mind on a pharmaceutical vacation once in a while? That maybe there wasn't any virtue in suffering and that the real test of a successful life was outsmarting the pain?

Am I still talking about Karmen?

I rifle through my files until I find her application to the exhibition. I read her proposal and flip through her preliminary sketches. She plans to title her piece "Pain Scale," mixed media sculptures of four body parts ranked in order of their ability to cause pain. She's submitted several spec sketches of each piece. What does it say that she considers the fist the least dangerous? She's drawn feet "for leaving or staying," she'd said. Then a mouth. In her sketches, the mouth is open and snarling, jagged teeth that she plans on fashioning out of metal and glass.

And finally, the most dangerous part of the human body in Karmen Bennett's opinion? The brain. She's sketched out a cutaway skull with a colorful, wrinkled canvas for the brain. She's made notes of details she'll incorporate but I don't read them. I want to see the work first. I like Karmen. I'm glad she came back to school despite the financial hardship. Yet another addition to the ever-growing list of reasons I'm glad I didn't sleep with Ellis. I feel like it would have been a betrayal of Karmen.

More than an hour has passed when Meredith leans against the divider. "I'm not getting anything done," she says. "You?"

"Yeah," I say, putting the file up. "I've pushed all these papers from that side of the desk to this one. I'm optimistic I can push them all back to their original position by the end of the day. That's my goal, at least."

"It's good to have goals." She pulls her sweater tighter around her body and shudders. "Do you think this building will be haunted now?"

"No."

"Really? Even after a violent murder in the basement?" I shake my head. "You don't believe in ghosts?"

"No." Not the kind you're thinking of.

She clucks her tongue. "I know, it's silly. This building is over a hundred years old. I'm sure plenty of horrible things have happened here and the only thing haunting these halls is the smell of old mop water." She doesn't sound convinced. "It's just that after what I've heard, I can't stop thinking some really horrible thoughts. I'm spooked. I know, I know, I shouldn't spread rumors, but these aren't technically rumors. I told you I have some friends at the police station and some information about Ellis's death has come out."

I can think of about a billion other things I would rather discuss at this or any other time, but Meredith shows no signs of stopping. Her eyes shine with held-back tears and she gestures to my office chair, asking for an invitation. I can't bring myself to say an actual yes because I do not want her to sit down and tell me whatever it is she's heard, but I can't refuse to hear her because she'll want to know why I don't want to hear it. She'll want to know why I'm not curious about whatever gruesome information she's discovered. That kind of curiosity is only natural for most people. As much as I don't want to talk about it, I want to explain why even less, so I nod toward the chair and she settles into place.

"Don't tell anybody what I'm going to tell you."

Not to worry.

She heaves a big sigh. "It's just bouncing around in my head and maybe if I say it out loud it won't keep morphing into this hell-beast that's haunting me."

That's not how hell-beasts work.

"Ellis was beaten to death." She waits for a reaction that doesn't come. "But that's not the worst part of it." She scoots closer to the desk and whispers, as if she doesn't trust herself to say the words too loudly. "He was also . . . damaged."

"Damaged." That's an odd word under the circumstances.

Her hands flutter as she searches for a way to say it. "He was partially dismembered." I don't even blink and she doesn't notice. "Anna, somebody cut off his hands. His hands! You can't tell anybody this because it's part of the investigation and my friend would lose her job if word got out that she'd let that slip. Seriously, you can't say anything. Promise me."

She doesn't need to worry. I can't move. I can't feel my lips and my face has been still for so long that it feels odd, like it's been put together wrong. My scalp is sweating and a wave of cool dampness flushes over my skin. None of this must show, because Meredith keeps talking.

"It's so horrible, Anna. She said it was like something from a horror movie. And that's still not the worst part."

I'd give anything to make her stop speaking.

"Whoever cut off his hands took them. They weren't in the basement. Someone cut off Ellis's hands and put them somewhere else. The police can't find them. They think that maybe someone took them as a trophy."

She finally stops speaking once I vomit in the garbage can.

CHAPTER 14

Bakerton, Missouri
Summer 1995
Anna Shuler, 9 years old

Anna sat at the kitchen table, coloring, staying out of the way. In the living room, Mom and Dad laughed loudly at something Yvonne Gilkerson said. Mom didn't really like Yvonne but the Gilkersons had let them ride along with them on the trip to Chicago so Mom was being nice. Dad told her the trip was part of Anna's birthday present but since she wouldn't turn ten until November, she didn't know if it was part of last year's birthday or this year's. She didn't care. The trip had been great. Mom and Dad laughed and sang with her in the back seat of the Gilkersons' Toyota.

They'd all gone up to see a special Gustav Klimt exhibit at the Art Institute in Chicago. It was the only thing Mom and Dad could talk about for weeks. They'd brought in books and posters and spent hours explaining to Anna what she would be seeing, why these works were so important. Mom helped her research the elements of Klimt's work, his Japanese influences, his use of allegory. Anna tried to pay attention. She fed off of their enthusiasm.

The paintings were beautiful. Anna preferred the ones from the Golden Phase over the Vienna Secession, even though her father told her not to be distracted by glittering colors. He told her to look deeper and try to understand the rules Klimt had broken in his creation. She tried as hard as she could but kept coming back to *the Portrait of Adele Bloch-Bauer I*, staring into the eyes that floated along her dress.

Anna had gotten bored. Dad and Yvonne were arguing over something about allegories and Mom was reading every single plaque on every single wall. She didn't know where Mr. Gilkerson was. Probably the bathroom again. So Anna wandered off, through gallery after gallery, until she discovered the painting that she considered her real birthday present.

The Bay of Marseilles, Seen from L'Estaque by Paul Cèzanne. Anna had seen pictures of it before. Dad had a lot of opinions about Cèzanne, not all of them favorable, and neither of her parents had ever remarked on this painting in any particular way that she could remember. But standing in front of it, alone, Anna felt herself falling into the water before her. She had the room to herself—the crowds were here for Klimt—and so she could be quiet and still and just look.

It was a simple subject—houses with chimneys clustered around the edge of a bay, mountains in the distance, a muted multi-colored sky overhead. It didn't glitter like Klimt's work. There were no naked people, no strangely bent bodies, none of the hypnotic swirling curves or lines, but she couldn't take her eyes off of it. She felt a fluttering low in her stomach when her gaze trailed over the crowded rooftops and into the blue-green-purple of bay and mountain and sky.

Away. That was the word she heard in her mind. *Away*.

To be away, to be in the blue, off the land, away from the crowded houses and across the blue water to the blue mountains to see the blue sky. So much space. So much motion.

Mom found her. She wasn't angry; her parents encouraged Anna to roam freely in museums and galleries. She took her hand and said that it was time to go but there was one more treat—a visit to the gift shop. Mom told her she could pick out one thing for herself, anything within reason, and Anna knew just what she wanted. It took her a while to find it—most of the books were hardcover catalog collections—but she finally found the coloring books.

Dad looked disappointed in her choice. He showed her the special edition "Klimt Your World" creativity set that came with metallic markers and little bits of glass and jewelry to paste on the pictures she could draw herself. Mom held up a poster of *The Kiss*, promising how nice it would look in her room, but Anna clutched "Color Cèzanne" to her chest.

As soon as they got home, Anna headed right to the kitchen and grabbed her box of sixty-four Crayola crayons. Dad had told her she wasn't ready for the student-grade oil pastels yet but Anna didn't mind. She knew the colors she needed. She could find them in the box with just her fingertips. So while the Gilkersons talked and laughed and let Mom and Dad thank them for the ride with cold drinks and pita chips and hummus, Anna colored.

Periwinkle, cornflower, cadet blue, orchid, burnt sienna, maize, sepia—color after color Anna drew from the box, coloring lightly, carefully, checking again and again where the light landed in the picture, where the solid shapes sat. She took the most time with the mountains—those she had to get right, those were what pulled her into the picture. The shapes of them, the shadows and the solidness and the mystery of them.

She knew she wasn't Cèzanne and these were only crayons but she could feel the colors blending and coming to life. She could see the balance of water and air and land pouring out beneath her careful fingers. She even got right the little scribbled gray smoke that puttered out over the water. While her parents and the Gilkersons drank and talked—their voices raised again over that allegory thing—Anna colored, replicating as precisely as she could the magic of the picture that had moved her.

"Whatcha doing, Peanut?"

Anna looked up and saw her dad in the doorway. He looked messy, like he had just gotten out of bed. His hair looked dirty and his eyes were dark and red-rimmed. His voice sounded nice, but it didn't go with the hard line of his lips. He looked like a thunderstorm standing there. His rages could roll in fast. Anna hoped he was just tired or that Yvonne Gilkerson had just really irritated him and that once she was gone, her dad would calm down. The storm would blow over. Mom was still in the living room. The toilet flushed so Mr. Gilkerson was still there too. Dad just stood in the doorway staring at Anna's hands.

"You're coloring," he said in a flat voice. Anna couldn't tell if it was a good thing or a bad one. She was glad she'd been so careful to get the picture right. It wasn't perfect. She hoped he wouldn't notice that she'd used the wrong green for the closest trees. She used too much plain green and had tried to cover it up with forest green but still the colors were off. She hoped he would see instead what a good job she'd done on the sky, the way the lavender and periwinkle sometimes blended, sometimes sat side by side.

He leaned across the table, his big hand pulling the book away from her and turning it so he could see it right side up. He looked from the left side of the book, where a photo of the painting sat, to the right side, where she had been coloring so carefully. His fingertips bounced from side to side, from print chimney to crayon chimney, from inked skies to wax. Finally he looked up at her.

"It's exactly like the painting."

Anna exhaled and grinned. She knew she was close. She'd been so careful. The periwinkle had been a good choice and she was just about to point out the tiny gray smoke when he smashed his fist against the table.

"It's exactly like the fucking painting!"

Anna froze, her hands balled up beneath the table, the worn periwinkle crayon breaking in her palm. She pressed the back of her head against the wooden ridge of the chair back, hard enough to hurt, away from his red face that leaned in close enough for her to smell the beer and feel the spit hit her cheeks.

"Do you know why we make art, Anna? Do you?" She couldn't answer. She couldn't move. "We express ourselves. Do you hear me? We express *ourselves*. Ourselves! Not what other people have created, not what other people tell us to see. I didn't raise you to be a monkey, to be an ape just coloring in the lines, following the rules!"

He screamed and pounded his fist against the paper and Anna made herself as small as possible, knowing how these storms went, knowing to stay low, to never be a lightning rod. But when he grabbed a fistful of crayons—magenta and orange-red and black, the colors she had set aside that didn't belong in the landscape—she tried to grab his hand. She yelled and jumped to her feet but he was faster. His fist scribbled across her beautiful bay. He ripped black and orange scars across her periwinkle sky. The magenta point tore a hole clear through her mountains.

"There! There! Now it says something! Now we're speaking the human language!" He screamed and scribbled, coloring the table as he ripped through the pages, unhindered by Anna's smaller hands, unmoved by her cries begging him to stop.

Mom came in and a full fight broke out. Chairs flew and glass shattered and all sorts of profanity was thrown at the Gilkersons, who finally left. Everyone stormed out of the house and porch furniture groaned as it was hurled into the street.

Anna didn't leave the table. Her hands shook as she tried to smooth the ruined pages of her birthday book. She scraped her bitten nails across the orange streaks over the Bay of Marseilles, trying to scratch off the damage, to bring back the mountains and sky. Her tears poured over the page, running into the hole left by the magenta point.

Nothing worked. The book was ruined. Not just the picture, the whole book. She couldn't stop petting the damaged sky. She wouldn't stop smoothing the crumpled mountains.

Her mother came back into the kitchen, swearing to herself. She grabbed a broom and dustpan, calling her father a crazy sonofabitch who needed to be put away, promising herself that she was done with his shit, that this was the last time he would act like that under her roof. She kept talking as she headed back to the living room. She still muttered when she returned to dump the pieces of a broken lamp into the garbage can by the door.

Anna didn't move. She kept her hands on the tragedy before her, waiting for her mother to notice it. It wasn't until her mother came back from mopping up something wet that she looked at Anna. She sighed and looked down at the book beneath Anna's hands.

"He ruined your book."

Anna nodded, trying not to cry.

Her mother sighed again, sounding exhausted. She reached for the book, shaking her head as she leafed through the ruined pages. "He shouldn't have done that, Anna."

I know, Anna wanted to scream. That was mine and I did a good job. You should have seen my sky and I got the smoke right and the water. She wanted to scream all of this but tears closed her throat. She wanted her mother to shout those things for her, to be angry on her behalf.

But when her mother spoke again, Anna couldn't breathe.

"He was right though." Her mother shut the book and looked Anna in the eye. "Coloring isn't creation. It's obedience." She headed back into the living room, tossing the book into the garbage on top of the broken lamp.

Anna wanted to scream, to throw a chair like her father did. She wanted to rage and scrawl crayons on the wall until the dingy kitchen disappeared under midnight blue and burnt sienna and brick red. She wanted to rescue her book, to pull it from the shards of glass and twisted wire and secret it back to her room where she would color around the scars.

But she didn't. She gathered up her crayons from the tabletop and the floor where they had fallen. She put them back into the box in their proper place. Even the broken periwinkle.

Then she closed the box and dropped it into the garbage can.

CHAPTER 15

I'm home now.

I don't remember seeing anything on my way home except my feet, step step step, through snow and mud, step step step until I finally made it up the stairs to my apartment. I didn't even stop to get my mail. I have enough on my plate as it is.

Bless her heart, Meredith handled my mess like a pro. She didn't flinch at the eruption and wouldn't let me clean it up. Of course she had towels and a face cloth on her shelves, cool water, breath mints, even a toothbrush still in the packaging that I didn't take her up on. She brushed my hair off my forehead and pressed a cold cloth to the back of my neck, whispering reassurances and rubbing my back. She apologized for upsetting me. She said she was ashamed of herself for being such a ghoul.

I said I wanted to go home.

Of course she offered to drive me. She offered to lay out a sleeping bag behind my desk and let me sleep a bit first, because of course she has a sleeping bag in there somewhere. When I said no to both, she revealed the depth of her worry and offered to call Jeannie to come pick me up. I must have looked like hell. The last thing I wanted at that moment was anyone hovering over me. The second to last thing was to have to explain to Meredith why I reacted the way I did. She didn't ask. She assumed good thoughts. She doesn't know me very well.

I assured her I just wanted to walk, that I needed the air. I apologized and worked on looking sufficiently recovered so that she finally let me leave. She walked me down the hall, still rubbing my back through my coat. She followed me out onto the walkway like I had wanted to follow Jeannie and she watched me all the way to the steps at the corner of the building. Like Jeannie, I didn't look back. I didn't wave. I just wanted to go home.

Now I'm home and I think I made a huge mistake.

For one thing, I stink. I haven't showered in more days than I want to add up and the sweet/sour hangover smell has been replaced by the sharp bite of flop sweat. Walking a mile uphill hasn't sweetened that any. I need a shower. I need hot water to power through the grease in my hair and thick clouds of steam to clean my pores.

You can do this, I think, staring at myself through toothpaste spatters on the mirror.

I peel off my sweater and my long-sleeved T-shirt and I unbutton my jeans. I'll have to unlace my boots and peel off my socks. I hold my reflection's gaze as I think about the steps I need to go through to accomplish this goal, but even these simple thoughts don't stick. Even my own eyes don't hold my attention.

All I can see is the tub behind me.

All I can think about is getting into that tub.

I know I cannot do it.

My reflection agrees and we break our stare-off when we collapse onto our elbows on the vanity. I grab a hand towel and shove it under the water and use it to scrub at my face and around my neck and under my arms. I wind up soaking my bra and I have the feeling I'm just pushing dirt around but that's all I can manage right now. I step over my clothes into the hallway and back into the living room.

The best I can say about my living room is that I'm suitably dressed for it. Jeannie and I left quite a path throughout the space, ratcheting up my usual level of chaos. Wine bottles roll circles around my feet as I step through them. An Oreo package sticks to a plate of dried enchilada sauce. For some reason, we threw clothes around the room—socks, T-shirts, several pairs of shoes. I grab a shirt that looks like mine and pull it over my head. My wet bra soaks through the fabric and there's a hole under the right arm.

It's damaged. Like Ellis.

My stomach lurches at the thought and the wave of nausea propels me out the door, into the cold air, hard against the railing outside. I knock icicles off onto the level below and the chill races into the damp spots on my shirt. Wind blows up from the parking lot, icy and wet, and I hold my face up to it, letting it draw tears from my eyes.

I'm in West Virginia now, I tell myself. Nobody knows me. I have no family here. It's almost March. I'm in the mountains now; I'm off the prairies and the farmlands. I'm high on rocks and buffered from wind. It's almost March and in March everything becomes okay again. It's almost March and I'm in West Virginia and nothing has followed me here.

To prove this to myself and to keep from freezing against the metal railing, I stalk the length of the walkway past the other apartments. I kick cigarette butts and coffee cups out of the way. Phone books in plastic bags lay abandoned and flyers for Gilead's only Chinese restaurant peek out of cracks and doorframes. Straight ahead, if I blink through my wind-drawn tears, I see trees. Pine trees and bare oaks rise up on the ridge across the road, deer tracks wind through rhododendron bushes bent under the snow and everywhere cardinals pop like Christmas lights against the white mountainside.

It looks nothing like Nebraska.

It looks nothing like Missouri.

I could stare at it forever.

My stomach cramps and I bend over against the railing, looking down into the less lovely corner of the parking lot where the dumpsters hold back the dirty mountains of snow plowed from the lot. More animal tracks, more garbage, more dirt. A gust picks up a 7-Eleven Big Gulp cup and bounces it across the surface of the ice. More wind blows and I lean out into it until I hear a flapping noise. Some sort of plastic sheeting has blown in from the road and gotten caught on the edge of the dumpster. Its frayed edges *snap-snap* in the sharp wind and that's all it takes to make my stomach heave once more. I paint the dirty snow below me with the watery contents of my stomach. I'm shivering and try to kid myself that I've got the flu.

The clouds part and a wide swath of sunlight falls onto the corner of the landing, striking my left shoulder and cutting me on the diagonal. The wind quiets and I close my eyes, feeling one side of my body warming, one side tingling in the cold. With my eyes closed, motors on the road sound like the ocean, and the snow cracks and slides off of tree branches and rooftops with whispers that almost sound human. I drift. Tears dry and glue my eyelids closed and I drift.

· · · · · · · · · · · · · · · · · · ·

"Ms. Ray?"

I jerk awake and my left knee buckles, banging against the metal railing. My hands ache with cold, and blood burns as it rushes into the indentation left behind from gripping the railing. How long have I been standing here?

I turn and the movement sets my whole body shivering. Whatever sun I'd been enjoying is gone behind the ridge but there's still plenty of daylight. Detective Hinton stands halfway down the walkway, Neighborgall several feet behind her. She approaches me slowly, her jacket open, her gun visible but her hands in front of her.

"Ms. Ray, are you all right?"

"Yeah." I almost stumble on my numb feet as I walk her way. Something flakes off the corner of my mouth when I speak and I rub my lips with icy fingers. I need to pull it together quickly because I remember what I look like. She's watching me so I go with the obvious answer. "Sorry, I think I've got the flu or something. Came home early. Needed air."

She nods as I approach and then pass her. "You don't look good."

"I don't feel good."

"Standing out in the cold probably isn't a good idea. Where's your coat?"

"In my apartment. I just stepped outside for a second to get some air."

Hinton and her partner might know that's a lie; they might have been watching me for a while. I expect them to follow me into my apartment but neither has moved.

"Did you want something, Detective? Did you bring me my phone?"

"We're not done with it yet."

"Do you want to come in?"

She glances at Neighborgall, who doesn't move, and then steps toward my door. "We're actually here for another reason. I wonder if you wouldn't mind stepping inside." That's when I see Neighborgall's glance flit to the door beside mine, his hand on his belt, close to his gun. Three uniformed officers stand on the stairs. All of them have their radios turned off, no telltale squawking giving their presence away.

"You're here for Bobby," I say.

"So you know who lives next door to you."

"I've never met him. I've never even seen him, but I've heard them enough to know it would just be a matter of time until you all showed up. Bobby is a nasty drunk."

"And Karmen?"

A lock clicks and Hinton spins away from me to stand with her partner in front of the door. I recognize Bobby's snarling voice.

"What the fuck's going on out here? You wanna—"

I step back out onto the landing, peering around to get my first glimpse of my neighbor. He's smaller than I expected, skinny. I guess after all the fights I pictured more of a big 'roided-up meathead. The cops consider him big enough, because Neighborgall and Hinton both have their hands very close to their guns.

"Robert Alistair." Neighborgall speaks loudly and clearly. "We are looking for Karmen Rene Bennett. We have a warrant to search your premises."

Bobby doesn't move out of the door. "What do you want with her?"

"Is Karmen Bennett here?" Hinton asks.

Why are they looking for Karmen here? Katie is Bobby's girlfriend. I'm waiting for him to explain that to them when he yells back into the apartment and solves the mystery.

"K.B.! K.B.! Wake up! The fucking cops are here looking for you."

Not Katie. K.B. Karmen Bennett. I've been listening to her getting slapped around for months. I remember the sound of glass breaking recently. I wonder if that was what happened to her foot sculpture.

Hinton and Neighborgall have pushed into the apartment, followed by the uniforms. Neighborgall shoves out a piece of paper that must be the search warrant. Bobby's not interested in reading it, giving way to the officers with disgust and what looks like familiarity. He stands there, shaking his head as they pass him, and then sees me on the landing.

"The fuck are you looking at?"

He's got a black eye, a bandage on his hand, and a massive purple bruise on his arm that disappears under the cut sleeve of his WVU T-shirt. I look him over from head to toe.

"I hope someone beats the shit out of you," I say and go back into my apartment.

They're searching the place. I hear kitchen cabinets slamming, silverware clattering. Karmen protests but it's not until she yells at Bobby to shut up that she sounds like the annoying neighbor I'm used to. It's strange trying to connect the two realities. I think of how many times Karmen sat across from me, bruised and cut, as I sympathized with her over a lack of sleep. I feel like a shit.

Stomachache or no, I think about opening a bottle of wine. I don't feel like drinking it and my stomach twitches at the thought, but this doesn't seem like a good time to break with tradition. I'm putting a lot of thought into this debate when I hear Bobby's door open. Karmen yells, "Call my dad, Bobby!" and I have to open the door.

She's not cuffed, but Neighborgall has her elbow. Hinton holds a cardboard box under her arm, and I can see several plastic bags sticking out the top. Evidence.

Neighborgall sees me first. "Go back inside, please."

Then Karmen sees me and her eyes widen. "Ms. Ray? Ms. Ray. Please! They're arresting me. They think I killed Professor Trachtenberg. Tell them I didn't do it."

"You're not under arrest," Hinton says, looking over her at me. "We just want to talk with you at the police station."

"After you took all my stuff?" Karmen looks like she's ready to bolt and Neighborgall holds her elbow more tightly. "Ms. Ray, tell them. I wouldn't do anything like that."

Neighborgall and Hinton both look at me, whether in warning or curiosity, I can't tell. I can't believe the words that come out of my mouth.

"Just go, Karmen. Tell them the truth. You don't have anything to hide."

How many times have I heard those words? They seem to comfort Karmen as much as they did me because her face goes dark, her mouth a hard line, and she shakes her head in disgust. At Neighborgall's prompting, they continue their path down the stairs and to the waiting patrol car.

Cigarette smoke blows in from the doorway beside mine. Bobby spits and steps back inside. Before he shuts the door, he says the first thing I've agreed with him on.

"Fucking cops."

· · · · · · · · · · · · · · · · · · · ·

I take a short break midway through the bottle. I'll call it a nap but all I really do is sit on my hideous sofa and stare at my front door. I'm not looking for anything or at anything; my front door is just the thing that's easiest to see from where I'm flopped onto my couch. Next door, Bobby comes and goes several times, punctuating his movements with door slams and yelled phone calls. He plays a little death metal at one point but can't commit to it. Silence wins out in the end.

My glass is empty and the room is getting dark but I don't move. My stomach growls and I have to pee but I still don't move. I definitely need to shower and now that my bra has dried, it's itchy and sticking to my skin, but that has to keep, too. I don't want to move.

If I move, I may think. It's like my body stands in a pool and my thoughts are silt around my feet. If I move, I'll stir them up and I don't want that.

Someone knocks on the door. It's not Jeannie. She'd just let herself in. If it's the cops, they'll find their way in eventually. Anyone else can go away. But they don't.

"Anna?" Meredith pushes the door open, peeking her head in and whispering. It takes her a minute to spot me amid the debris and shadows. "Anna, are you okay?"

"Yep."

She closes the door behind her and picks her way over the clutter to sit beside me on the couch. Her hand is warm on my knee.

"Anna? Are you okay?"

"Yes." I hope in vain that this is the extent of the conversation. I can do this all night.

"I'm sorry I upset you today. It was thoughtless of me."

"I'm okay."

It feels nice where she rubs my knee. "Can I get you anything? Something to eat? Maybe I could run you a bath?"

Air rushes out of my mouth until I catch it and turn it into, "No. Thank you."

"You know, it might not be true what I heard about the crime scene. It might just be a stupid rumor that someone was spreading. It might just be an exaggeration someone told to make an already awful scene that much worse." I nod as she talks and focus on the warmth of my knee beneath her hand. She leans in closer and I look up to face her.

Meredith's eyes get soft as she looks at me—no judgment, no anger, just compassion and worry and friendship. As I watch her expression shift through these soft emotions, I think, *she knows. She can see it all right there in my face.* I think that she must, that maybe everybody can, but out of some arcane social nicety nobody points it out, nobody calls me on it. Or nobody is looking for it but when they see it, they know me.

It's impossible to me that only four people who ever walked the face of the earth know the truth about me. Two of them are dead. One of them is in prison. And one of them is about to burst into tears and throw herself into her boss's arms and beg her to admit that she sees it, that's it's not a secret anymore. That I can put it down.

Meredith starts to speak and I hold my breath, waiting to hear the words. Instead she says, "You were in love with Ellis, weren't you."

"Oh for fuck's sake." That gets me moving. I push myself off the couch and send a wine bottle spinning somewhere beneath the coffee table.

"Anna, wait."

"Are you kidding me, Meredith? That's what you think?"

She holds her hands up in that surrender pose that I've been seeing a lot from her lately and it's starting to get on my nerves. I grab my wine glass off the table and empty the bottle into it. Naptime is over.

"Anna, talk to me."

"And say what? That I was secretly in love with Ellis and now I'm going to have a Hallmark moment mourning him? You want me to weep into a lace hanky and wear black?"

"You usually wear black." I'm ready to pounce on that when I realize she's trying to lighten the mood. "C'mon Anna, you have to admit you're acting a little weird. I'm worried about you. And you know, it's not unheard of to be attracted to a man. Even when you're grieving, it's nothing to feel guilty about. There's no sin in it."

I've got nothing to say to that. She follows me toward the kitchen. I stand at the sink, pretending that I'm going to wash something. She perches on a bar stool on the other side of the island. "You can talk to me. You know that. You can tell me anything."

When I look at her, one of those ridiculous curls has broken free again. It jumps out wildly like a spring over her left ear. When she talks, it bounces and twists and reminds me why students find Meredith so easy to talk to. She's a tireless champion of the underdog, a true advocate. I admire those qualities until they're turned on me. I need to put her mind at rest.

"Tuesday was the one-year anniversary of my husband's death." I almost say *suicide* but I don't want to go there. I want to wrap this up. "He died suddenly and it was very hard. I tried to put it all behind me when I moved here but sometimes I think that maybe I changed everything too quickly. I didn't give myself time to grieve, time to process it all." I'm making this up as I go along. I'm doing a hell of a job at it, too, because my throat tightens. "I wanted to build a new life here. Then Ellis started coming on to me and I kept thinking how tacky that was, how insensitive. Couldn't he see how much I was grieving? Couldn't he tell? It was all over my face, but he didn't see it."

I force a mouthful of wine down my closing throat. It burns but makes speaking easier. "Of course he couldn't see it. It's not like I was wearing a mourning veil. I didn't tell anyone. I didn't want to talk about it. I didn't want to be 'that person,' that griever." I catch myself before I add the word *again* to that sentence. Meredith nods, her eyes soft and a little damp.

"And so," I say with a flourish of my glass, "I resented Ellis Trachtenberg for not being psychic and for having the audacity to think nice things about me. And that concludes my essay for admittance to the nut house."

Meredith smiles. "You're not nuts. You're human. You're allowed to be human. Things hurt. Sometimes they hurt so much that you can't think about anything else but making the pain stop. You do crazy things. We all do. Pain makes us crazy and nothing causes more pain than love." I watch that curl shimmy and flip.

"I wish you drank." It's the most honest affection I can convey. "You won't join me?"

She shakes her head and stands. "I appreciate the invitation but no, thank you. I just wanted to make sure you got home safely and that you're okay. Are you sure you're okay drinking alone?"

"I'll muddle through."

"I bet you will." She throws me a scolding look as she gathers her purse and jacket. Her rogue curl hangs down over her eye as she focuses on her zipper. "Just out of curiosity, did you happen to tell your cousin about Ellis flirting with you?"

"Yeah, I did. Why?"

"How did she take it?"

"She took it fine."

"Good." She smiles. "I'm glad. I know you two are close. Some-times something like that can cause friction between people. Even when people are like sisters, feelings can get hurt."

"Jeannie's not like that."

"Good." She says it with a smile that gets less convincing each time I see it. She hesitates before heading to the door and I get the feeling she's trying to find a way to say something. Before she can manage it,

Jeannie strolls in, phone to her ear, and holds up a hand to silence us as she wraps up her conversation. Meredith's smile gets a little twisted.

"Yeah, okay, thanks. I'll check in on Monday." Jeannie ends the call and dumps it into her huge purse with a dramatic sigh. "It's just one damn thing after another. I'm not gone a week and the whole world falls apart."

"Please," Meredith says. "Don't let us interrupt your important work."

There's that withering look again. "Oh Meredith. How nice to see you. Again."

I grab another bottle of wine. "Hey, if you guys want to start punching each other, that's okay with me. Let me get my glass out of the way."

Meredith gives me an injured look but Jeannie just rolls her eyes. "I'd have been here sooner but I went by the police station to get your phone. They wouldn't release it to me."

"Did you see Karmen?"

"Who?"

"What?" Meredith drops her purse. "Why would Karmen be at the police station?"

"The police picked her up to question her." Time feels weird, like this happened days ago. "They had a search warrant."

"How do you know?" Meredith asks. "Did she call you?"

"No." I wrestle with the cork, trying to sort my thoughts. "How weird is this? It turns out Karmen lives next door to me. At least her boyfriend does. Bobby something. They're the ones that make all the noise."

"Ooh," Jeannie says, "you mean finger-in-the-butt Bobby?" I laugh at that but Meredith looks horrified.

"Do you mind, Professor? That's disgusting."

I want to laugh again but I remember what we're really talking about. I remember the look on Karmen's face when Neighborgall led her away. "They said they weren't arresting her but they wanted to question her about Ellis's murder. They had a search warrant and a big box of stuff."

"Oh my god," Meredith says, "that poor child. Did you go down there with her? I should go down there to make sure she's okay. See if anyone called her parents. They certainly can't believe she had anything to do with that horrible crime. She's a child."

Jeannie takes the glass I offer her. "Is this that waitress we're talking about? I told you the cops were interested in her. It's got something to do with that book. I know it."

I'm grabbing my own glass when Meredith's hand comes down hard on mine, not a slap exactly but not a gentle gesture. "How could you not know that Karmen Bennett was living right beside you? How could you not know what her boyfriend was doing? He's a thug and piece of trash who has done nothing but give that girl trouble and you didn't do anything to help her?"

"I didn't know that was them. I never saw them. How was I supposed to know?"

"She is your student. She is your responsibility. She counts on you for help."

I'm getting really irritated that I can't drink my wine. "She is not *my* student, Meredith. She's one of the students I work with. She's an adult. She has her own parents." I jerk my wine glass free of her grip. "We are not their mothers. What they do outside of school is none of our business and it's certainly not our responsibility. You need some boundaries."

She looks more disgusted at my words than when she looked at the puddle of vomit I left in our office. She gathers her purse and glares at both me and Jeannie.

"Well, thank you very much for that sage advice. I appreciate your candor. It must be very comforting to hold that worldview. Now if you will excuse me, I'm going to see if there is anything I can do to help out a young woman in trouble." She stops in front of Jeannie and stares at her. "If it's all the same to you, I choose to place my boundaries elsewhere."

Jeannie toasts her with her wine and Meredith turns on her heel and storms out. As soon as the door is closed, Jeannie flips her the bird with her glass-free hand.

"How can you stand working with that woman? She's such a sanctimonious busybody."

"She's okay. She means well."

"Oh please, she's a barnacle trying to be a ship. She attaches herself to everybody's business and acts like she belongs there."

A headache makes itself known behind my eyes. "She's right, though. I should have known that was Karmen living next door. I should have recognized her voice. I should have asked where she lived. I knew she was in a bad place and I didn't try to help her."

Jeannie sets her wine glass down in front of me. "There are a lot of bad places in this world, Anna. Some of them you have to get through on your own. Even if someone is helping you, some of that stuff you have to handle on your own. You know that better than anyone." I nod and she pats my arm as she moves past me. "Now go sit down and let me clean up this kitchen. What the hell did we do in here?"

I do as she says and flop back down on my couch. In minutes, water is running and baking sheets are clanging. Jeannie is sweeping and picking up garbage, folding clothes and stacking magazines. The movement and noise make my headache grow ferocious.

"Jeannie, stop."

"What?" she hollers over the running water.

"Are you doing your laundry in there? For god's sake, turn the water off."

She does and comes into the living room drying her hands. "What's the matter with you? I'm just doing the dishes."

"You're taking forever!" I hate the whine in my voice. "It's just that I've got a headache and you're running around doing all this stuff. Just stop. Stop."

"Okay." She drops the towel. "What do you want to do? You want to watch TV?"

"No. I think I'm going to go to bed."

"Are you going to take a shower first?"

"What? No." My right temple throbs.

She grimaces. "You need a shower. Like, badly."

"I'll take one in the morning."

"You really ought to take one tonight."

"Fuck off, Jeannie!" My own voice lodges the spike of my headache deep into my eye. "God, you're as bad as Meredith. I don't want a fucking shower. I want to go to bed."

"All right," she snaps back. "You don't have to bite my fucking head off. Go to bed. Wallow in your filth. Have at it." She grabs her purse and heads for the door. Before she leaves, she turns back to me. "You know, Anna, you don't always have to be so unhappy. There's got to be a point where you're allowed to get over it. All of it—your dad, your mom, Ronnie. At some point, you're allowed to be happy."

I lie back on the couch and put my arm over my eyes. I hear her sigh and I hear her leave. I don't hear anything for a while after that.

. . . .

I wake up when I hit the floor. I've fallen off the couch. I land on that wine bottle I kicked under there. Almost under there. My apartment is dark. I thought I was in the tub when my arm pressed against the side of the couch. I yank the bottle out from under me and lie on the floor a moment, figuring out where I am, pushing the dreams out of my head. I thought I heard a door open and I sit up, making sure it wasn't mine. If it was, whoever opened it is gone. There's no noise from next door.

I climb back on the couch and I'm gone.

. . . .

Now the garbage truck wakes me. The sun is mostly up and I hear the beeping of the big truck as it backs toward the dumpster. It seems a little aggressive to me to have garbage service so early in the morning on a Saturday, especially around college students. Maybe it's Gilead's way of paying them back for the beer bottles and trash the students leave everywhere on Friday nights.

There's no noise except the garbage men but they make enough for the entire apartment building. The beep of their truck, the rumble of the big diesel engine, their yells and laughter will lead up to the tormented sound of the huge metal dumpster being hefted, turned, dumped, and returned. I lay with my eyes closed, waiting for the crescendo when the noise changes. The rhythm breaks. More yells, less rumbling. Different yells.

It can't mean what I think it means.

Why would my mind even go there?

I sit up on the couch, hoping to hear the rest of the dumpster-dance song but all I hear is a chatter of male yells, truck doors slamming, and then just the rumble of the diesel engine. I don't know how but I know I'm right.

I take my time. I pee, brush my teeth, pull on shoes and grab a jacket. I've got to be wrong but I know I'm not. I know that tone the men speak in. I've heard it before. This can't be happening but I know it is. I make my way out the door, down the walkway in front of the other apartments, all of which are quiet. Everyone tries to sleep through garbage service.

At the end of the walkway, I lean over the railing like I did yesterday. The dumpster isn't where it should be; it's still in the arms of the sanitation truck, hovering in the air undumped. The reflective green jackets of the garbage men stand out bright against the dirty snow where they're gathered around the open space left by the dumpster. They're vivid but not as vivid as what they're staring at.

A body sprawls out across the dirty ice like a snow angel. I recognize the cut WVU T-shirt. It's my neighbor, Bobby. He looks even smaller from up here. It looks like he's pulling a huge red sheet behind him in his left hand but when I look closer, I see that's an illusion. He isn't holding anything in his left hand. That's blood pouring out beside him.

His left hand is gone.

I bend over, pressing my forehead against the railing. Its rusty edge cuts into my skin and a thin stream of saliva drips down from my open mouth. I'm panting. No, my body is panting. I feel nothing. That nothing feels familiar.

My knees hit the walkway and my face scrapes the metal spindles below the railing as I fall. I turn, sit, press my head back between the bars and close my eyes. When I hear sirens, I think I should go back to my apartment. I should close the door and pretend I saw nothing, pretend I just woke up, pretend to be shocked when they come asking about Bobby's death. But there's no point in that, I figure. I'm not that good an actress. I can't even tell the truth well.

I know things. The same way I knew what I would find down there, I know the way this will look. I know the way the cops will look at me. It will be the way they looked at me in Nebraska. The way they looked at me in Missouri. They'll look at me and they'll see me.

I wonder if they've seen me all along.

CHAPTER 16

Chattam, Nebraska
2014
Anna Shuler Ray, 28 years old

They had been happy. She had been happy. Ronnie made Anna happy in ways that startled her. He was funny and silly and smart. He looked gorgeous in his jeans and even better out of them. He made her laugh and got her sense of humor. His poetry could be uneven but he didn't take himself too seriously. He laughed at his own shortcomings and teased Anna about her criticisms.

But he listened to her. He came to her for advice and listened to what she said. For the first time in her adult life, Anna began to trust someone other than her cousin, Jeannie. It liberated her and made her optimistic for the life ahead of her.

For the first time she could remember, she wasn't just playing at normal. She felt normal. She thought maybe she felt the way normal people felt—relaxed and content, safe and included. Ronnie had a lot of friends and they accepted her without question, pleased that their funny, talkative buddy had found someone who seemed to make him so happy. They didn't ask Anna why she was so quiet; Ronnie was a talker. It took experience to get a word in around him.

But he listened to her. When they were together, when he calmed down from the giddy high crowds sent him on, he would focus on her with an attention that took her breath away. He didn't frighten her; he didn't pry. He listened. He looked at her and accepted what she had to give him and he gave her pieces of himself back.

When did it fall apart?

Anna used to think it was when she told him everything, when he coaxed her secret from her, something no lawyer or cop or therapist had ever managed. Even Jeannie hadn't gotten this out of her, but Ronnie had. Those big hazel eyes and soft lips, his thin, strong hands and that one crooked front tooth had hypnotized her. They had relaxed her and opened her in every conceivable way until the only thing that lay hidden was the worst of her.

But that wasn't how it started. Not really.

Ronnie gave her a lot of room. He liked to hike, his energy seeming endless and frenetic to his much more sedentary girlfriend. He would go away for days, always letting her know he'd be gone but never feeling the need to check in. In truth, Anna loved Ronnie as much for his absences as she did for his hand-holding and the funny, filthy poems he'd leave in her underwear drawer.

He asked her to move in with him and she ignored the alarm that went off in her head.

That was the first mistake.

For the first time in her life, Anna walked a normal path and she knew that path led to cohabitation because that's what normal people did. She and Ronnie loved each other. They should live together. That's how this went and so she told herself that the clutch of panic she felt in her stomach was the result of a lifetime of fear. A habit of mistrust.

Love trumped distrust. Isn't that what everyone is supposed to know?

And so when Ronnie got the job teaching English at a community college in Nebraska, Anna quit her job and moved with him. She packed her stuff, he packed his, and they headed off to a little house Ronnie had rented within biking distance of the school. The house showed all the signs of a long-time rental property—shabby yellow paint, a crooked porch, uneven floors. It looked so much like the house she had grown up in, Anna could only stare, trying to blink, trying to break the link to the past and locate herself in the present.

Ronnie thought she didn't like it. He ran from room to room, chattering, wide-eyed, pointing out the space he would have for an office, pointing out the tiny laundry room hanging off the back of the house, pacing out the bigger-than-expected bedroom and the big-enough kitchen. Then he took her by the hand and dragged her to see what he thought would be the selling point for Anna.

A tiny bathroom with an old claw-foot tub.

She turned from the bathroom and kissed him, closing her eyes to the sight and her ears from the alarm clang-clanging inside of her.

He pressed her up against the bedroom door and banged the anxiety right out of her.

Moving in brought the second warning. They each packed secrets that neither wanted unpacked but the house was small and they couldn't be avoided. Anna saw Ronnie's first—a battered leather bag that looked like the shaving kit Jeannie's father used to keep under the sink. Ronnie tucked his there, too, back behind the Drano and the extra pack of toilet paper. Anna found it when she went looking for a bandage and, not knowing it was a secret, pulled back the zipper. No real reason. She thought she'd see his razor, maybe find the shaving soap that made his skin smell so delicious. Instead she found bottles, short orange plastic bottles with labels covered in strange prescription names and long dosage warnings.

Seroquel. Clozaril. Zyprexa.

She didn't know what they were for but she knew she'd never seen them before. She zipped the bag and shoved it back under the sink just as Ronnie stuck his head in around the door. He saw the cabinet slam shut and stared at her for a second with no expression.

Then he grinned, that crooked tooth winking at her. "Hey babe, let's clear some of those boxes out of the living room so we'll have a place to crash tonight."

Ronnie stacked boxes of books high against the wall to the kitchen—they had way too many books for the tiny house—and Anna waited until he was bent to the task before opening the two cartons she'd packed and carried in herself, boxes with "personal" written in solid red letters on the tops and two sides. Those she dragged over to the hall closet that sat just where it was supposed to and held nothing more than a few wire hangers and a broken umbrella.

She felt a twist of anxiety when she examined the closet. It was tall, its walls extending high up into the crawl space with deep shelves over her head. Closets weren't supposed to be so high, not hall closets. Not this closet. She looked out at the cartons she needed to unpack. They didn't hold enough to build the wall.

There was nothing to be done about it now. More boxes would come.

She opened the first carton and started unpacking the smaller boxes. These she stacked in the back of the closet, side by side, tight in the narrow space. The two oldest were the largest. They were from when she still lived with Jeannie's family. They nearly filled the bottom row. The smaller boxes came next. Anna had to shove one into the gap between the bigger boxes and the wall. She had to wedge it in there. That was okay. They needed to be steady. They needed to stay put.

She worked quickly, stacking the boxes, three on the next level—stack, wedge, align. She fitted shoeboxes and small cartons together like a puzzle she assembled every time she moved. Every year the puzzle gained another piece. Every year she made it fit. The ninth and final box she set on top of the second row. The box wasn't full, none of them were.

The cut-off dates couldn't be altered. Full or not, the boxes were closed on March 1 and another box was brought in. Eventually she would have enough to build a wall.

"Hey, babe." Ronnie knelt beside her and she jumped, almost knocking the top box over. Her fingers dug into the cardboard. "What are these?"

"Letters."

"Really? That's a lot of letters. Who are they from?"

"My mother."

"Do you want to put them somewhere else?"

"No."

He suggested moving them to the office they could share. He offered to put them in the crawl space where they would be safe or even to buy her an actual file cabinet. He reminded her that the vacuum cleaner and coats and boots went there as well.

"This is where they go." She didn't look at him. She couldn't take her hands off the cardboard wall in front of her. "They go in here like this. This is where they go."

"Okay," he finally whispered and leaned in to kiss her temple. "That's where they go."

And so they moved their secrets in with them.

It worked for a while. They found their places within their new home, bumping into each other here and there, finding room for each other's comforts and private spaces. They were happy and Anna told herself that most couples probably went through those same awkward adjustments going from dating to living together.

So when it came time to adjust from living together to getting married, Anna had grown so accustomed to the occasional run-ins and missteps, she hardly noticed the alarm clanging deep in her gut. She made up half of a couple now. She had a place. They had been dating for eight months, living together for two. She had gotten accustomed to normal, even if she wondered if maybe they weren't getting it exactly right.

Ronnie wanted a Christmas wedding. What could be more normal than that?

He said his family didn't celebrate any holidays and that he wanted a real reason to celebrate Christmas. He wanted to invite his friends from Illinois and make it a long celebration. Ronnie hadn't made many friends in Chattam yet and Anna knew that it bothered him more than he expressed. He went on longer and longer hikes and bike rides even as the Nebraska winter bore down on them. She heard him talking to himself more than once and started noticing that he often wouldn't sleep through the night.

She didn't say anything to him about it. What could she say? Since moving into the little yellow house in Chattam two months before, he had found her asleep in the tub no fewer than half a dozen times. He would lead her back to bed and kiss her. He loved her and she loved him but it seemed neither of them had the tools or the inclination to examine these odd edges.

Ronnie decided to try before their wedding.

Three days before Christmas, two days before their wedding, and the day before Jeannie, her husband, and all of Ronnie's friends would descend upon their home, Ronnie pulled Anna into his arms. He led her to the doorway to their bedroom, the first place they had made love in their new home. The space had an intimacy about it. The gateway to their couple-space, they often bumped into each other in this doorframe and almost always shared a kiss there. Here they weren't in the bedroom, they weren't in the hall. They weren't anywhere but with each other and both relaxed under the stained pine molding.

She let him pull her down to the floor where they sat cross-legged, backs against either side of the doorframe, hands tangled up in each other's. He looked into her eyes and smiled.

"This is it."

She nodded, breathy and nervous.

"We're doing this," he said, squeezing her fingers. "We're getting married."

"Yeah."

"Are you ready?"

The clang-clang-clang she'd grown so accustomed to grew just a decibel, not enough to silence her. "Yeah."

"Me, too." He leaned in to kiss her. "I need to tell you something. Something you already know but I need you to hear it from me. I know you've seen my medication." She nodded. She had never said anything about the pills. "I've been under treatment since high school. I got sick in middle school."

He rubbed her hands as he told her about the breakdowns, the bizarre behavior, the terror and the pain he had caused his family. He told her about the shame his mother felt having to commit him his second year of college and how hard he worked to ride out the misdiagnoses and incorrect medications. He told her that he became a teacher because he was afraid to have children of his own and thought that would be the closest he would ever get to being a father. He promised that he would work every day to stay well enough to be the man who could love her for the rest of her life.

He cupped her face in his palm. "You make my life worth living."

There it was—his wedding gift to her. The black leather bag underneath the sink with his secret in it was worth more to her than any diamond ring. He didn't ask for anything in return, either. He just wanted to tell her the truth; that was the kind of man Ronnie Ray was. He loved her and he trusted her and she trusted him.

So she told him.

She told him everything—all the details, all the parts she could remember, and did her best with the parts that remained cloudy. She talked and talked until every last bit of it was out of her and he took in every word. He didn't interrupt; he didn't comfort her. He just listened in that way that had made her fall in love with him in the first place. When she finished, she stopped talking. She waited for him to leave, to recoil, at least to reconsider joining his life to hers, but he didn't do any of those things. Instead he kissed her.

The first February after they were married was the first February in sixteen years that Anna Shuler wasn't afraid. She didn't have to bear its dark weight alone. This was good since neither of them was fully prepared for winter in Nebraska. Icy wind, snow drifts, the low, dark skies combined to drive them both indoors, together, close and quiet. Weather kept Jeannie from being able to visit in February and Ronnie took care of her. He let her talk when she needed to and left her alone when she wanted. He woke her up in the tub and led her back to bed whenever he found her there.

By spring, the clamor of alarm within Anna had fallen all but silent. By summer, she began to hear it again.

Ronnie made new friends—a cycling group that took impossible journeys over hundreds of miles. They would be gone for long weekends, pushing their endurance, pushing each other. His new friends encouraged Ronnie to work out more, to become a vegetarian and worship his body, even while they urged him to party harder. They smoked a lot of weed and invited Anna to join their drumming circles and sweat lodges. They formed bands and held poetry slams. They made manic plans for food co-ops and art colonies and government protests that never got past the yelling and smoking stage. Ronnie seemed to enjoy it and he didn't pressure Anna to join in.

By August she could see the dark circles under Ronnie's eyes that hadn't been there before. In September, she noticed he didn't keep his leather bag of pills under the sink. In November, she began to ask him about it and in December he told her he had found a new doctor and was trying a new regimen.

He had more energy, she had to give him that. His body hummed beneath her fingertips. He ran and cycled and lifted; he ate organic everything and only drank microbrew beer and locally sourced wine. His temper grew edges.

She didn't help. She didn't know how. Not only that, but the bang-bang-bang of internal warning had numbed her affection and she found herself provoking him. She'd spit out the (admittedly hideous) locally sourced boysenberry wine in front of him. She laughed at his new devotion to rhyming haiku, arguing the absurdity of practicing an art form that by definition did not exist. He threw a drawer across the room during that fight. She answered by whipping a volume of Basho's poetry at his head.

February was right around the corner. She knew how fast it would come in and in those dark moments, a part of her longed for it. As terrifying as it was, she knew it. It knew her. The intimacy she had felt with Ronnie now seemed like a dream, the kind of delusion prisoners must conjure when rotting at the bottom of a hole.

The hole was reality and it was just a matter of time until she was blown back into it.

Jeannie called her a lot. She talked about coming in, asking Anna if she needed her. Anna knew she did but couldn't say the words. It hurt Jeannie's feelings, being cut out of this role in her cousin's life. Anna wanted to comfort her, but something about that low Nebraska sky kept Anna's mouth shut. Something about the sharp lines of Ronnie's drawn cheeks told her that there was no shortcut off this path.

As January wrapped up, he started asking her about it. He brought up details and asked questions under the guise of comforting her, encouraging her to talk about it, but Anna saw through him. This wasn't concern. Ronnie fixated on details, he chewed on them the way he chewed on his gluten-free bagels and vegan Nori wraps. He hungered for them and Anna decided to let him starve.

February 17, Ronnie left for school early, riding his bike despite the sub-zero temperature. Anna called in sick, glad for him to be out of the house. She couldn't relax once the afternoon rolled in, knowing he would be home, knowing what he would want to talk about. So she warmed up the car and drove down to the BW3 on the other side of town.

Beer, wings, trivia, sports—the bar was packed and loud. Nobody noticed the woman in black in a corner booth, a trivia console in front of her as a decoy, a pitcher of beer in front of her as a mission. The waitress had eyed her curiously on her first pitcher, suggesting she order some wings or mini corndogs. When the second pitcher ran empty, the waitress stopped asking. Ronnie would have argued with her over what he called "shitty American piss beer." For Anna, it went down as smoothly as champagne.

She decided to go home. Driving carefully down the dark, flat roads, Anna thought about what they were doing to each other. It wasn't enough to say she didn't know any better. She should try to know better. She should try to break the cycle of destruction that she had internalized. Jeannie loved her and that had never led to pain. Aunt Gretchen and Uncle John had made their marriage work despite all sorts of craziness nobody outside the marriage could know.

She pulled up in front of the little yellow house, the house so similar to her childhood home. But this wasn't that house. This wasn't that life. This was her life, the life she was making with Ronnie. It didn't have to burn just because her mother's life had.

The lights glowed in the window, looking so cozy. She wanted to go in. She wanted this to be home, her home, their home. A real home. But when she opened the door, she knew she was wrong.

What did she see first? The note? Or the shadow from the closet door? All sounds fell away as the clang-clang-clang within her hammered at the inside of her skull. A poem. Ronnie had left her a poem—a jagged mess of ugly words scrawled across the back of an envelope. Not just words—rhyming haiku. His last jab at her? Not quite. It wasn't just any envelope. This was a letter from her mother.

That's why the closet was open. He had opened a box—the tenth box, the new box. He had dismantled her wall. She looked only at the boxes when she pulled open the closet door. White cardboard picked up the faint light of the living room, cut with the shadows of the heavy weight dangling in front of them. Shoes. Cycling shoes, toes turned toward each other, swinging.

A carpet of white envelopes splayed from the spilled box. Not perfectly white. Blue ink marched across the fronts of them; red stamps broke up their smooth surfaces. Something else now, too. Black. Red. Brown. Stains. Spatters. On the envelopes, on the boxes. Blood soaking into them. Or was it seeping out of them? She didn't know. She couldn't tell. She couldn't see anything but envelopes and boxes and cycling shoes dangling off of legs that swung, all that hard-won muscle useless now.

Her eyes would go no farther than his hands. Those beautiful long thin hands that had reached for her and opened her up. That had held her and worn the ring that promised that she made his life worth living.

She had to call the police. She had to call 911. She wanted to call Jeannie. She walked without looking, wanting to find the phone in the kitchen. Instead, she found herself in the bathroom, plugging the tub, running the water.

CHAPTER 17

"Ms. Ray?"

Hinton stands in front of me again, her hand near her gun.

I nod and rise to my feet. "Okay."

"Okay."

She escorts me to the patrol car.

. . . .

Gilead's police station looks more like a down-on-its-luck insurance office. Dropped ceilings, cubicles, tan paint on drywall and industrial green carpeting make the open front room feel dead even though phones are ringing and three officers in uniform march about energetically. Behind a glass wall, an older officer nods at Hinton and buzzes us through a metal door. The detective waves me through in front of her and guides me to a smaller version of the front room. Metal table, plastic chairs, same ugly tan walls.

I take the seat she points me to as she closes the door.

"Do I need an attorney?"

"Did you kill Robert Alistair?"

It takes me a second to place the name. Robert Alistair sounds so dignified, not fitting for my neighbor Bobby. "No."

"Okay." Hinton picks up a cardboard file box from the corner and brings it to the table. Of course she's not going to tell me to get a lawyer. Just because I have the right to one doesn't mean it's encouraged. "I have a few questions for you."

I probably should ask for a lawyer but I don't. All my energy goes to keeping me from dropping my head onto the table and pretending none of this is happening.

Hinton puts the box to the side and leans forward on her elbows. "Where is Karmen Bennett?"

That's not what I'm expecting. "I thought she was here. You brought her in."

"For questioning, yes. We didn't charge her with anything. Her father came to pick her up last night. Have you seen her?"

"No."

"What is your relationship with Karmen Bennett?"

"She's a student. I'm a student advocate"

"So your relationship with Karmen Bennett was strictly limited to the college." I nod. "Like your relationship with Professor Trachtenberg."

What the hell does that mean? I say nothing and Hinton pulls a manila envelope from the box. "Professor Trachtenberg gave you gifts."

"He lent me a book."

"He had a gift for you on his person when he was murdered." Oh yeah, the rosemary. Hinton opens the envelope. "Did Karmen ever give you any gifts?"

"No, why would she?"

"Nothing?" Hinton asks with her hand in the envelope. "No little tokens, pieces of artwork, nothing like that?"

You've got to be kidding me. "She gave me a few doodles she'd do while she was at my desk. She's a very talented artist."

"Doodles, like . . . what? Sketches? Of what? Of you?"

It sounds weird in this context but I nod. Hinton pulls out a torn sheet of sketch paper and slides it across the desk.

"Like this?" It's a charcoal rendering of my profile.

"I guess, yeah. Nothing big."

"And this?" Another sketch, this time a more detailed full-face shot in colored pastels. "And this?" Pen and ink. "Or these?" Sheet after sheet, Hinton lays out versions of my face in an array of mediums, a spectrum of colors and treatments, a variety of styles with only two things in common—my face as the subject and the scrawled "KB" in the lower corner.

She waves her hand over the gallery. "What did you say your relationship is?"

"Not this." I can only shake my head at the array. "I have no idea what this is."

Hinton's expression is impossible to read. She reaches into the box again and pulls out a plastic bag holding a thick book that I recognize. She holds it up so I can only see the back cover. "Is this the book Professor Trachtenberg gave you?"

"It looks like it."

She turns it over and lays it on the table. The front cover is smeared with brown stains that I know were not brown at first. "Does it still look like it?" My stomach sours and the detective keeps talking in that nice voice of hers. "This was one of the weapons used to kill Ellis Trachtenberg. We believe he was struck with this first to disable him, then he was beaten to death with a wrench that we found on the floor. A third weapon was used for other injuries. We haven't found that weapon yet."

She's talking about whatever cut his hands off. I cover my mouth just in case my stomach continues to rise in my throat. Hinton leaves the bloody book in front of me.

"How tall are you, Ms. Ray? Five-ten?"

"Five-nine."

She nods. "Professor Trachtenberg was six-one. He was tall. Judging from the angle at which he was struck, we know the killer couldn't have been over five-six." I guess this should make me feel better but all I can do is look at the blood stain. "Whoever killed him was able to get very close to him, so it was probably someone he knew, someone he would have no reason to fear. It would be someone he wouldn't be surprised to see carrying the book he lent you."

I tear my gaze away from the tabletop. "I didn't grow three inches last night."

"No, of course not. I don't think you killed Ellis Trachtenberg or Robert Alistair. But I do think you're involved." I decide it's time to find an attorney when Hinton holds up her hand. "Let me finish."

I nod and sit up straighter.

"Have you told anyone around here about your past?" It takes a great deal of strength to get my head to turn back and forth. "Nobody? At all?"

"It's not much of a conversation starter."

"No, I wouldn't think it is. I would imagine those are details you would like to keep private, but we have reason to believe someone knows a good deal about you." She's watching my face. I wonder if she can see that I've drawn blood biting the inside of my lower lip.

"Why would anyone care about that?"

"That's what we're trying to figure out. When we asked around about Professor Trachtenberg, several people mentioned his interest in you. A few confirmed what you told us about not reciprocating that interest. Turning down a date is not a very good motive for murder. There were plenty of other people with better motives. Trachtenberg failed a lot of students every year. And he didn't just fail them. He had a reputation for demoralizing them, insulting them, and generally being a condescending prick to them." She doesn't hide the anger in her tone. "Most dropped out and left town. Karmen Bennett was one of the few that stuck around."

"She was talented," I offer.

"She was pissed. Karmen has a history of violent outbursts. She's been in trouble since middle school. Her parents have the money to send her anywhere but they made her stay close to home and made her pay her own way. They hoped it would keep her out of trouble."

My headache has blossomed from a pinprick of pain into a full-skull cap. It's blending with the ache in my shoulders and I can't hold up my head any longer. I wonder if the police invest in special mind-melting lights. I collapse forward on my elbows, holding my chin up in my palms. "Why are you telling me this?"

"I think Karmen Bennett is obsessed with you. I think she was angry and humiliated by Trachtenberg. When you began working in the Advocate's Office, you were kind to her, encouraged her, and I think she became attached to you. She wanted to be like you. She wanted to matter to you."

"It doesn't mean she killed anyone."

"There are two bodies in our morgue. Evidence points to both men being killed by the same person. One of those men was pursuing you; the other was making your life unpleasant as a neighbor."

"You can't be serious." I rub my eyes. "How many people live in Gilead? Seven hundred? Two thousand when school's in? Surely Ellis and Bobby share more connections than their proximity to me."

"They sure do. They share one big connection—Karmen Bennett. We already know she hated Trachtenberg; she'd written him several nasty e-mails and had threatened him publicly. Maybe she found out he was asking you out. Maybe she was jealous."

"Don't you need some kind of evidence?"

Hinton points to the bloody book. "Her fingerprints are on the book."

"So are mine. Are you going to arrest me too?" I can't believe those words just came out of my mouth. "Karmen picked up the book when it was on my desk. I saw her. Surely there are other prints on there as well. It's an old book." .

"There are other prints. We're running them but so far we've only identified three sets—yours, Karmen's, and Trachtenberg's. There is something, Ms. Ray, something we've been keeping out of the public record. Something about the crime scene." She reaches into the envelope and pulls out a photocopy.

"Do you recognize this?"

It's a sketch of a human hand, anatomically correct, with notations and scale markings.

I see the "KB" signature at the bottom.

I shake my head. I know where Hinton is going with this but she has it all wrong. "This is for her submission to the Rising Tide Exhibition. She's doing sculptures of different body parts. Any artist knows you need to learn the anatomy to sculpt it correctly."

Another photo. This one a close-up of the bloody stump of an arm. Then another photo of another arm without a hand.

Then a close up of the scene I witnessed over the dumpster, focusing on Bobby's arm.

"You're handling this very well, Ms. Ray," Hinton says in that nice voice of hers. "That would have surprised me if I hadn't seen this." I close my eyes when I hear her reach into the envelope again. How many pictures can that fucking envelope hold? At least one more. I hear it slide across the table. I open my eyes.

It's copy of a newspaper article printed out on copier paper. I don't need to look at it to know it. I don't need to squint to see what part of the picture has been circled in red marker. I think my neck must creak with the tension shooting down my spine. When I swallow, I think my throat might crack open.

Hinton folds her hands and watches me. "This article was found in a plastic bag left under the windshield wiper of a patrol car the evening after Professor Trachtenberg's body had been discovered. It was left after the first snow had stopped but before the second snow started. That's a pretty large window. Our officers were busy, understandably distracted by the murder."

She holds the paper up by the edges. "I'm assuming you recognize this picture." Wisely, she doesn't wait for me to respond. "You say you didn't tell anyone about your past and yet someone knew enough to give us this article. There are several interesting things about this piece of paper, Ms. Ray. Would you like to know what they are?"

I would not.

"For one, this was downloaded from the *Bakerton Herald* newspaper from Bakerton, Missouri. Do you know why that's interesting?"

Because I accidentally hit my head and have woken up in hell?

"It's interesting because it wasn't downloaded from Wikipedia. You do know you have a Wikipedia page, right? It's not under your name; it's under Plasti—"

"Please don't say it." My mouth is very dry. "Please don't say it out loud."

Hinton nods. "I understand."

Like hell.

"Anyway, my point is this: It wasn't hard to find information about you online. Unfortunately there are plenty of people in the world who are fascinated by grisly stories like yours." There's that word again. "Lots of people are comfortable with search engines. That doesn't point to Karmen, though it's true she did get a job in the library's research department after Trachtenberg cost her the scholarship. With her skills and resources, she might've sniffed out the archives of a small Missouri newspaper more quickly than a casual user, but it's true, anyone can get online. But there is something even more interesting about this copy. Do you see these stains in the lower corner?"

I do not. I will not.

"At first we hoped it would be fingerprints, but no dice. It's rare to get that lucky. So we examined the stains and it turns out they're grease stains. Cooking grease. Just plain old vegetable oil, the same kind of oil that the cooks use to fry the pickles at Ollie's where Karmen Bennett also works. Where she serves you drinks. Where she asked you about helping her out with Professor Trachtenberg. Where she asked to borrow the book so that she could maybe get some extra credit from a professor with the reputation of never giving second chances."

This is too much to take in. "What about Bobby? Why would she kill him?"

"Funny you should ask that, Ms. Ray." She steeples her fingers together. "There are plenty of reasons someone would have killed Bobby Alistair. He was a punk and a dealer. He owed money and ran his mouth. He didn't have a lot of friends. He was tough to like. After all, even you said, and I quote, 'I hope someone beats the shit out of you.' I heard you. We all did, including Karmen."

Her steepled fingers tip forward, pointing at me. "Ms. Ray, dismembering a human body is not your average crime. It takes a certain mindset. It's not shooting someone or beating someone over the head in a heated moment. It's a very singular act that requires planning and precision.

"Ellis Trachtenberg was not hacked at. Whoever removed his hands did so carefully, precisely, and with an understanding of how to do it. They had the knowledge and they had the proper tools. Knives sharp enough to cut like that aren't just lying around in a maintenance room. Whoever killed him knew they were going to take his hands. We know this, not only because of the precision of the cuts, but because there was no spattering or dripping of any kind around the body. Whoever cut off Ellis Trachtenberg's hands had a plan—not just to remove the hands but to remove them from the crime scene. We believe whoever killed Ellis Trachtenberg brought with them the knife and a container to store the hands in."

I haven't blinked in so long my eyes burn. I shut them hard. It's easier to talk without seeing Hinton's serious face.

"And was it the same with Bobby?"

"No. Well, same type of head trauma. And we think it's the same knife. But the knife-work was rushed, messier. Only one hand was taken. It looks like a rash decision."

My eyes stay closed. "Why would she make that decision?"

"To impress you. Maybe to warn you."

I open my eyes at that.

"Ms. Ray, the murder of Ellis Trachtenberg required more than planning. It required rage. Not hot, sudden rage or passion. It took a deep, long-burning rage to carry out a plan like that. Someone was incredibly angry. That kind of anger usually comes from loss—lost love, lost pride, lost reputation. Someone blamed Trachtenberg for that loss and I believe you are the catalyst for them to act upon that rage. Maybe they love you; maybe they resent you. Maybe both. Maybe they were literally telling Ellis Trachtenberg to keep his hands off of you."

"How does any of this tie back to Karmen? Why would she kill her own boyfriend?"

"Think about it, Ms. Ray," Hinton says, like I'd be thinking about anything else. "Trachtenberg pursued you. You rejected him. She kills him. You voice your obvious disapproval of her boyfriend, so he dies the same way. Two women, two unsuitable dead men. Now you're the same."

"That is such bullshit." I shake my head, feeling like I'm waking up from a dream. "So what's the logic behind leaving that newspaper article or using the book Ellis lent me? She loves me so much that she frames me for the murder?"

Hinton watches me like she's expecting me to come to some conclusion she has. I don't and she picks up the newspaper article, holding it up facing me. "She wants to be like you." That twitchy finger of hers taps on the photo. "Maybe she wants you to know that she is like you."

"Fuck you." The words slip out on air but get stronger as I repeat them. My mind is spinning out brilliant arguments but my mouth only forms one phrase over and over as I push back from the table. "Fuck you and fuck you. Are you charging me with something? Are you arresting me? No? Then fuck you and fuck you."

She rises and stands between me and the door. I can't be sure what will happen if she forces me to move her. "Ms. Ray, aren't you curious why I'm telling you this?"

"Because, fuck you, you're a fucking cop and a fucking ghoul."

My tirade doesn't faze her. "I'm telling you this because we cannot locate the missing hands and we believe that Karmen will reach out to you."

"Fuck you." It's all I have to say.

"I've upset you."

"Fuck you!"

"Karmen Bennett is dangerous." She shouts over my profane chant. "Don't be fooled by the fact that she is young and small. She's smart, she's strong, and she's focused. She is angry and unstable and she is dangerous. Listen to me."

I stop yelling.

"Whoever is doing this and for whatever reason they are doing this, I don't think they're done. I don't think they've accomplished what they set out to do. We believe you are in danger. I think we both know that you are aware of how dangerous people can be." She lowers her voice to its usual nice tone. "But, Ms. Ray, believe me when I tell you this. If it turns out that you played any role in these murders, if you encouraged Karmen Bennett in any way for any reason, if you used your influence over her to incite her to violence, I will take you down, too. Believe me."

I take a deep breath. "Fuck you."

CHAPTER 18

I call Jeannie as soon as I'm outside. Detective Hinton gave me my phone back and offered to have a squad car drive me home and I responded to both with my interjection du jour. I like to keep my rides in cop cars to a minimum. I get Jeannie's voice mail, which I ignore. Instead, I text her. If she's on the phone, she'll text me right back—Jeannie is a master multi-tasker—but no text comes back. I start walking home. The police station is on the far end of town from EAC but thankfully Gilead's downtown takes up less than two miles at a straight shot.

I pass the Sheetz and Tudor's Biscuit World. Speedway's pepperoni rolls must just have come out of the oven because I can smell them from the sidewalk until I walk into the smell of Kroger's fried chicken. A wintry Saturday in Gilead and all anyone seems to be doing is eating.

It's so normal. People are probably watching football and making chili, drinking with their buddies or playing with their kids. Down here at the bottom of Gilead, it's hard to imagine that two people were murdered up on that hill. But Hinton is right. I know how dangerous people can be, even in normal towns. I look across the street at Ollie's Tavern. It's still impossible for me to believe that Karmen Bennett is one of those people. But what the hell do I know?

If Karmen Bennett didn't kill Ellis and Bobby, who did it? Surely Ellis Trachtenberg knew plenty of people and in a town this size surely some of those people knew Bobby Alistair, so surely there are other directions for Hinton to be looking. There have to be other theories she is entertaining, right?

But it doesn't look like it from where I'm standing.

Why am I fighting so hard against the idea of Karmen as the killer?

I focus on not falling through the ice and filthy snow stacked up along the roadside. I check my phone—still no word from Jeannie. She picked a hell of time to be MIA. I'm halfway up the big hill to campus when I almost regret not taking Hinton up on her offer of a ride home. There's no way I would have agreed to it, no matter how worn out I feel. Hinton is sharp. I won't let myself call her dangerous, because I have to remind myself that she isn't dangerous to me. I'm not hiding anything from her.

I catch the flaw in my logic—just because I'm innocent doesn't mean she believes me. I'm not a little kid anymore. If the police think I'm letting someone take the fall for me, they won't let me off the hook. If Hinton thinks Karmen is covering for me, if she thinks I'm somehow pulling her strings, if she believes I am involved in the deaths of these two men, Hinton will never stop. I know the type. She's smart and she's patient and she believes she is on the side of justice.

As I stomp over the packed snow covering the parking lot of Everly Place, I let the reality of the situation flood through me: Hinton is dangerous to me. I am in danger.

Welcome to the Fucked Up World of Anna Shuler Ray. There's a small, pissed-off, hand-hacking butcher running around the edges of my world, and it's the cop I'm afraid of.

. . . .

My apartment is cold and dark and filthy. Home. I kick a sweatshirt out of the way, ignoring that it lands in a bowl of French onion dip. A wine bottle rolls away from my foot as I slog through the wreckage. All I want to do is lie down. The couch is out of the question—that miserable monstrosity is as inviting as a coffin. I want my bed. I want sleep. But even I'm not so far gone from basic hygiene that I don't recognize how filthy I am. I step into the bathroom, just the thought of hot water and clean clothes making me relax.

Until I see the shower curtain is drawn.

I wonder if it's possible to die from adrenaline poisoning as I stand in front of my bathtub staring at the ugly blue plastic shower curtain drawn out in front of me. I've never really looked at it, because I only see it from inside the tub. I never draw the curtain after my shower. I never hide my tub. I don't like to see it, but I never, ever let it hide from me.

My hand feels separate from me as I watch it drift out toward the shower curtain. A dismembered hand is an image I don't need to bring to mind right now, but there it is. My brain won't translate the sensation of the plastic crinkling beneath my fingers and I don't think I'm breathing as I draw the plastic curtain along the bar.

Karmen Bennett is in my bathtub. Crouching. Holding a knife.

She only moves to tighten her grip on the kitchen knife. She's tense, compact, drawn in like a frog in a hole. A frog with a knife.

My hand falls away from the curtain and I sit back hard on the sink.

"I'm faster than you," she says, her gaze darting toward the door.

"I don't doubt it." My hands feel heavy where they hang at my sides.

"Are the cops with you?"

"No."

She rises from her crouch, relaxing a little at that, which seems foolish to me. Why would I tell her the truth? I mean, I am, but why would she believe me?

"What are you doing?" I ask.

She waves the knife in her fist. "What does it look like?"

You don't want to know, I think.

"How did you get in?" A stupid question. Even locked, the doors on Everly Place can be opened with a brisk sneeze. Obviously, I'm not the only resident aware of this. "What do you want?"

"I need your help. Do you think I killed Professor Trachtenberg? Or Bobby?"

My adrenaline has drained away. I'm not sure what's taken its place but it's not fear or anxiety. Standing in the tub, Karmen looks small, smaller than Jeannie even. She's lost her layers of clothing and I never realized how slight she is, how young she really looks. Without the black eyeliner her eyes actually look larger. She looks scared.

"It doesn't matter what I believe."

"It matters to me!"

Small or not, she looks very comfortable with that knife. I think of the array of drawings Hinton showed me, pictures of me drawn by this scared girl in the tub. I think of that newspaper clipping stuck under that cop car wiper blade. "Detective Hinton has some theories about why I matter to you."

"Fuck!" Karmen presses both hands to her forehead, the knife jutting up like a headdress. Her fingernails are dirty and her breathing is loud in the small bathroom. "Fuck! Those pictures. You weren't supposed to see those pictures. She's wrong. She's got it all wrong. It's not like that. Fuck. You weren't supposed to see those. Those were mine. Those were for me."

She's rocking on her feet, her fingers digging into her skull. I want to comfort her, to pull her out of that dark space, but the shaft of that knife flashes next to her head as she rocks and her knuckles are white around its handle.

"Why do you have a knife?" I ask. I suppose, under the circumstances, this should be as obvious as how she got in. But I know very well that circumstances aren't fact. Besides, she doesn't seem keen to use it. On me at least. "It's me, Karmen. Talk to me." I keep my voice soft and calm. "Not the police. Me."

"Everything is so fucked up." Her voice is small and broken on her sobs. She's leaving marks on her forehead from her grinding fingers. The knife is coming very close to her face. "It's all so fucked up," she says again. I'm inclined to agree. "And Bobby and my project . . . you always helped me and now . . ." I want to reach out to help her again but before I can, her head snaps up, her eyes narrow with rage.

"Don't look at me like that! Everyone is looking at me! My dad, that cop. Why is everyone looking at me like that?"

She's scratched red lines into her skin that make her look like a wild creature. Her eyes are glossy and I wonder if she's high.

"Maybe you should put down the knife."

"Why?" she snaps. "So you can kill me, too?"

I know she's armed and probably high and that makes her dangerous, but in that moment it is all I can do to not slap the shit out of her. I keep seeing that newspaper clipping. I keep seeing that red circle drawn on it. God damn it, Karmen.

I keep my voice low. "Karmen, don't assume you know me. Whatever you think you've found out about my life, whatever you think you're going to prove about what's going on here, you're wrong. You are wrong."

Her eyes widen, a kaleidoscope of emotions playing over her face—fear, confusion, anger. It settles on sadness. "You were wrong about Bobby," she says and sniffles. "He wasn't that bad. He didn't deserve that."

"No, he didn't."

Karmen heaves an exhausted sigh and nods, then scrubs her nose hard with the back of her hand. Her free hand, that is. Whatever emotions she's warring with haven't distracted her from keeping the blade ready.

"I just want to go," she says in a small voice. "I don't want to talk to the police. I won't say anything. I just want to go. I just want to get away from here. Away from all of this."

"Karmen." Her shoulders sag when I say her name. Surrender, I hope. "You need help."

The kaleidoscope shifts again. Rage. The eyes on me are filled with all the fury of trapped alley cat.

She climbs out of the tub, the knife back in full-weapon mode. She's sweating and talking very quickly. "You got that right. I need help and you're going to give it to me. You're so good at helping, aren't you? You and Trachtenberg—so smug, so smart. Having such a good laugh at the stupid hillbilly." She rolls her eyes, showing a lot of bloodshot white, as she raises her voice to a syrupy falsetto. "'Oh Karmen,'" she says, waggling her head, "'where did you get that bruise?' 'Oh Karmen, your work is so powerful.' 'Oh Karmen, let me help you with that application.'"

She's tiny, almost a foot shorter than me, but that knife, now up tight under my chin, makes up for the difference. "You never gave a shit about me. You laughed at me. You only pretended to help me. Well guess what? Here's your chance to make it up to me. You're gonna help me get the hell out of here."

I speak carefully, mindful of the knife point touching my neck. "How am I supposed to do that?"

"Money." I can't help but snort at that and she shuts me up with a little jab. "No, I'm not robbing you. I've seen your apartment, okay? I'm not blind. Bobby has money hidden next door. The cops didn't find it but I know where it is. You're gonna help me get the money and I'm getting out of here. You're going to stay right next to me while I get that money out."

"Where is it hidden?"

She sneers at me. "Where do you think?"

My stomach drops and my palms sweat against the vanity. I can see that newspaper photo. I can see the red circle she drew on it. My voice has no body. "The hall closet."

"What? No." Karmen looks at me like it's the stupidest thing she's ever heard. "Who hides shit in the hall closet?" Before I can give her the obvious answer, she points to the wall behind the toilet, the wall our apartments share. "It's in the plumbing wall. Why do you think I was in the bathroom in the first place?"

She yanks my arm, disrupting the rapid descent my thoughts were taking, and I stumble against her. She reads it as aggression and before I know it, the knife is back at my throat and Karmen is hissing in my face.

"Don't even try it. I'm not scared of you."

Keeping the knife pointed at me, she crouches down, reaching into the tub and pulling out a hammer. Then she's standing there in front of me, wild-eyed, scared, holding a knife and a hammer, and still, somehow, my fear won't rise. It can't get any traction. It keeps slipping on her question.

Who would hide something in the hall closet?

She wasn't taunting me with that question. She didn't know. How could she have read that article and not known?

She must see me relax because she nods. Maybe she thinks she's gotten me in line. She tips her head toward the toilet, gesturing for me to step in front of her. The only space there aside from sitting on the toilet is the little spot at the end of the tub where a normal person would probably keep a hamper or maybe a magazine rack. All I have there is a pack of toilet paper.

"Stay where I can see you."

I realize that's going to be a problem before she does. She's staring at the wall in front of her, probably trying to reconcile it with the identical bathroom on the other side of the wall. The toilet sits close to the wall on the right. I'm standing in the narrow open space to the left that, judging from Karmen's troubled expression, must be close to the spot where Bobby hid his money. If Karmen plans on knocking a hole in the wall, she's either going to have to move in front of me or give me the hammer. Neither one of those works well with her plan.

I'm no street fighter, but even I know a hammer requires a lot less finesse than a knife.

Unfortunately, she comes up with a solution. She sets the hammer down on the toilet seat, glaring at me while she slips the knife into her back pocket. Then she lifts the heavy ceramic lid off the back of the toilet. She holds it like a baseball bat and nods at the hammer.

I'm not a mechanical engineer, either, but I can calculate which one of us is going to get the most bang for her buck with our respective weapons. Looks like I'll be knocking a hole in my wall.

Karmen points to a spot beside the toilet.

"Right there. In there somewhere between the studs. In a canvas bag. Bobby put twenty K in there for safekeeping. It's his getaway money."

"He obviously won't be needing that anymore."

She rears back with the ceramic lid and I pick up the hammer. One hard whack and I succeed in putting a hole the size of the hammer head in my wall. I have to yank hard to free it. Two more swings and I'm just dotting the drywall. Karmen screams at me to hit it harder but it's not until I start dragging the hammer down after my blows that the wall begins to crumble. Old plaster and god knows what else crumbles loudly within the wall and dust blows out everywhere. Karmen keeps screaming at me to hit harder but all I can hear is the warning voice in my own head telling me not to think about this, not to think about knocking holes in walls, not to think about the space between the studs, about things that can be hidden there.

Finally she shoves herself against me, knocking me into the wall. I haven't realized how much drywall I've cleared but she's seen a red nylon gym bag sticking out from between a stud and the water pipe and is jerking on it to free it. She's gripping it with both hands when it slips out of its hiding space. Her look of triumph is short-lived when we both realize that she's holding a bag; I'm holding a hammer.

I'm holding a hammer up high, over her head. All I have to do is swing down.

Karmen stands before me. We're close. Where her arms wrap around the nylon bag, she almost touches me. Her eyes stare up at me, wide and bloodshot, but all I can see is how she clutches that bag to her chest. I remember clutching my backpack like that when I was a kid. I remember the panic of hanging on to something that you cannot let go of.

I lower the hammer and Karmen starts to cry.

That's when I realize we're not alone.

"Don't move." Detective Hinton stands in the doorway, gun trained on Karmen. "Ms. Ray, drop the hammer and kick it toward me." I do although it gets caught in the bathmat in front of the tub. She steps farther into the room until she can reach the hammer with her foot. She drags it toward her and then kicks it behind her out of the bathroom.

Karmen drops onto the toilet, her face buried in the bag. Sobs make her shoulders shake. Hinton nods at me but I don't know what she means by it. I don't know anything right now.

"Karmen Rene Bennett," Hinton says in that nice voice of hers. "You are under arrest for the murders of Ellis Trachtenberg and Robert Alistair. Anything you say can and will be used against you in a court of law." She holsters her gun and draws out a set of handcuffs. I don't listen as she tells Karmen her rights. I don't listen to Karmen's sobs. I hear the handcuffs lock in place and I close my eyes.

Then I'm back in a rerun of a hell I know too well. Cop radios squawking, uniforms standing around, someone taking notes, and as always one cop watching me. This time it's Hinton. We're sitting together on the couch. I wonder if I'll remember her name after a while or if it will vanish in memory like the other cops' at the other scenes.

"Ms. Ray, just a few more questions."

I nod and watch her write. How long has this taken? I can't even begin to guess. Karmen is long gone, taken out in a squad car. Hinton's partner is wrapping things up with the uniformed officers. They've taken pictures of my bathroom, put the bag of money into evidence with the knife and the hammer, and check that the police tape sealing the apartment next door is undisturbed. My phone buzzes in my pocket. Still not Jeannie. It's Meredith texting me.

Just drove by your place. What's with the police?

Hinton is answering a call on her radio so I type back.

Karmen arrested here. Had a knife. Long story. An understatement, but I don't feel like typing anything longer. I have no doubt Meredith will know more about this than I do before long. She doesn't text me back and I can only presume she's on one of her fact-finding missions.

Hinton signs something on a clipboard and hands it to a cop who takes it and heads for the door. At a nod from her, he pulls the door closed and we are alone.

"We're about done here, Ms. Ray. I may have some more questions for you as we close out the investigation and you will have to make another statement for the trial. You will most likely be called as a witness."

I nod, not really listening to her words, just waiting until there's space to say my thoughts out loud. "Why were you here? How did you know she was here?"

"We've had a car watching Bobby's apartment, waiting for Karmen to show back up. When you left the station, I radioed out and asked whoever was on watch to let me know when you got home. The kid called back and said you had gone into your apartment five minutes before." Hinton shook her head. "Unless you are one hell of a ridge-runner, there was no way you got home that fast, so I headed up here in an unmarked car to see who it was. I beat you here. I watched you go in and I followed you."

"You followed me into my apartment?"

She nods. "These doors are the same pieces of crap they had been when I lived here. Not exactly tough to open. First I listened outside the door. I knew it had to be Karmen inside. Your cousin is at the gym in Elkins—we've been keeping tabs on her, too."

I let out a disgusted laugh. "I don't suppose you were keeping tabs on the fact that Karmen had a knife. And a hammer. Were you going to keep tabs on how many times she stabbed me? Or smashed in my skull?"

Hinton shrugs. "I had to know if you were working together. I had to know if she was coming to you for help and if you were going to give it to her. I was outside the bathroom when she started yelling at you. I heard the whole conversation. Surely you can understand my curiosity about what was hidden in the walls. You of all people should know what an interesting question that is."

I'm this close to resuming my earlier profane chant. I want to tell Hinton what she can do with her interesting questions. I want to suggest that she use both the hammer and the knife to lodge Bobby's bag of money deep into one of her orifices, but I don't. There's no point.

"So now do you believe me? That I had nothing to do with it?"

She gives me a look I can't read. "We believe Karmen was acting alone."

Not quite the same thing, is it? There's no point in asking her that, either.

CHAPTER 19

The cops are gone. The sound of radios squawking fades away but the memory of it rings in my ears. I'm alone in my apartment, trying to catalog the massive inventory of things that are fucked up about this. I don't know where to start. I'm drowning in a sea of dark details and the only thing close to a bright side is that I'm not currently in handcuffs.

Police. Arrests. Handcuffs. Weapons. Reports. So many familiar details. One very noticeable detail is missing.

Where is Jeannie?

Someone taps lightly on the door and pushes it open and I think, Oh, here's Jeannie. But I'm wrong. It's Meredith, tiptoeing into my apartment again, looking just as worried as the last time she found me sitting here on my couch, numb and dumbstruck. She stands in front of me, hands on her hips, huge purse slung over her shoulder, an almost cartoonish mom-face going on.

"Tell me what happened."

So I do. I tell her about Karmen hiding in the tub. I tell her about the knife and the hammer and money in the wall. I tell her about Hinton following me home. I gloss over the basis for Hinton's suspicions and

I leave out the newspaper article altogether. I don't mention it but I'm thinking about it. I'm thinking about it hard.

Meredith scowls. "How could Karmen have killed Bobby? She was in custody."

I shake my head. "They let her out. Didn't have enough to charge her."

I don't listen to her complaints about how that's impossible, how there has to be a way to prove that Karmen is innocent, that Karmen is just a child. I'm not listening because I'm thinking about Karmen's reaction when I mentioned the hall closet. She didn't know what I was talking about. How could anyone who had read that article, who had found that newspaper photo and left it for the police, not know why I was talking about the hall closet?

But if Karmen didn't leave that article for the cops, who did?

Who knows about the closet?

Hinton certainly does. She made no bones about her curiosity about me and secrets hidden in walls. Someone else had to know, too. Someone angry. Someone strong.

My phone buzzes, shaking me from my stupor. It's a text from Jeannie. *On my way.*

Meredith is still talking, her voice buzzing in my head. She's talking about hiding things and finding things and being wrongfully accused of crimes and needing to bring people to justice. I would dearly love for her to shut up but I'm afraid of where my thoughts might go if I'm alone with them. My phone buzzes again.

Need anything? I can stop by Kroger.

I know what I have to do. I have to look in the closet. There won't be anything there but I have to look in the closet before Meredith stops talking, before Jeannie gets here, before my thoughts can poison me.

Eleven boxes.

I count them off from memory—two larger boxes on the bottom, on top of them, eight smaller boxes—shoeboxes and cardboard cartons—stacked and fitted together like a puzzle.

On top of them, the new box. A boot box from American Eagle. The newest box. On top, in the center, not full. It's almost time to pick up the letters, to scoop them up without straightening them and shove them into the box to seal it up on March 1. I know it's half-full now. I know it will hold at least two more handfuls of letters.

Eleven boxes all in place. Almost waist high. Almost half a wall. I hear my breath reedy in my nose as I count the boxes. Everything is in place. Everything is just as I left it.

And then I see the stain.

On the new box. The eleventh box. Brown. Reddish brown, seeping, staining. Like the stain on the tenth box, the box that had been on top last February in our little yellow house in Chattam. I remember staring at that box since I couldn't stare at what was right in front of me. I remember wondering if the stains were on the outside of the box soaking in or on the inside of the box seeping out.

I'm shaking, jerking, my shoulders are hitched high against my neck as I reach for the box. I have to force myself to look up, to look around in the closet, but this time there is nothing to see. This closet has a low ceiling, no high recesses to attach a bar strong enough to tie a rope. My cardboard wall is higher and my closet ceiling is lower but still that same stain is seeping and I have to see what it is.

The envelopes rattle inside the box, my hands are shaking so hard. I back out of the closet. I can't figure out how to hold the box and open it at the same time. It's impossible that this box can be held in one hand. It's so heavy. It doesn't hold anything except envelopes but it feels like it weighs a ton.

"What's in the box, Anna?"

I think Meredith asks me that. I can't be sure since my breath is so noisy in my head and I'm shaking so hard I think my bones are going to break. I set the box down on the coffee table and it takes me a second to figure out that I have to let it go to put it down. My fingers are attached to the cardboard. They grip the edges tight but leave plenty of room for the stain.

The cardboard almost tears when I yank the lid off. I look into the box, expecting to see straight into hell, but all I see are envelopes. Just envelopes piled up in no order. A few spill out over the lip of the box.

But that's not right. This box shouldn't be full.

And envelopes don't seep.

I don't have the control to do this well. I shove my hands under the envelopes and my fingers grasp something soft. Something familiar. I lift the bundle from its hiding place, knowing the slippery feel of plastic and the sickening slide of flesh within it.

A hand in a plastic bag.

The bag is leaking.

I was right. I opened the box and looked right into my hell.

Meredith screams. She jumps back from the table and is fumbling in her purse. I can't let go of the bag, the hand. It's dripping and I'm shaking so wetness is spattering until I finally realize what's happening. I drop the bag, toss it sort of, and it bounces on the rug, flopping over until the hand is palm up.

The human hand is palm up on my carpet. Blood seeps from where the seal is open.

I make it as far as my garbage can before vomiting.

Then Meredith is there again, rubbing my back, pulling my greasy hair off my forehead. I can feel her hands shaking through my shirt but her voice is calm. Well, calmer-sounding than my panting and retching. She helps me to my feet and makes sure I'm steady against the counter before she lets me go.

"The police are on their way," she says, like that's going to help.

"Oh fuck, oh fuck." It's all I can say. I grip the counter, trying to control my shaking, when I see a solution for my nerves. I reach for a half-full wine bottle Jeannie and I must have forgotten about. I have no plans to pour it into a glass. I want it straight down my throat, but Meredith yells and grabs it from me.

"No, no, no! No, Anna. Not now."

I would stop her if I could make my hands work but she gets the bottle away from me. She sets it out of my reach and holds me by my shoulders.

"Anna, listen to me. You need to be sober now. You need to get a grip and get ready to tell the police what happened. How did that hand get there?" She's watching me with that cautious look I've seen before. "Anna, do you know how that hand got there?"

You know what's weird? I haven't asked myself that question. I'm shocked that the hand is there, but in a way, I don't wonder why. My hell is in those boxes. Of course a hand would wind up there. I can't say this to Meredith.

She guides me back to the couch, taking the long way around the coffee table to avoid the mess on the carpet. She pushes me to sit, reaches into her bag, and pulls out a plastic bottle of Dr Pepper. "Drink this."

Gross, I think. I hate soda. It occurs to me that I might be going into shock. Meredith unscrews the cap and I take a deep drink. The bubbles burn my throat and it tastes like medicine but I keep drinking. The old habit of shoving something in my mouth for comfort kicks in. Meredith calms down as I drink, as if my thirst were the only concern in the room. She kneels in front of me as I drink, nodding, breathing loud sighs of relief.

"Okay," she says, "okay. This is under control."

That's an odd way to look at it, I think, but I just keep drinking. My phone buzzes. Meredith holds her hands out to me, a wordless command to stay, as she picks it up. She doesn't ask permission; she just reads the message.

"Your cousin is on her way."

"Good," I say. That makes me relax. I'm glad Jeannie's on her way. It's always better when Jeannie is around. My shoulders slump, the mostly empty soda bottle weighing a hundred pounds in my lap. I let my head fall back against the cushions.

My relaxation must reassure Meredith that I'm not a danger to myself anymore because she stands up, hands on her hips, and nods her head. Another curl breaks loose and I smile at it.

"You feel better knowing your cousin is going to be here, don't you?" I nod and she heads to the kitchen, talking to me over her shoulder. "Of course you do. Everything is better with family, isn't it? There's nothing more important than family." I nod. My breathing evens out and relief rushes in. I even close my eyes. I'm so tired. These past few days, the police and the questions and blood and boxes all tumble together in my mind until it makes perfect sense that I would have found that hand in the box. It feels inevitable.

I jerk awake at the question that pops into my head. "Whose hand is it?"

Before Meredith can answer, Jeannie storms through the door. She looks pissed.

"Why aren't you answering my messages?" She's wearing gym clothes. The world's going to hell but she still gets her workout in. She jabs a finger at Meredith. "And why are you here? *You* don't need to be here, so why don't you leave?" She marches into the room, staring at me. "What's wrong? What's wrong with you?"

Nothing. There's a severed hand in a puddle of blood in a plastic bag on my floor but at this moment it doesn't seem to bother me. I don't move as she steps closer. I don't ask her to repeat herself when I can't hear what she says. It's weird; I don't even react when I see her fall.

Jeannie has fallen to the floor and she's bleeding. Meredith is just standing there watching her. Oh, no she's not. She's holding something. A frying pan. That heavy one I never use.

She smiles at me and then swings the pan again like a hammer down where Jeannie is.

Then I understand. I know what's happening. I've been drugged. I've felt this before.

CHAPTER 20

Bakerton, Missouri
February 17, 1997
Anna Shuler, 11 years old

Anna woke up in the tub. She jerked awake and splashed water over the sides. She couldn't remember how many times she'd done this—wake up, drift off, wake up again—but she must have been doing it for a while because her fingers were pruny and the water was getting cold. Her teeth chattered and she forced herself to sit up with her knees against her chest.

Her eyes burned and her hands hurt. She wanted out of the tub.

Her body felt so heavy she almost couldn't do it. She had to bend over and hang on to the edge of the tub to haul her feet out. Even then, once they were on the fuzzy mat, she couldn't stand up right away. The room spun and Anna feared she would throw up. Again.

Her throat felt raw and she tasted blood. Her tongue found scratches along the roof of her mouth. They hurt and her tongue wouldn't leave them alone.

She wanted her mother. All the towels in the bathroom were wet and piled up around the tub, so Anna walked out into the hallway naked. It was freezing out here, an icy wind rushing down from the living room like an indoor tornado. Her teeth chattered and wrapping her wet arms around her body did little to warm her. She wanted to go to bed. She wanted her mother to put her to bed. She was too old for that, but she wanted it.

Something banged against the floor somewhere in the house. Anna leaned against the wall, her eyes closing despite the shivers wracking her body, and listened. It came from the back of the house, the closed-in porch her parents used as their studio. Her mother would be there, Anna bet. Her mother would get her a warm towel.

In the living room she found out why the house was so cold. Some-one had opened all the windows. Mom was going to be pissed when she found that out. She and Dad always argued about the heating bills. She said the house had to be insulated; he said it was a rental and wasn't worth it. They must have had a fight, Anna thought, and Dad won because the windows were all open and she could hear the old furnace going.

Maybe Mom wasn't home yet. Dad had come home, hadn't he? She couldn't remember. She couldn't really think any clear thoughts. Even the cold didn't feel right, like her body could feel it but her brain didn't care.

They must have had a big fight because the living room was wrecked. Someone had pushed the couch back crooked and the easy chair was knocked over. It had broken the lamp. There was a big stain on the carpet but without the lamp on, Anna couldn't see what it was. She didn't want to, either. She didn't want to be in the living room. It smelled terrible. It smelled like the gas station. Then she saw the red can Mom used to fill up the lawn mower. Someone had thrown it against the wall. That must have been some fight.

She followed the banging sound coming from the back porch. She could see through the glass in the door that her mom was working on something; she was bent over on the floor and her arms were pulling at something. All the windows were open in there, too. Anna's hands were almost too cold to turn the knob but she finally managed to get the door open. If it were possible, it was even colder in here and it smelled worse, even with the windows open.

"Mom?"

When her mom spun around, Anna screamed. She looked like one of those voodoo priestesses Anna had read about in *National Geographic*. Her blond hair stuck straight up from her face, dark with sweat and streaked with something brown. Her arms and neck and face were streaked with black and shiny with sweat. How could she be so hot when it was so cold in here?

Anna started to cry.

"Oh Anna, no no no no no." Her mom rushed to her, grabbing her with her filthy hands and pulling her close. Anna pressed herself against her mother's warmth, wrapping her arms tight around her, crying now in relief. She wanted her mother to make a fuss over her. Her mother didn't do that much and Anna couldn't believe she'd gotten so lucky to get her mother's attention when she needed it so badly.

Her mother rocked her for a moment and then pulled back. Anna was scared her mom would be mad that she had disturbed her but instead she pulled an old Indian blanket off one of the shelves and wrapped it tight around Anna. It smelled like sawdust and turpentine and it scratched her skin, but it felt good to be covered. Her mother wrapped her tight and rubbed her hands quickly over her arms, warming her through the blanket.

"You can't be in here, baby. You have to go. You have to go."

"I don't want to be in the tub anymore. I'm cold."

"Okay, okay." Up close, Anna could see her mother wasn't just sweating. Her face was smeared up because she was crying. "Everything is okay."

"Are you okay?" It was a dumb question because her mom had just said that, but she didn't look okay. "I don't feel good." Her mom petted her hair and pressed her hand against her cheek and Anna opened her mouth wide. "My mouth is scratched."

"I know. I know." Her mom talked really quickly and her voice sounded hoarse. "I'm so sorry about that, baby. I'm so sorry I scratched your mouth, but we had to get the bad stuff out of you. We had to get your tummy empty and I had to put my fingers back there so you'd feel better. I'm so sorry I hurt you but I had to get your tummy empty."

Mom was talking to her like a baby and Anna was embarrassed by how much she liked it. She wanted to be babied. She wanted to be wrapped up and put to bed, rocked and sung to sleep. She kept crying and her mom kept petting her.

"Here's what I want you to do, okay, baby?" Her mom held her face in her dirty hands and looked into her eyes. "I want you to go to the kitchen and eat some bread." She talked over Anna's protests. "I know your tummy hurts but you need to eat something. You need to eat as much bread as you can. You can have all the white bread you want. Will you do that? Will you be my good, good girl and go eat bread? And soon as I can, I'll come in with you and we'll eat all the bread. Okay? Will you do that? Will you be my good girl, Anna? Please? Please?"

She didn't want bread. She wanted to feel her mother's hands on her face and she wanted her to keep looking at her like that. But she was afraid to say no. She was afraid her mom would get mad and stop looking at her at all. So Anna nodded.

She was glad she did because her mom kissed her forehead hard.

"Oh, you're such a good girl, Anna. You're the best thing that ever happened to me. I love you so, so, so much. I love you so much."

Anna would eat bread until she exploded to hear that.

In the kitchen, however, with the bread in her hands, it was hard to keep that promise. Her stomach cramped at the first bite and she almost couldn't swallow it. She pulled the milk out of the fridge and drank straight from the carton. It felt good on her throat although it also made her stomach hurt. It was warmer in the kitchen since none of the windows were open and Anna felt herself getting sleepy again. She wanted to lie on the rug under the table and sleep, but her mother had told her to eat and she wanted her mother's praise again. She wanted that even more than she wanted to sleep, so she stuck the bread under her arm, wrestling to keep the blanket over her shoulders, grabbed the milk with her free hand, and headed back to her parents' studio.

Mom had closed the door behind her but the latch hadn't caught and Anna was able to sneak back in unheard. She sat on the top step leading down to the porch and set the bread and milk down beside her. She pulled out a slice of bread and watched her mother's arms working. Her mother had strong arms, Anna knew, from working with clay and metal and stone. She could bend any matter to her will to create the sculptures and figures that she said filled her dreams. Anna liked to watch her work but she couldn't see from the step what she was making.

A hose trickled into the drain in the center of the floor. The whole floor was wet and Anna could see where someone had mopped a wide streak through the water. She wondered why the water didn't freeze with that cold wind blowing over it. Her mom knelt in the water like she couldn't even feel it. That wasn't unusual. When mom worked on her art, the whole world disappeared around her.

A hacksaw clattered to the side where her mom dropped it. She heard her mom grunt with exertion as she pulled on something. Anna finished her slice of bread and reached for the milk. Her stomach felt a little better and the cold air helped clear her head. It also made her nose run and when she sniffed, her mother spun around, eyes wide.

"I told you to go to the kitchen!"

But Anna didn't hear her. She could see what her mother had been cutting.

Then she remembered.

. . . .

Dad had been gone for two weeks on one of his rages. She was glad he was gone. Mom had thrown him out and Anna had relaxed.

But she missed him. And she worried about him.

Anna was home alone that night. Mom had a gallery showing. It was no big deal; Anna was eleven. She wasn't a little kid and this wasn't the first time she'd been left alone. She was working on her hieroglyphic drawings when she heard her father come through the front door. She heard him talking to himself and moving stuff around in the living room. He wasn't breaking anything or yelling and Anna hoped his rage was over.

"Anna? Anna, sweetheart, are you here?"

She dropped her pen and ran to him. He wrapped her up in his arms and squeezed her tight, kissing the top of her head.

"I missed you," she spoke into his shirt.

"Did you? Oh you sweet, sweet girl." He held her even closer and began rocking her back and forth. "Do you have any idea how much I love you?" She didn't answer, just let herself be crushed against his scratchy sweater. "You're the most beautiful piece of art I've ever made."

Anna giggled at that. He always called her his masterpiece. He kissed the top of her head again. "I brought you something. It's in the kitchen."

She followed him into the kitchen and sat down at the table with him. He was crying and she put her hand over his. "Don't cry, Dad. It's okay. I'm glad you're home."

He laughed through his tears. "Home. We have no home, Anna. There is no place for us, not here, not anywhere." She didn't know what he meant and she was afraid his rage wasn't over. But he didn't yell or knock over his chair, he just cried and looked at her hand over his. After a moment, he went to the refrigerator and pulled out the orange juice. He grabbed two glasses and set them on the counter. He had his back to her but Anna could see him pull something out of his pocket. He poured the juice, returned to the table, and handed her a glass.

"Let's make a toast." He held up his glass and clinked it against hers. He smiled. "To art, the cruelest mistress."

"To art," Anna said. They always toasted to art. She took a big drink of her juice but when she started to lower the glass, her father put his finger under it, tilting it back up. She had no choice to but to keep swallowing until she'd emptied the glass. He smiled at her.

"Good girl." He took both of her hands in his. "Do you know why we make art, Anna? Do you understand?"

"To create beauty?"

"No, sweetheart. No."

Crap, she'd never get that right. No matter how many times they asked her this, she never got it right. They kept changing it on her.

He didn't seem disappointed in her though. He just seemed sad. "We can't create beauty. It exists in its own right, it exists at the heart of everything, burning like a coal, glowing within it, waiting until it can come into its perfect form. Beauty seethes, it smolders beneath the surface of everything. It can never be held, it can never be seen in its truest form because it would incinerate us. We would burn to ash if we knew beauty. You are beauty, Anna. I see that now. I see your eyes and I see the world through them and there is no beauty here, no beauty for you."

She had no idea what he was talking about. She tried to follow his words, to think of something intelligent to add to the conversation. She loved hearing him speak and she had missed him so much, but his words had begun to swim in her head. Her eyes felt so heavy and she tried to hide her yawn but he saw it. He saw it and he smiled.

"Yes, relax. Let's go to the living room and relax."

She could only nod as he led her to the couch. She was too big to sit in his lap but he let her cuddle up underneath his arm. His voice was soft as he kept talking his strange monologue and petting her hair. She didn't move when she felt him get off the couch. He pulled her from a dream when he wrapped her wrists together with wire. She struggled to open her eyes when she felt wetness splash over her T-shirt.

Her eyes burned and she spit when another splash hit her face.

"Dad?" she sputtered and had to squint to see through the fumes. She wished he would stop whatever he was doing and let her sleep. She was sleepy but the smell assaulted her nose.

He stood in front of her, sobbing. "Go to sleep. Go to sleep. And when you wake, my beautiful girl, the world will have burned and all will be beauty."

She didn't want to talk about beauty anymore. Her wrists hurt and the smell was so bad. It took everything she had to force her eyes open and she saw him dump water over his head. Not water. He had the gas can for the lawn mower. In the living room.

"Sleep, sleep, Anna. And beauty will burn through us all."

She couldn't keep her eyes open anymore, even when she heard the front door open.

Everything was jumbled up after that. She remembered screaming, her mother jerking her across the floor, cold water hitting her skin, her mother's nails scraping the back of her throat until vomit roared out of her like lava. Through it all, all she wanted to do was sleep, to close her eyes and drift, but her mother kept slapping her and screaming at her. She scrubbed at her skin and raked rough hands through her hair. Anna tasted shampoo and soap and something that tasted so bad she threw up again.

Finally it ended. Her mother lowered her into a warm tub and Anna relaxed. Her mother shoved towels all around her torso, under her arms, propping her up in the water so Anna could truly relax. Her head fell back against the tub and her eyes finally closed.

. . . .

"He said beauty would burn down the world."

Her mother's hands hung down by her sides. "Anna, any idiot can burn down the world. Only art can rebuild it." Then she crouched down in front of her. "Do you know why we make art?"

Anna shook her head. She wasn't going to fall for that trick anymore. "Because we're fucking nuts. Now go to bed."

"No."

They stared at each other for a long moment. Her mother looked away first. "Okay," she said. "Okay. We're going to see to this and then we're going to put it away." She went back to her task. Anna took out another slice of bread.

She watched the hacksaw cut. She watched the drain take away the wetness. She watched the wide plastic sheeting wrap around and around each piece. And when every piece was wrapped, she watched her mother carry them to the front hall and stack them there on the floor. She watched her open the closet and move the vacuum cleaner and pull out the coats and boots and umbrellas. She watched her take a sledge-hammer and knock away the wall in the back of the closet.

She ate her bread and watched her mother stack the pieces between the studs of the exposed wall. She drank her milk as her mother brought in white painted boards from the studio that had been shelves. Her mother lined up the boards and hammered them in place, her strong arms working steadily until a new wall appeared in the closet, a white wall that grew from floor to ceiling and put their secret away.

Anna watched every nail go in that wall. She watched her mother return the coats and the boots and the vacuum cleaner. She watched her close the door.

· · · · · · · · · · · · · · · · · · ·

Eleven months later, Anna was home alone again when a fierce winter storm blew in on a Tuesday afternoon. High winds and hail buffeted the house and Anna curled up snug under her bedspread, reading about the evolution of textiles. The wind gained power and finally toppled the old pin oak that had been secretly rotting within for a decade. In the weeks that followed, the news outlets referred to it as The Judgment

Tree, granting it some sort of supernatural sentience, claiming its trajectory was directed by destiny. Had it fallen twenty feet to the left, it would have hit their neighbor's pickup truck. Had it fallen twenty feet to the right, it would have crushed Anna where she lay.

Instead, it hit the corner of the rental house and demolished the front porch. It crushed the corner of the house and peeled the vinyl siding off like old skin. One thick branch snagged on the roof for a moment before finishing its journey to earth and clawing a jagged hole in the wall.

Ken Bearson, the owner of the spared pickup truck, heard the impact of the massive oak and ran outside to survey the damage. When he saw the destruction next door, he grabbed his camera. He had always wanted to see one of his photos in the *Bakerton Herald* and thought the image of the little house crumpled beneath the huge tree would surely earn him a spot.

When he finally got the strap around his neck and his lens cap off and found a site sheltered enough to get the picture without rain blowing straight into his face, he started snapping shots. He saw the girl who lived next door, the weird kid with the long hair and the big eyes who never spoke or went to school. She was weird but that weirdness would only enhance his image and he snapped her again and again as she clambered over the tree trunk, over the crumpled siding. He thought maybe he should warn her to be careful but these pictures were going to be amazing so he let her climb.

She made it over the trunk. She made it through the branches. She made it to the hole in the side of her house and then Ken Bearson got the picture that made him famous.

He caught twelve-year-old Anna Shuler holding a bundle of plastic, trying to shove it back into the wall. From that plastic, the camera picked up the clear image of a human hand.

CHAPTER 21

She's dragging Jeannie across the floor. I'm dreaming of enchiladas when my head snaps up and I see Meredith, my boss, with her arms hooked under Jeannie's armpits, hauling my unconscious cousin across the carpet. Blood runs from the side of Jeannie's face.

"Meredith?" That's what I try to say. It comes out as mostly an *mmm* sound.

She hears it though. "You awake? Go back to sleep."

As much as I'd like to, there's not a drug on earth strong enough to let me sleep through this. I haul myself up higher on the couch, or I try to, at least. My head weighs a lot right now and I succeed only in tilting myself to the side on the couch, compressing my left hip, my right foot sliding forward in a way that's going to get uncomfortable very soon.

Meredith drops Jeannie in front of the open closet and straightens herself up, hands on her hips, breathing hard. "Whew. She's heavier than she looks." She crosses the room again to her purse. I think she's singing to herself until I realize she's talking through her plans. She snaps on latex gloves and begins unpacking—a belt, a knife, a box cutter. She lays them out on my counter, her hands fluttering over them in that fussy way she has.

She picks up the rope first, twisting it into some sort of slipknot, her voice cheerful. "Let's get you up there first, Professor," she says to Jeannie. "I may have to lift you in stages. I'm not as young as I used to be." She laughs a girlish laugh and slips the noose over Jeannie's head.

"What the fuck?" I try to yell and succeed in shifting my body so that somehow my right hip slips over the edge of the couch and I feel myself sliding, collapsing ass-first onto the floor. Meredith drops the rope and comes to stand over me.

"Do you mind?"

"Why?" That word comes out just fine.

"Justice." She sighs and shakes her head, turning back toward the counter. "And because we all know nothing ever goes according to plan, I think I'd better take a few preventative steps and take care of you first." She picks up the box cutter.

It's a little easier to move on the floor. I have more to push against. Of course, I landed on a wine bottle again—how many are there down here?—and I'm able to kick myself to the side until it rolls out from beneath me. Unfortunately, that kick is against the coffee table, which scoots farther from me. If I can get my hands on the table, I think I'll be able to push myself up, but Meredith beats me to it.

I think she's going to slash me with the box cutter but she just pushes my left shoulder with her foot and I go down easily. She gives me that look that says I'm trying her patience.

"I can't hit you, Anna. I can't leave any signs of a struggle. That's not the narrative. The narrative is you got the drop on Jeannie. You got the rope around her neck and you hung her and then killed yourself. Your fingerprints are all over the bag with Ellis's hand. Oh!" She snaps her fingers. "I've got to remember to put Bobby's hand somewhere. Maybe the refrigerator. I'll save Ellis's other hand for something special. Maybe your suicide note. Or maybe I'll leave it in your desk."

My hands burn against the carpet as they slide uselessly, trying to drag my heavy body along the couch away from my boss, away from that box cutter.

"Meredith, don't."

"You sound drunk." She doesn't look up, concentrating instead on getting the blade to push out. "How does this work? Oh, here we go." The whole blade slides out and Meredith fiddles with it, adjusting it. "It has to be this way, Anna. It's justice."

"For who?"

"Whom," she says with a prim pucker that I'd love to slap if I could get my dead limbs to function. "Guess you're not as smart as you think you are, which is the whole point." She leans in, her face very red and very close. She screams, "You are not special! None of you are special!" The heat and hatred in her eyes burns into me, giving me a jolt that helps me push away a few inches, but she grabs my left hand and jerks it toward her.

"Karmen Bennett is an innocent child who will *not* go to prison to cover your crimes." She's jerking my arm in rhythm with her speech. "You killed Ellis Trachtenberg and you killed Karmen's boyfriend and now you're going to kill your cousin and yourself and prove that that child is innocent."

That's what she thinks? I let her keep my hand and focus instead on getting these words out clearly: "I did not kill Ellis." I forget the words when the box cutter slices into my wrist where it meets my palm. Meredith pushes the blade in deep and drags it toward my elbow.

She squeezes my arm, watching the red flood rise. I'm panting, wanting to jerk my arm away, but not wanting to further the damage. "They call that a 'mean it' cut, when someone is serious about suicide."

"I didn't kill Ellis!"

"No, no, I know that." Her tone is warm, motherly. "But you did kill your dad and everybody knows it. You let your mom take the blame for it and nobody can blame her for that. That's what mothers do. We take on burdens for our children. That's why this is so perfect." She presses her thumb against the edge of my palm, staunching the bleeding long enough to see where the skin is untouched. Then she pushes the blade in again less than an inch from the first cut. I'm screaming and trying to pull away but she's stronger than she looks.

"It's a perfect example of justice." Her voice stays calm and warm, the helpful advocate calming a desperate student. "Ellis Trachtenberg destroyed my son. My beautiful Derek. You saw him. He's such a beautiful boy, but no, the Professor failed him, humiliated him, crushed his lovely artistic soul when it should have been nurtured! It should have been nourished and cherished." She's crying hard now and the blade makes a jagged turn that is setting my arm on fire with pain. Blood is everywhere and I can see blue spots blossoming in front of my eyes. I'm going to pass out soon.

Meredith is still talking. " . . . Found out about your colorful past . . . background check doesn't give the whole . . . newspaper . . . just so perfect. Perfect."

My neck is bent, my chin pressed against my chest as my body splays, trying to get away from the agony that is my left arm. My right hand claws at the carpet beside me, under the couch, around the debris, grabbing on to what it can.

"You let them arrest Karmen Bennett. A child! Not that children don't kill. Heaven knows you're proof of that." Oh my god, there's so much blood. "So I had to kill Bobby, which is also your fault. If you had met your responsibilities as a student advocate and stayed with Karmen when they took her to the police station that first time, you could have called me and let me know she had been released. I wouldn't have killed Bobby if I'd known she was out of jail. The whole point was that it should happen while she was in custody. It didn't do her any good. You could have saved the boy's life."

Meredith takes my face in her free hand, holding my chin. She wants me to hear this.

"Think of it this way, Anna. Now you can finally have peace. I know why you drink so much. Now you can finally face your demons and know that justice was served. You didn't pay for your father's death, so you can pay for Derek's. You can pay your debt and let Karmen Bennett be free. She *is* in custody, this time. They're children, Anna. They deserve a chance to thrive." Tears drip off her red cheeks. She's leaning over me now, her tears hot where they fall on my face.

"My Derek had a beautiful heart that the world will never get to know. What do you have, Anna?" She's screaming again, twisting my damaged wrist. "What do you have to offer the world that's better than my son's heart?"

I sigh. "Another hand?"

The wine bottle connects with Meredith's temple with a satisfying crack. It's not enough to knock her unconscious but it gets my injured hand free and gives me room to kick off of her. I crab scramble backward on my elbows but she grabs my ankles, jerking me forward and slamming the back of my head against the floor. My legs are stronger though and one booted foot clips her under her jaw. Her teeth slam together and she falls to her back.

I make the mistake of trying to crawl. The first ounce of pressure on my left wrist and I face-plant into the carpet, howling. I roll onto my right, still kicking the carpet like I'm swimming to the door, and I see Meredith rise. She looks unsteady. She looks insane.

I must have broken some of her teeth or maybe she bit her tongue because when she pants, blood sprays out like a mist. Unlike my blood, which is pouring out like an oil spill, making everything around me wet and slick. I haven't made it very far by the time Meredith gets to the counter and picks up the knife.

That's a big knife. She won't have to be very close to me to get that into me. She won't have to cut me very much, either, since I'm probably mostly done bleeding to death. I won't let myself say that I've reached the end of the line at this point but I have to admit I can see it from here. It looks ugly. It looks bloody and I really wouldn't mind sleeping through it.

I roll onto my back, my arms splayed wide. My injured arm lands on a dirty plate and something scratches me, adding a fresh jolt to the pain. It's insult to injury. My filthy habits conspire against me. Then the fingers of my right hand find another wine bottle.

Man, I drink a lot.

Meredith makes her way toward me, circling the coffee table. She pauses to check on Jeannie and then she smiles at me.

"You bitch," I try to say, but my lips don't work that well.

"I think I'm going to take care of your cousin first." She keeps smiling. "She gets to die, too. Professor Fitzhugh-Conroy—so important, so smart, but she'll bleed to death just like you. Unless she asphyxiates first. Maybe you'll be conscious long enough to watch. Yeah, I'm going to kill her first. That way, just in case someone does a really thorough autopsy, they'll know that she died first. You fought, she got a few good licks in, but you triumphed. You're a killer and you finally decided you couldn't live with it anymore."

I want to scream. I want to stop her but I can't move. I can't get my feet under me so I use the only weapon I have left. I focus everything I have on my right arm and I whip that wine bottle toward her head as hard as I can.

Of course, it misses her. It doesn't strike her in the eye or knock her out. Life doesn't work like that.

But sometimes it works like this.

Meredith sees the bottle. She dodges it easily, laughing, seeing it coming from a mile away. What she doesn't see is the hand lying on the floor in the plastic bag. I don't think she ever sees it. She steps on it. Her heel lands in the palm, her feet fly out from beneath her, and her skull smashes against the heavy wooden arm of the sofa.

She doesn't bounce. She just sort of crumples.

Blue flowers blossom in front of my eyes.

I hope she landed on her knife.

CHAPTER 22

Gilead, West Virginia
February 22, 2015
Anna Shuler Ray, 29 years old

Jeannie settles back in the tub with a sigh. My bathroom smells like jasmine and the bubbles make tiny music as they pop. God, even her baths are better than mine.

The Days Inn only had shower stalls, so we're back at my place. I sit on the mat beside the tub, my back against the wall, my feet stretched out toward her head. This means I have to stretch out my injured left hand along the edge of the porcelain to reach Jeannie's, but I don't mind. She made sure to lay a towel underneath the bandages so it wouldn't get wet.

She looks like hell. The right side of her face is swollen and purple. Both eyes are black and she has to breathe through her mouth, but seeing her in front of me, seeing her alive, she is the most beautiful thing I've ever seen. I think about how close I came to losing her and it makes it hard for me to breathe. I don't think about my own injuries. All I can think about is what I would have lost if I'd lost Jeannie. How close I came. How we both owe our lives to a clipboard.

One of Hinton's patrolmen had left his clipboard on my counter. A three-dollar piece of plastic and a cheap ballpoint pen. I don't know what paperwork was on that clipboard but it was important enough for the cop to come all the way back up Everly Road to get it. Fortunately he thought it important enough to open the door even when nobody answered his knock. None of us could get to the door. All three of us were busy dying.

All three of us survived. They kept us in the hospital overnight. Jeannie's concussion wasn't as bad as they feared. My stitches took a while and I needed quite a bit of blood but I'll be okay. Meredith is still unconscious. I hope she's dreaming about me. I hope she's screaming in her sleep.

"That crazy bitch." Jeannie reads my mind. "I never could stand that bitch."

"I liked her," I say. I did.

"You've always been a terrible judge of character."

I laugh. "Maybe I just like bad people."

She grips my hand, careful not to squeeze hard enough to hurt. "How did she know about you? I still don't understand that."

"Well, they ran my background check when I was hired, and she knew I was your cousin. Right about then, her son got arrested for heroin possession down in Nashville. She blamed you and Ellis for flunking her kid out of school, so she probably started digging into all three of us, looking for whatever she could use. Then when he OD'd over Christmas, she really went sideways, and started planning. She was right, I never should have underestimated her ability to find shit out." I lay my head back against the wall and close my eyes. "I guess when you hear my backstory, bloody thoughts come to mind."

She squeezes my hand hard enough to hurt, hard enough to stop my train of thought. I finally told Jeannie everything, all the things I told Ronnie, all the things I remembered—the gasoline, the wires on my wrists, the puddles of blood draining in my mother's studio. Like Ronnie, she didn't pull away. I'm hopeful that, unlike Ronnie, she won't use it against me.

"Why didn't your mom just call the police?" Jeannie asks. "He tried to kill you. It was totally justified. I mean, who would blame her for killing him? She saved you."

I shrug. "I don't know. We didn't talk about it. I tried a couple of times. I tried to be normal and find a place to put all that. I asked her once if we could call the police and tell them what happened. Do you know what she said? That a murder/suicide was just too pedestrian."

She stares at me for a moment. "Only our mothers," she says, "would have a social classification scale for violent deaths." Then we're both laughing.

In a heartbeat, my giggle becomes a sob. My throat catches and I hang on to my cousin's hand, ignoring the stitches pulling at my wrist. "She just didn't want me to be weird. She didn't know any better. She didn't want to saddle me with being the girl whose father couldn't love her enough to let her live."

"He loved you," Jeannie says quickly.

"He loved me badly. But yeah, he loved me. And so did my mom. She thought she was sparing me something. Instead she saddled me with being the face of the Plastic Bag Murder. And the worst part? It's not that everybody thinks I killed him." I sigh. "It's not even that everybody thinks he was hurting me, that he was molesting me or something. He wasn't. He didn't. He did love me, Jeannie. And I loved him." I'm losing my voice to my tears.

"Jeannie, the worst part is that sometimes I wish he'd finished it. I wish he'd gotten that lighter—"

"Don't say that!" Jeannie splashes water on me when she sits up in the tub and scoots toward me. She yanks my head back by my ponytail and shakes me. "Don't you ever say that. Ever again. Do you remember what I told you when you came to live with us? All of this, everything that's happened is just something that happened to you. It's not you. You are not these events. Do you hear me?" I nod as much as I can, which isn't much since she's got a serious grip on my hair. She lets me go and settles back in the tub.

"You are my cousin, Anna," she says. "If you need a title, if you need a role, that's it. Got it?"

I nod and she closes her eyes.

"Are you hungry?" I ask.

"Starving."

I slip out of the bathroom and head to the kitchen. My apartment is a disaster. I didn't think it was possible for the space to be any dirtier but the crime scene unit took the filth to new heights. Fingerprint dust is everywhere. Sections of the carpet have been cut out and two of the couch cushions were taken into evidence for blood stains.

Fortunately Meredith never got near the refrigerator and the pan of leftover enchiladas is just where I left them.

Jeannie yells from the bathroom. "Are you reheating the enchiladas?"

"Yes."

"Turn the oven on to three-fifty. You can put them in while the oven heats up."

"Okay."

"And keep the foil over them until they're heated through."

"Okay."

"There's extra cheese in the blue bowl in the back and sauce in a jar but don't add them until you take the foil off. They'll burn—"

"Shut up, Jeannie!" I yell. "You're not the boss of me!"

"Yes, I am!" she yells back. I hear her say more softly, "I am too the boss of you."

I laugh. She's right. She probably always will be the boss of me and I'm okay with that. I do as she says with the enchiladas. There's nowhere to sit but on one of the stools at the counter. I look at the couch and I think about Ronnie. Before he went off his medication, when we were still happy, he always said the same thing when something bad happened. He'd always say, "Something good will come out of this." I think he really believed that.

There are twelve bottles of wine still in the box at the end of the counter. I would dearly love to open one but the doctors said Jeannie can't have any alcohol for seventy-two hours after the concussion and I don't doubt the violence she would bring on me if I tried to drink without her. I don't know how much longer we have to stay sober but Jeannie does. She set the timer on her phone. There's no point in pretending we're anyone we're not.

I'll have to clean up the apartment. I'll have to pick up the envelopes. The police will eventually return the box where Meredith stashed the hand. Of all the gruesome things I've seen, of all the violence and the violations, the thought of her opening that closet door to plant the thing in there unnerves me the most. She must have had Ellis's hand with her that whole day at work. Maybe she kept it in one of her refrigerators in our office. She must have had it in her bag when she drove me home. I had clementines; she had a human hand.

God, I know some crazy people.

She must have been in so much pain. Losing her son, first to drugs, then to the overdose. She must have felt so helpless, so angry. So alone.

I never gave my phone number to the students because I believed I was setting clear boundaries. Do I set them with everyone? Did I set them with Meredith? Was I just walling out her pain? Had she ever shown it to me? Or had she already set her plan in motion? If she had shown me, would I have let it in?

I put my forehead down on the counter. My wrist throbs from moving around so much. The doctor gave me pain pills but I've decided to stick with Tylenol. I've had enough drugs. The enchiladas smell delicious as they warm up and I'm drifting off to sleep. I shift my good hand and feel something sharp jab my wrist.

A white number ten envelope. Neat lettering slanted to the right. Red stamp from the Jefferson City Correctional Center.

I have fifteen years' worth of unopened letters in those boxes. I remember when I stopped reading them, when I stopped taking my mother's calls. It was when Jeannie went away to college. Aunt Gretchen never forced me to open the envelopes or ever pick up the phone. She thought I was trying to adjust, but that wasn't it. Not really.

I couldn't do it without Jeannie. I couldn't read my mother's words or listen to her voice without Jeannie there holding on to me. I was too young, too small, to bear the weight of all that worry, to withstand the force of my mother's intensity when it was funneled through an ink pen or a phone speaker. She poured herself into every message, and every time I was blasted back into that tub, stinking of gasoline, tasting vomit and blood from her fingers scraping my throat. Every "I love you" awakened the memory of that wire cutting into my wrists; every "Oh, Anna" sounded like the clattering of the hacksaw dropping onto that blood-soaked floor.

Without Jeannie there to hold on to me, every message from my mother blew my world to pieces. So, when Jeannie left, I stopped reading them. I put them in boxes; I kept my answering machine on. I started building a wall of my own.

But what am I keeping back there? What am I walling in? It's not protecting me or anyone I've ever cared about—not Jeannie, Ronnie, Karmen. Not even Meredith. Crazy Meredith, pushed over the edge by outrage for her wronged son.

I'm not eleven anymore. Surely to god I've seen enough horror for a lifetime and I'm still standing. Besides, Jeannie's here, too. She's singing in the bathtub, probably making sure no stray demons try to swoop in on me.

My mother's handwriting hasn't changed in fifteen years. I wonder if she still worries about me. I still worry about her. Pain shoots up
my arm as I grip the envelope with my bandaged hand. I hear Jeannie
whistling as I slip my finger under the paper flap.

The envelope opens with a whisper.

ACKNOWLEDGMENTS

Writing a book is a solitary endeavor. Getting a book out into the world takes the help of many talented people.

To my development editor, David Downing: I'm running out of original ways to sing your praises. It is much easier to write bravely knowing I have you to keep me from looking stupid. Now if I could only find a way to parlay your abilities into my everyday life.

Hannah Buehler had her capable hands full with copyedits on this beast. You are a trooper!

The team at Thomas & Mercer keeps impressing me with their professionalism, generosity, and enthusiasm. Many thanks to JoVon Sotak, Anh Schleup, Alan Turkus, Gracie Doyle, Tiffany Porkony, and a special holler to Jacque Ben-Zekry who has the unfortunate task of being my designated adult. I don't envy you.

Thanks to my agent and friend, Christine Witthohn, for putting up with all my shit.

Sergeant Kendra Beckett of the Huntington Police Department did all she could to keep me from looking like an idiot when it came to the police stuff. All mistakes are my own. Seriously, she did all she could.

My sister, Monica Rimer, has long since given up expecting any normal questions from me. Thanks for being a font of gruesome information.

Huge thanks to my cousin, Meredith Michener, who just gamely offered up her good name to my book of mayhem. You are an optimist, my dear.

Deborah Reed, Helen Smith, Nancy Rommelmann: I will never be able to thank you enough for your eleventh-hour support. Dream Balls, indeed.

I wouldn't be able to do this without the friendship and support of The Hitches—Debra Burge, Angela Jackson, Tenna Rusk, and especially Christy Smith, who let me assault her with some of the most insane ramblings I've ever uttered. You all are the best.

And finally, much love to friends and family, near and far, who keep me human.

ABOUT THE AUTHOR

Photo © 2015 Toril Lavender

A fifteen-year veteran of morning radio, an avid traveler, and a so-so gardener, S.G. Redling currently lives in West Virginia.